COURTING DRAGONS

Also by Jeri Westerson

The Crispin Guest Medieval Noir series

VEIL OF LIES
SERPENT IN THE THORNS
THE DEMON'S PARCHMENT
TROUBLED BONES
BLOOD LANCE
SHADOW OF THE ALCHEMIST
CUP OF BLOOD
THE SILENCE OF STONES *
A MAIDEN WEEPING *
SEASON OF BLOOD *
THE DEEPEST GRAVE *
TRAITOR'S CODEX *
SWORD OF SHADOWS *
SPITEFUL BONES *
THE DEADLIEST SIN *

Other titles

THOUGH HEAVEN FALL
ROSES IN THE TEMPEST

* available from Severn House

COURTING DRAGONS

Jeri Westerson

**SEVERN
HOUSE**

First world edition published in Great Britain and the USA in 2023
by Severn House, an imprint of Canongate Books Ltd,
14 High Street, Edinburgh EH1 1TE.

Trade paperback edition first published in Great Britain and the USA in 2023
by Severn House, an imprint of Canongate Books Ltd.

severnhouse.com

British Library Cataloguing-in-Publication Data
A CIP catalogue record for this title is available from the British Library.

ISBN-13: 978-1-4483-0987-0 (cased)
ISBN-13: 978-1-4483-0989-4 (trade paper)
ISBN-13: 978-1-4483-0988-7 (e-book)

All Severn House titles are printed on acid-free paper.

MIX
Paper from
responsible sources
FSC
www.fsc.org   FSC® C013056

Typeset by Palimpsest Book Production Ltd.,
Falkirk, Stirlingshire, Scotland.
Printed and bound in Great Britain by
TJ Books, Padstow, Cornwall.

For Craig, because he's a fool for love.

And thorns shall come up in her palaces, nettles and brambles in the fortresses thereof: and it shall be an habitation of dragons, and a court for owls.

Isaiah 34:13

GLOSSARY

Battlement – defensive architecture on the upper walls of a castle.

Bauson – badger.

Bench-whistler – idler.

Beshrew – to invoke evil upon. To blame as the cause of misfortune.

Biliments – the decorated border of a French hood.

Bodkin – a dagger.

Bring-a-waste – an insulting term.

Buckram – a stiffened fabric as a precursor to a corset.

Close stool – a small cabinet with a padded seat for a chamber pot.

Cock lorel – rogue, reprobate.

Cod – a man's genitals.

Crenellation – wall on the roof of a castle or palace as a battlement with alternating upward projections and gaps through which arrows or other weapons of war can be launched outward.

Cross-biter – a swindler or trickster.

Doublet – an inner close-fitting coat worn under a fuller, longer coat.

Embrasure – the open part of an alternating crenellation on a battlement.

French hood – not actually a hood, but more of a headband for women where a cloth veil is attached to the back.

Galapines – food preparers.

Hartichoak – artichoke.

Hose – for men, stockings attached to a pant, the whole akin to tights, which ties to the bottom hem of the doublet with laces called 'points', with the codpiece attached to the front.

Jesu – archaic form of the name Jesus, pronounced zhay-ZOO.

Kennel hood – headgear for women, so-called because of its resemblance to a dog kennel, with its pointed, roof-like top. A cloth veil would be pinned to the back.

Kirtle – a fitted bodice with a skirt, an overdress that split in the front at the skirt to allow the underskirt to show through.

Lady-in-waiting – the senior attendants of a noble lady or queen, usually married.

Maid of honor – the younger member of a noble woman's or queen's attendants, unmarried.

Manchet – a small loaf of bread, round like a roll.

Marry – an interjection expressing surprise, outrage, etc., now archaic. Probably a variant of 'St Mary!'

Merlon – the upward-projecting parts of a crenellated battlement.

Motley – distinctive clothing of a jester, with bells attached, and a hood or foolish hat with bells.

Mummery – a highly stylized play, usually with a religious theme.

Nef – saltcellar.

Parapet – low protective wall along a roof.

Pate – the head.

Pillicock – penis, or vulgar term for a boy.

Points – laces that attached from the bottom hem of the doublet to the top portion of the hose, to keep them up. A precursor to suspenders.

Sirrah – insulting form of 'sir', to those of lower rank.

Truckle bed – a trundle bed that slid under a larger bed.

ONE

The king laughed, thank Christ.

It wasn't always an easy feat, though I had only been at it for four years, I knew well what King Henry liked. I could also read his face and by the tilt of a ginger brow and the flicker of a lash, I knew he was not in need of his jester at the moment, for his eyes lingered not on his wife, Queen Catherine – stuffed away so he would not have to look upon her – but instead on her erstwhile maid of honor, Anne Boleyn. In fact, she was no longer required to serve the queen, and we at court had little doubt as to what that might mean.

King Henry tapped his foot to the rhythm of a merry song plucked out by his musicians. He sat at the head table facing outward toward all, and his chair was under the Cloth of Estate, a canopy that climbed up the wall and hung over his royal self so that all would know exactly where he was in the room. As if they wouldn't know.

And so, as quiet as a man can be with bells sewed to his person, I slipped away.

I wore my usual blue doublet, a short-waisted and tight-fitting garment that covered my chemise, with long, tight sleeves. My yellow hose was tied to the doublet's hem with points – laces, that is – tipped with silver. Silver-tipped because Henry paid me enough and I was vain enough to want it. I also wore a hood of party colors of yellow and green, and there would be no mistaking me for a courtier or a servant whilst wearing such. There were also a few tiny bells sewn to my doublet's sleeves and the hood, for it was easy to caper about in only this as I was always rolling on the floor or climbing onto tables, or simply gamboling about. But more often than not – because the palace was so cold – I wore my coat overall. It was of green wool with many pleats at the skirt that reached

down to m'knees, because I fancied myself a courtier and had
the coin for pleats, for the more pleats a man had, the wealthier
he was . . . or *appeared* to be. And at court, it was as much
about appearance as competence; the former overall, and the
latter not a wit. And aye, I was be-belled upon the sleeves of
my coat as well. But the fewer the better, was my thinking on
it. For the tiny silver bells were a constant reminder that I was
set apart. Not quite a servant but not quite a courtier. Merely a
shadow of one or the other, always trailing after, hiding. But
a presence nonetheless. A jester walked a fine line between
distraction and destruction.

At least I wore my motley – my fool's garb – on the outside.
Far too many at court wore them concealed under fine slashed
velvets and brocades. And many more under chasuble and
miter.

I scanned the great hall, its space as big as a cathedral's
insides, or nearly. Open wide for the laying out of trestle tables
for meals for the many – as they were now – it easily served
as a place for ceremonies of state for all of court, or nearly
so, to attend and view the king and ministers and foreign
officers or any other gathering that needed bodies crushed
together to prove the majesty of the king.

Great arched windows above on both sides showered the
hall with light, for the ceiling above in its carved wood of
arches and pendants was dark so as to direct the eye to the
many intricate tapestries lining the walls. There they depicted
hunts, and dances, and country scenes of royalty observing
the farmers at play. Idyllic scenes to remind all and sundry of
what it meant to rule and who was being ruled.

It was Monday late afternoon, and there were candles – oh
so many candles like the stars in the night sky – in chandlers
and raised coronas hanging from the ceiling. It was lavish
beyond the most covetous of dreams, for just as I had bells
sewn upon my coat, so did courtiers have jewels sewn upon
theirs and they sparkled with celestial light. It was a sight to
behold, one a mere lad from Shropshire, as was myself, had
never seen before.

I moved with impunity through the crowd. There were
dancers in the center – courtiers showing off a well-turned

leg. A table with food groaned under the weight of Henry's indulgence, for he loved a merry court and it hadn't been very merry for the past few years under his frowning brow and stiff queen. To be fair, the queen and the Princess Mary were often cosseted away from the king's strange wrath, and it was scarce her fault that she had been so stiff of late. For she was beyond the years to bear the king sons. I knew it. The court knew it. But most importantly, Henry knew it.

He had only been a lad of ten, after all, when he first met Catherine of Aragon on her way to marry his brother Arthur . . . who later died. And almost immediately, the *former* king and Henry's father, the late King Henry VII conspired . . . oh, forgive me. For the word is *contrived* . . . a new treaty with the King of Spain to marry Arthur's Spanish widow to his English son, Henry, now the heir to the *English* throne. King Henry VII was supposed to have been a tricksy man with a contract.

Can this be the moment the trouble began?

I had heard Henry rejected the idea of marrying his brother's widow when he was still a lad. And so our poor Catherine languished at court, a widow to the boy prince, Prince Arthur. And in danger of becoming Henry Seven's new wife, an old man; for sly and greedy Henry Seven would not return Catherine's dowry to King Ferdinand of Spain, nor would he return *Catherine*.

It was said that Henry Eight only took her up again once his father died to spite him. But it was also said that it was a happy court. Indeed, when I arrived four years ago, it was a festival every day.

The king used to indulge his daughter, the Princess Mary, when she was young, calling her his Pearl. And yet, as the years wore on and Mary grew and his wife failed to give him living sons, he was not enthralled at the prospect of a queen to rule after him. A man needs sons, and a king needed them most of all.

Soon there were rumors. Salacious, ugly rumors that he would put away his wife to get him a new one who *could* bear him sons. It had become a very Great Matter.

As for me, I like to discover about the men and women

who are here for all their greed and ambition . . . and any other thing I can use to jest about. And when the court gathered, as it did this afternoon, it was *my* time to feast.

The rest of court, those who were not cavorting in dance, stood at the perimeter. Like mussels and barnacles, they clung tight to what they believed was a sturdy pier as the tide washed in and washed out again. But this pier was a false hope, for in most instances it was to another courtier they clung, believing them to stand upon a higher rung of the king's ladder. Foolish to put your hopes in such, for a ladder does not only go up, but it has a descent as well. For four years I watched men climb, cling, and clatter down. There were very few men who survived it for any length of time . . . except me.

And even so, I have never counted myself secure.

As much as I amused His Majesty and kept him smiling, I had it in the back of my mind that it might only be a matter of time till his anger could not be placated, and I would be the recipient of it. Oh, he cuffed me, often. And kicked. Mostly in good nature. Once or twice in true anger. And yet, His Grace well knew that I am no carry-tale, no whisperer, nor flattering insinuator. I tell the truth to shame the Devil and woe be to that Devil who tries to shame me back. I am always Henry's man, no matter what. It is my gift . . . and my curse.

A fool's work is never done, I mused. *For look. Here comes Cromwell.*

He was the corpulent Cardinal Wolsey's assistant and, as Wolsey stepped lower on the ladder's rungs, so his lickspittle Thomas Cromwell moved up it. Where His Grace the cardinal had moved comfortably through the crowds, Cromwell did not, for he came from low estate. Like me. But at least I admitted to being a fool.

His manner was not as oily as Wolsey's, for the cardinal had cajoled the king when Henry was younger and was given many favors. But unlike the boisterous cleric, Cromwell was quiet, like a ghost, and very like a spirit he appeared most inconveniently. He was a lawyer and a member of Parliament. He was a man in his middle years of some discretion. I didn't know if his excessive reading caused the perpetual squint, but he always seemed to be calculating something. A dark man, a shadow, for he was emerging from Wolsey's shadow as his own man and the king had noticed full well.

And though he had a sharp eye like any predator, he once again failed to notice me, for surely his sneer would have been all the more pronounced. Instead, I waited for the opportune moment to startle him, and I was not disappointed when I stepped into the candlelight and with a huge sweep of my arm and a cascade of tinkling bells, I bowed low.

'Good Master Crumbled-Well. Whither do you go?'

'To my duties, Fool. Why do you skulk so?'

'It is *my* duty, good sir, for to seek amusements for my king.' I cast a glance toward the dais where King Henry nodded to the dancers. 'And they might be in a room filled with people making merry . . . or in locked chambers where plots are hatched.'

Cromwell muttered something unintelligible and tried to push past me. I snatched the leather satchel from under his arm and earned a muffled exclamation from the man.

'Will Somers, give that back at once or I shall . . .' He dropped his voice, but even so, others near us could not help but notice us and smile under their hands.

'Or what, sir? Idle threats, Master Crumbled-Well. You and I both know our Uncle Harry would have words for you on the matter. But what have we here?' I began unlacing the flap. Cromwell reached, but I, more agile than the lawyer in his long gown, managed to keep it just out of his grasp. The courtiers within our hearing laughed. Oh, how Cromwell hated that, hated to be made a fool of.

Cromwell's secretary, Ralph Sadler, finally took hold of the satchel I wasn't trying very hard to keep from him and handed it to his red-faced and ruffled master. The man tucked it tightly under his arm again. He stabbed a finger into my face. 'You had best watch yourself, Master Somers. Your day will end like any other man's.'

'Oh, but until that day, Master Crumbled-Well, I can sit at my king's feet and give him good cheer. A man who cheers the king is longer-lived than one who frowns and gives him sour milk. If I were you, master, I'd sweeten my milk.'

'Rot in hell!' said his secretary, turning swiftly with his master Cromwell, as they both continued through the laughing crowd.

'You *will* lead the way, won't you, good master?' I called after them.

My courtiers laughed and applauded. I bowed to them, bells jangling from my sleeves.

Yet soon enough, they turned away. Fickle. As long as I entertained them, I was like a pouch filled with gold. Once the gold was spent, what was I but an empty pouch?

And so, I finally found my moment of leisure. Crossing my arms, I leaned against the warm wainscoting and watched the dancing, the musicians. I gazed at the crowd, ticking in my mind 'what next, what thing would please the king?' Always was I at such occupation.

My old master, a wool merchant by name of Richard Fermor, had made note of my judicious eye and wit. He himself had presented me to the king whilst we were in Calais. And even after all this time, comparing my life should I have stayed in Shropshire with either my father or Master Richard to my life now at court . . . I cannot to this day decide which was the better part.

'You *are* a witty fellow.'

I startled. It wasn't every day I did so, for I was always alert. I didn't fancy getting caught at it now but I had the advantage of playing it to the extreme to hide my lack of attentiveness. I jumped back, my hand to heart, my face a dramatic mask of fright.

The dark-eyed stranger chuckled at my antics, his smile serene, his eyes flashing with interest.

I sobered and smiled back. I doffed my motley hood and swept it back to my head. 'I thank ye.'

The man sidled closer, mirrored my crossed arms, and leaned against the wall beside me. 'I had not realized that the English court would be so full of amusements.'

Ah, I now detected a Spanish accent but his English was very good. He had obviously spent some time here. Casting a glance over my shoulder, I took in the man once more. Handsome features of dark brows, a pointed nose, plump and shapely lips, a strong, shaven chin. Rings on his fingers, a gold chain round his neck. Bauson fur on his doublet.

'Forgive me, good sir, but I do not know you from court, do I?'

'Indeed not. I am with the imperial ambassador and the Spanish contingent.'

'Oh? Spain would not seem to be the flavor this month.'

He smiled ruefully, a most charming aspect. It creased his cheek in a dimple. 'But Spain hopes to be as appetizing as it once was in England, if only the king could find a taste for it again.'

Our poor Spanish queen. Would that Henry *could* find his tastes in Spain again and leave his taste for French pretenders behind. But then I began to wonder. Why was this man talking to me? I was the jester, the king's fool. It wasn't worth a man's time talking to me, for I could offer him nothing but a jest or prank at his expense. And so it was common to find a moat about me when in such a crowd. No one sought the jester, so why did he?

I could not help the quickening of my heart as I slowly turned toward him. I appraised him boldly this time. 'I am Will Somers.' I lifted an arm and the bells there lightly tinkled. 'As you can plainly see, I am the king's jester.'

He smiled and ducked his head in a bow. 'So I do see. And I am Don Gonzalo de Yscar, aid to Eustace Chapuys, ambassador to the Holy Roman Emperor.'

'Now there's a name with gusto.'

Gonzalo lowered his face, a grin perched perpetually on his face. 'It is easy to pronounce.'

'Says you.'

He rolled against the wall toward me. 'Let me instruct. It is "day iss-CAR" . . .' He repeated it, rolling his 'r'. 'Can *you* say?'

I gathered the spit in my mouth and tried, 'Day IS-car.'

He laughed. I liked the sound of it. 'Yes. And then. Gon-ZAH-low.' He gestured toward me and I dutifully repeated it, watching that dimpled cheek the whole time.

I shook myself loose from his smiling eyes. 'And now you. Repeat, if you will. Somers . . . as in many warm days.'

'SOM-ers. A sunny disposition to go with the name.'

'Oh indeed. And then, of course, Will. For there is always a will where there is a hope to succeed.'

'Will,' he said, pronouncing it a bit like 'weel'. 'Will,' he said again, thinking. And when he looked up, he said firmly, 'Will . . . you meet me later?'

'Yes, now you've got it . . . Oh!' I had not mistaken him. His attention was solicitous for a reason. I raised my head and surveyed the crowd. No one was taking note of us. I looked toward the king and surmised by his smile and laughter that he would not need me for some time yet.

Still, even as my heart fluttered and my cod firmed, I took another cautious perusal of the room. 'Whither shall we go?' I said quietly. And then for the sake of any with keen ears, I added, 'You of course wish to talk to me of English music.'

'Of course,' he said shyly. It was utterly charming. I had already begun to calculate how long I could be absent.

'I . . . attend to the king. I am at his beck and call.'

'He does not need you once he has retired, does he?'

'No, he does not.'

'Then meet me in my apartments. I will be awake.'

'So I shall.'

The man smiled, gave a little nod, and strolled away.

As it was, the feasting and dancing went on for some hours more, but His Majesty finally called for his groomsmen to take him to bed. Who might be in his bed tonight did bear speculation. If I were to wager, I would say it was to be that Bullen woman. Though rumor had it that she continued to put him off. In my estimation, the rumor was true. I spent almost as many hours in Henry's bedchamber as Henry did, and I think I would have known if that Nan Bullen had already been there.

I followed all the groomsmen – for it was for me to follow – and we entered Henry's Donjon tower chambers. First the watching chamber – a large hall for those waiting to see the king, then through to his presence chamber, a slightly smaller room where Henry would receive visitors, and then his dining chamber, then privy chamber where he meets with his privy council, then the withdrawing room, and finally his bedchamber. All were magnificent rooms with tiled floors, tapestries, elegantly carved furniture of sideboards, coffers, and the like. But his bedchamber had a bed fit for an entire family. It was wide, wider than any bed I have ever seen, with carved posts reaching to the heavens, and was all enclosed with heavy curtains and a tester above of carved wood polished to a sheen, like the paneled walls. His blankets were embroidered, as were his pillowcases, with large aitches all in florets, unicorns and lions. A resplendent room, much too large for a bedchamber, but he did seem to entertain his close companions there as well sometimes. The room was quiet because of all the wood panels on walls and ceilings. In one corner was a screen to keep his close stool private. It was a solid room, a comfortable room, for there were chairs, footstools and lounges, and there was plenty of room for his many groomsmen who were all at various tasks; some unfolding his night clothes from coffers, some removing the layers of what he was wearing, and brushing out the velvets, the furs, handling the jewelry for the Keeper of the Jewels to store away under lock and key. All of Henry's life was a whirr of business and crowds.

I didn't know how a man could stand it.

He was jovial with his goblet and laughed and jested with his men. I perched myself on his bed (for it was allowed me by my status) and I pretended to bless it with my jester's staff. I incanted a rustic prayer, sounding as much as I could like Cardinal Wolsey with his slow and measured drawl. Henry threw a goblet at me and I made a dramatic fall from the bed onto the floor, legs up like a dying frog. That, too, made Henry laugh, as his men dressed him in his night-shift. He was a fine figure of a man, all wide and muscled shoulders. And with blazing ginger hair and beard, he always stood out among men. His presence was more to the point, for no man was worth a farthing when King Henry was in the room, whether in his night-shift or in his finery.

'Get out with you, Will,' he said to me, kicking at me but not striking. 'Go make your mischief in your own bedchamber.'

'Oh, sire! Is that a command? For merry mischief I will make.'

'Ah. Who's the lass, Will? Some wench from a farm?'

'Hmm,' I thought, a hand to my cheek. 'What day is it?'

He laughed, waving me off. 'Any woman who makes merry with you . . . well. I shudder to think.'

I smiled. There *were* many a wench, truth be told. But also many a lad. My tastes were like that somehow.

When I was free at last of his grace, I left for my own chamber some few passages away. There, I was free to doff my motley. My rooms were fair, especially so for a man like me and whence I came. Oh, our farmhouse was a goodly size for the manner of my father and his lands, but it was not as fair as these carved and tiled palaces that Henry had in his possession.

I was pleased to have a withdrawing chamber where I entertained friends with a dining table and sideboard, and in the private chamber, a coffer, a table, bed and tapestries – a few of which Henry himself had commissioned for me. The windows were large and faced the courtyard, not the garden. But I have heard that some jesters lived in their master's suites on truckle beds, which is not that bad a thing. Still, I was honored to be given these rooms for my own purposes. And indeed, I stored much of my foolery here. Puppets, and costumes, and musical instruments. I had learned to play many, for I was a quick study. It pleased the king, and I could always make a jest with them, following courtiers around and playing sounds that seemed to imitate them, for instance. It made the king laugh . . . though it often made the courtier vow vengeance in some way. It seldom happened, for they must have thought about it, then knew they would be punished by Henry for ill-treating me. And who would be the fool then? Though I'd gotten my share of black eyes and bruises. Men have such short tempers. I wouldn't know. I never had a temper.

I dressed myself in a clean, simple green doublet and blue hose. No hat or hood for me. Most of my hats had bells and I wished a stealthier venture through the palace. I donned my green coat, the one that had no bells, secured my belt and pouch and set off.

I stuck my head out my door to the corridor and, finding no guard nearby, I stepped into the passageway and headed out toward where the foreigners and ambassadors were usually housed, past the grand courtyard. I passed through a garden and glanced at the cleverly trimmed bushes, some in the shape of cones, some in balls. It was an art that eluded me but delighted the king, to make yews and other such plants into these interesting shapes.

The Spaniard's quarters were not hard to find. I knocked, a servant answered, and I asked him where Lord de Yscar was, and he took me there to his apartments. When he left me in his withdrawing room, I knocked at his bedchamber door, and Don Gonzalo opened the door himself. He carried a goblet and was dressed in only a chemise and hose. The chemise was untied and left open in a most enticing fashion.

'Will,' he said softly. 'So you are here. Come in.'

I closed the door behind me. He strode to the sideboard and poured another goblet, bringing it to me. 'Here. Drink.'

I lifted the bowl to my lips and tasted. It was good Flemish wine and I cleansed the taste of court from my mouth. Being cautious, I only sipped a bit and strolled about the room, taking in the bed with curtains, coffers, table, chairs and fireplace. 'One wonders what a Spanish gentleman could want with a jester so late at night, when even the king was abed.'

Gonzalo frowned. He walked toward me and stood very close. '*Do* you wonder, Will?'

I waited. This was such delicate work with men. With women it was far easier, for they knew what men wanted and they'd offer it easily. But a man facing another man – the business must be weighed and measured. To do or say the wrong thing could bring disaster down upon one's head. The king did not know, after all. If he suspected, I'd never serve him again. Why then did I not spare myself and stick to wenches? It was my curse, to be sure, to enjoy the wench as well as the fragile company of men. Under any circumstances was dangerous, but to do so under the nose of the king . . . was folly.

But I was a man who had never shied from folly. If I were, I would never have agreed to come to the king's court in the first place. It was the making of me.

Gonzalo edged still closer. 'How do you like the wine?' he asked when I had replied nothing to his last query.

'It is sweet and light.'

'It makes the breath sweet and light, does it not?' He leaned toward me and breathed on me. I smelled his breath and nodded.

'Let *me* try,' he said, closing the distance.

His lips were wet with wine and his mouth and tongue did taste sweet. We partook of each other's mouths for a long while. He kissed hard and deep, and his hand clutched roughly at the back of my neck to keep me close. I didn't mind.

When he drew back at last his eyes traced over my face. 'It's late,' he said. 'Most everyone in the palace is abed.'

'Then so should we be,' I breathed.

The bolster was soft, the bed-curtains heavy with privacy, his sighs and grunts were music, and his cod steely and strong. Our coupling was eager, rough, but we settled softly afterward, he lying back against his pillows, me at an angle near his shoulder. I was sleepy and felt him stroke my hair.

'Such short hair,' he commented.

'Yes, I keep it close-cropped for my antics. Often I wear wigs for to amuse His Majesty with imitations of people at court.'

He chuckled, a lovely deep sound. 'Do you? Who does he favor most?'

'He likes my Cromwell and my Wolsey. I see I shall have to fill in the alphabet presently.'

He chuckled again, still stroking my nearly shaved head, and bringing his stroking fingers down to my cheek. 'What makes a man want to become a jester?'

'I don't think any man sets himself to become a jester. It happens. I was naturally a foolish fellow and brought to the king's attention by my master. It is a marvelous place to be, before the king's attention. For I make him laugh, I make him merry. And sometimes, I even make him think.'

He touched my chin, lifting my face for a soft kiss, for he was spent as well. 'You make him think?'

'About this and that. His councillors have one opinion that may not be the best for the realm. For they are men and have their own pursuits and interests.' I gave a soft chuckle. 'But I mustn't speak of that. I shouldn't like the gossip in Spain to be that the king takes his advice from fools. But of course, they must know that already.'

Gonzalo laughed again. 'I can see why the king took you in.'

'Can you?'

'You are a merry fellow.' He sighed. 'Would that I could steal you away to my country to keep me amused.'

I touched his face, my thumb passing his lips. He sucked on it.

'It would be lovely . . . but impractical. I doubt you would pay me what the king does.'

'You saucy fellow. Would you have me pay you?'

'I'd need to live in some fashion if I were far from home.'

'I see. You don't need me to pay you now?'

I slapped his face lightly. 'I'm not a whore. Just a fool.'

He kissed me again and we didn't talk much after that. But early in the morn, before daybreak, I slipped out of his apartments and made my way back to my own. I washed, I ate a bit of bread, I changed into fresh braies and doublet, and as I made my way through the darkened corridors, the sounds of little brass bells followed, reminding me all too keenly of who I was.

Tuesday passed.

I didn't see my Spaniard except as he hurried through the passages with purpose, and wearing a disagreeable frown.

That Boleyn woman – I mean, the *Lady Nan* was here and there and everywhere Henry was. Out riding, dancing, prattling in the gardens. I pushed my way into my lord's apartments where he and his fellows – along with Lady Nan – were playing at cards. I made a big show of setting up a chessboard and the pieces. But I made frowns and sounds of discouragement before Henry, chuckling, asked me what the matter was.

'I'm trying to play chess, Uncle. But I'm confounded.' I moved pieces about on the checkered board. I doubt Henry noticed just yet that they were all the same piece.

'Why is that? Why confounded?'

I shook my head and gestured toward the pieces. 'There are too many queens in play.'

A jester measures his achievements through laughter, but sometimes also through the silences. And as I knew this would create silence, I was cheered that the arrow had struck true.

And truer than I thought. Lady Nan cast her cards down and, in a flurry of silks and brocades, stalked out of the room. Henry watched her go with a frown. 'Get out,' was all he said to me. I gathered my tools and did so, but not before leaving two queens for him on his sideboard.

I snatched a look at his fellows. Only one or two smirked at my jest.

I would have liked to have shared the moment with Don Gonzalo, but I did not see him all the day, nor did I receive a missive. Such things were expected. A wench would often tread after you once you bedded her, but a man contented himself with the one night . . . or oftentimes one moment in a darkened alcove.

The rest of my day was filled, at any rate. I had a puppet to repair, and I sat in an opened window in my chamber with borrowed needle and thread, fixing the poor creature's hand. And then I had a new song to learn, and I spent some hours with my lute and fingering it out, for I could not read musical notation. When I was certain I had it in my mind, I embellished it with extra notes and a trill to my voice. One of the lads who cleaned my chamber smiled at me for the good music and I nodded to him. Later, I took a journey to the kitchens, for one of the galapines told me there was a dog that had pups weeks ago, and I was now the proud owner of a little furry brown whelp, already weened and trained, who had a tangle of whiskers on his face and who stuck his nose into everything, including the skirts of the ladies of court. I dubbed him Nosewise.

I next went to the harness-makers at the stables round the back of the palace, and a good fellow there cobbled a collar and a leash for him. He didn't much like the leash at first, but I worked at it for several hours, even teaching him a quick trick that he took to easily, and then brought him in to see Henry later in the afternoon.

Henry was merry again, no doubt after a thorough consolation from the Lady Nan. 'What by the saints have you got there, Will? You call that a dog?'

'He's my new companion, my liege.' The little fellow took

one look at Henry and piddled upon the floor. 'And look! He's all ready for the privy council.'

'Clean that up, you knave,' said the king, turning away to stride out of the chamber.

'You heard him,' I said to Francis Bryan, one of his privy councillors. 'Isn't that what you lot do? Wipe up piss, leave shit for others?'

He sneered as he walked by me. They were all in a foul mood today, making Henry foul of a sudden. Henry didn't want me in his privy council meeting either. That meant some secret thing was afoot. As if I didn't know what that might mean. He needed to find a way to have in play one less queen.

I dreaded to think it. Queen Catherine did nothing to earn his vexation. It isn't a crime to give birth to a daughter. Yes, I know a king needed an heir, but a strong-willed daughter could do much as queen.

Aye, me. I did worry over the Princess Mary. She must be as sorely hurt by it as much as her mother. I miss our evenings together in the withdrawing room, when Henry would sit in the big chair, I at his feet on a cushion, playing the lute or some other instrument, Queen Catherine in another chair doing her sewing and tapping time to the music with her foot, Princess Mary sitting upon the floor with her dolls. Such happy times.

I miss our family.

Ah well. A jester could only do so much. It only meant more time with Nosewise to teach him some tricks. That would take my mind off it.

Little Nosewise got to know me and I found him to be a quick study. He could stand on his hind legs and jump forward. It was a useful trick, and I spent some time fashioning him a hat, very like the king's favorite, feathers and all.

It was late when I tried to practice my songs. I thought little Nosewise would sleep by now, but it seemed he was my greatest critic for, wide awake, he howled at each strum of my lute. 'You disagreeable hound! Though it's funny some of the time, the rest of the time it's plainly annoying.'

He sat before me, tongue lolling, mouth open in an irresist-ible smile. 'Oh, you charmer.' I scooped him up, gave his muzzle a kiss, and set him down. 'I suppose it's time to walk you again. Let's get the leash.' He'd already learned what that meant. He ran in circles, yipping and jumping, so that I could scarce get it attached to his collar.

'Becalm yourself, dog. I'd not have you piddle on my floor. Save that for the king!'

We walked the quiet corridors of Greenwich when all were in their beds. I thought of Gonzalo, my cod twitching. I gave it a squeeze as Nosewise and I reached the courtyard. The passing thought to venture nigh his window titillated before I crushed it underfoot. It wouldn't do for me to seek him out without an invitation. I knew my place. But it galled nonetheless. Perhaps I could be eased with a visit to a male servant. Edward always welcomed me there. Though some deemed me frivolous and ugly – for I could not be called beauteous, not as Henry was beauteous, what with my silly face and crooked back – but there were a few who loved this fool just as he was. Perhaps they were more calculating, cannier, surmising the coin I made and the place I took up at court. Truly, it didn't matter to me.

Marion might welcome me, though it had been over a fort-night since the last time. I had a soft spot in my heart for her. The bastard daughter of a courtier who spent her time sewing for others, Marion was my bosom companion, the only woman I had fallen in love with.

After Nosewise had done his business on King Henry's carefully coifed lawn, I decided to try out the tricks we'd learned.

Nosewise was only shin-high to me. He was a mix from several different breeds, so I was told. But the hound-keeper said he'd not get much bigger than he was. He had the face of a hunting terrier only furrier all over, like he had a mustache, and he was mostly light brown, with a dark spot on his back.

I raised my hand and gave it a quick jerk, and Nosewise was up on his hind legs. I tossed him a little sliver of crust from a pork pie I had in my pouch and he snapped it down. Next, I twirled my arm and he ran in circles. 'Good boy, little hound,' I said, and tossed him another bit of crust.

I decided to let him run and took off the leash. 'Off with

you! Pretend you are on the hunt.' And damn me if he didn't, streaking down the lawn and onto the gravel path, deep into the darkness. I could hear him distantly, scrabbling about over the gravel and into the brush of the gardens. He growled and wrestled with some shrubbery before scrambling off in some other direction.

I yawned and rolled my head on my shoulders. It had been a long day, full of this and that. My constant vigilance to be available to Henry meant that my leisure was stymied. Even a session in the latrine needed to be hurried lest the king be delayed in his entertainments. Henry could be at his stool for as long as he liked, but the jester must not.

It was a silly life indeed, full of its rewards, but also full of its strangeness. I could have stayed in the employ of Master Fermor, though I did not take to the wool trade. Or, perhaps even become a gentleman . . . Bah! This life made more sense to me. And that in itself was the most absurd of all.

Nosewise growled, barked, and made a nuisance of himself outside someone's darkened window. 'Nosewise!' I hissed into the dark, for I could not see him. 'Come here! Where have you got to?' Had he got hold of a rat? I shook the leash, but that did not bring him running. He continued to growl and I followed the sound. And there he was, standing in a slice of moonlight and barking at the lawn.

'That's no way to treat the king's grass, you cur.' But when I got closer, I sensed something strange. In an alcove of hedges and beside a bench there appeared a great lump of something. At first, I thought it might be a pile of branches and twigs left behind by the gardeners.

When I got closer, it wasn't the leavings of hedges, but a man. I sputtered a laugh, for he appeared to be lying on his side on the wet grass. 'What, sirrah, are you doing there?' I said, my voice seeming too loud and echoing into the garden from off the stone walls. But nearly the moment the words left my lips, I knew that man *would* not, *could* not speak.

I rushed forward and knelt beside him. It was Gonzalo! I recoiled. Those lips I had so recently kissed were slack and cold. Those eyes that had gazed so merrily at me were glassy and still. His dark hair was wet with dew and slapped against my hands as I held his head, painting my palms with a tangle of damascene.

I passed my hands over his body, felt no quickening. 'What . . . what . . .?' I couldn't seem to speak, to form the thought. My throat was hot and clenched, crawled up behind my eyes and stung them. I glanced around, looking for help. There was none.

Nosewise whimpered behind me as if in mourning for my loss. Indeed, I might have whimpered too. Because for once in my life, I knew not what to do. I cradled him, rocked him, whispered a prayer over him. Any chance that a priest might bless him had expired.

But when his head tilted back, I could clearly see in the moonlight that his throat had been slit. And what I had taken for dew-wet grass . . . was blood. Tankards and tankards of blood.

TWO

I puked. I'd never seen the like before. His neck was split from ear to ear and it gaped like a macabre smile. He was soaked in crimson all down his doublet and coat. The fur at his lapels was wet and matted with it.

Somehow, I was able to raise the hue and cry and they came running from all over the palace. First the guards with their spears. They stood over us and stared, until I roused one of them and demanded he get help. Then more came, and finally some courtiers, bearing burning cressets.

The next was a blur. I answered their questions as honestly as I could. I stood away from the . . . the body, clutching Nosewise to my chest. I tried not to look at the corpse as they carried it away. And soon the chamberlain came and questioned me again. He wanted to take me to the sheriffs, but someone had the presence of mind to remind all and sundry that I was the king's and that they'd need ask *his* permission before taking me away.

'Anyone can clearly see he had naught to do with it,' said one courtier, and thank God he was believed, even though I was covered in blood. In Gonzalo's blood.

I was let go and I trudged back through the darkened corridors to my chambers, with Nosewise clenched in my arms. I thought of lovely Gonzalo and his lovely hands and his lovely mouth, who would tease me no more. When had it happened? At what hour had been his murder, for it plainly was that. He was wet with blood but also with dew, so he had been outside since at least nightfall. And his body was loose, not stiff as bodies became when dead. How long did that take?

I remembered my father's farm – a sprawling estate in Shropshire with its green plains and humble manor house. I walked the grange and found a cow once. It had been alive only that morning, but poorly. It had died on the hill and lain there all night. Its legs stuck out before it, as if it were carved stone and someone had merely toppled the strange statue. But as I had observed it, the limbs eventually loosened again. So, by that vision of a cow so long ago, I reckoned that either Gonzalo had just died hours ago, or over twelve. It seemed unlikely that he would have gone unnoticed, lying there as he was in a courtyard. It must have been mere hours.

And why had they done it? Why kill *him*?

I consoled myself by hugging the dog until I got to my chamber. And by then there was a cadre of maids and manservants milling there, waiting for me.

'Will!' cried one of the kitchen boys. 'We heard you found a body.'

I scrubbed my hair, dappled with wet. I didn't want to talk, only longed for my bed. I opened my chamber and sent Nosewise in as the others followed, before leaning on the closed door. 'I did, God help me.'

'Who was it?' asked one of the laundresses with whom I used to tumble before I met Marion. Alice was her name.

'The imperial ambassador's man.'

They exchanged looks with one another. 'Who'd want to kill him?' asked one of the cocks, with whom I'd also tumbled from time to time; Edward. 'I'll wager it was a duel!'

'It wasn't a duel,' I said, and even now I could not get the look of him out of my head. 'He was murdered.'

There were exclamations all around. They wanted to ask more questions. I wanted to be rid of them. 'It's late,' said Marion, pushing her way through the crowd. Because she was the daughter of a courtier her orders held weight. And thank God for that. 'Can't you see how vexed is our Will? Surely your masters and mistresses will be awakened early because of it. You'd best go to bed.'

I was grateful to her. She had a good head on her shoulders, did Marion. She shooed them all away and remained when all was silent in the passage again. 'Do you need anything, Will?'

'Nothing. Nothing but a little peace.'

'And you shall have it.' She leaned in and planted a pecking kiss to my cheek, gave me a nod, and turned to leave. But I grabbed her hand and pulled her toward me. She held me close, a safe, warm presence, before she pushed me back. It was then she saw my doublet.

'God's wounds! Look at the state of you! We must get these off.'

She pushed me into my chamber and closed and barred the door. I stood there like a child as she unlaced the doublet, untied the points at my hose, and peeled it all away, the material already stiffening with the drying blood. She said nothing, only glanced at my face from time to time. She folded it and set it aside. 'Hose, too,' she said, in her no-nonsense tone.

She poured water from the jug into the washtub I used for bathing and laid the doublet and hose within. 'There's no amount of brushing these stains. They'll have to soak. Then I'll get at it with powders and lye.'

'How do you know as much as a laundress?'

She sighed as she unpinned and removed her sleeves, rubbed the wet material together and finally left it alone in the rosy water. 'You know as well as I do that I must often make do.'

'But your father is Yeoman of the Records.'

'And little he is paid for it. He shares what he can with me, gives me my allowance, but he has a household to maintain. Clerks and servants. And an image before the king, too. As long as I am thrifty, he can stay in the king's company. *You* of all people know that, Will.'

I did. Only those in the finest array – be they lord or lowly courtier – can gain the king's presence. He did not like to look upon those of poorer garb. Marion was an exception. For even though the woolens she wore were modest, she was a master at embroidery and that was what elevated her mere woolens to something more sumptuous. She was a prize, was my Marion. She was therefore allowed to be part of the company of maids of honor, first for Queen Catherine . . . and now Lady Nan. She did most of the work, but she also taught the ladies new stitches who wanted to learn.

'Your father is an important man,' said I, 'and Harry knows it.'

'Well, God willing he stays in his position. You know how he worries so.'

I had disrobed enough times in her sight that I didn't cringe at it. I divested myself of the blood-stained chemise – which she took and lowered into the bath – and stood before her in only my braies.

She clucked her tongue at the water blushed with blood. 'I'll wash all these myself.'

I was about to object, but then thought better of it. It would be best that no laundress saw them as they were.

'You are the most forlorn fellow I have ever seen,' she said, shaking her head. 'For a jester.' Even though it was late and the others had been in their shifts, Marion still wore her small French hood that cradled her auburn hair and covered her ears, with its modest biliment edge of gold-threaded embroidery. It might have been the only one she owned, for I never saw her with another. She was no rich courtier's daughter to be wearing pearls or gems on her person. Her kirtle with its low, square neckline was made of bombazine, and her only ornament hung on her girdle of embroidered fabric; a bone needle case, inlaid with ebony. 'Shall I stay with you tonight?'

I felt the fool asking her to . . . but then again, I *was* a fool. 'If it would content you.'

She said nothing more. She laid out my night-shift on the small bed, and set to preparing various things about the chamber; banking the fire, opening the window a crack the way I liked it, even seeing to Nosewise that he had his water in a bowl. I slowly began to dress and I watched her out of the edge of my eye. Her face did not betray her heritage with a blunt nose and small eyes. Instead, it was every bit as noble as her father's, with an elegantly sloped nose and wide expressive eyes and the rusty hair so admired in court. Her skin was properly pale and not in the least tanned by work in the sun, nor were her hands blistered and raw from rough scrubbing of floors or laundry. They were long-fingered and genteel, as was Marion's manner. She *should* have been a noble, but she never complained.

She unpinned the black veil from her headdress first and then laid both aside, unpinning and shaking out her long, straight tresses. I always thought she was the prettiest maid, with a proper blush to her cheeks and lips, those two buds that twisted when she heard tales of my exploits but were also always ready with a kiss, even after hearing of my more intimate exploits, for she knew me well, better than anyone. Better than any man.

She folded the sleeves and then undid the laces at the side of her bodice, stiff with buckram and, once having loosened them, she shimmied out of her kirtle, underdress, and petticoats, letting them cascade to the floor in a soft whoosh. Only in her shift, she gathered them up in a heap and set them on a chair, laying it out as if it were a second skin. But the thought of dead skin made me shiver, and I quickly climbed into my bed.

The jingle of Nosewise's collar traipsed through the room before he leaped to the bed, curled into a ball, and slept against my side nearest the wall.

Marion fussed with her shift a bit before dousing the candle. Darkness swept into the room, with just the faint glow from the hearth lighting her profile and outlining bench, chair, and coffer. She climbed in beside me, gathered me in her arms as I laid my head upon her bosom, and sighed. 'I worry about you,' she said after a time.

'I worry about me too.'

'Oh, Will. How did such a thing happen?'

'I don't know. I can't believe it. It was only last night that we . . .'

'Oh, I see.'

'He was so sweet to me, Marion. You would have liked him.'

'Did you talk to him today?'

'No. I doubt I would have seen him again. He's an important man. *Was* . . .'

'You're a butterfly, aren't you? Fluttering from here to there, from man to woman.'

'Only to you, Fair Marion. Only back to you.'

She resettled, holding me close. I inhaled her scent of sweet marjoram and rosewater. 'You love me. And I love you. Why do we not settle together?' she asked.

'Because even though you are a bastard, your father would never agree to you marrying the king's fool.'

She sighed again. 'Aye, I know. But it's also so you can have your men.'

'If I married you, I'd still have men.'

She slapped my head and I muffled an 'Ouch' before she tugged me close again. 'I wonder if I'd be a good enough wife to let you.'

'Would you? That *is* sweet. I don't love them. I only love you.'

'Then you must like about them what *I* like about them.'

I reached up and kissed her softly. 'Of course.'

'I've never understood your ways, but I have no argument for it. Especially . . .'

She fell silent, but I finished her words for her. 'As long as I come back to you. And I always shall.'

We said nothing more that night. She was gently breathing after a time, but I stayed awake, watching the red coals glow and radiate. Even so, she was a comfort, her warm presence, her arms about me. I needed it just then. For I could not help but run the thought over and over in my mind: *How the devil am I to be merry for the king in the morning?*

But merry I had to be. For the king must never know that I had aught to do with the dead man or that I even found him, though word might have gotten back to him already. I hoped not.

It must have been quite late when I finally dropped off, for Marion had left sometime before I awakened, and the clothes that had been bloody the night before lay draped over some chairs set near the fire, damp but clean. Fortunately, I had several changes of clothes.

I prepared a pig bladder full of air on a stick with which I planned to harry the men of court, but Henry told the court to subdue themselves in deference to the Spanish and imperial ambassador's mourning. And then Harry gave me the eye, and by that I knew that *he* knew I had found the corpse.

I did manage to smite a few men with the bladder, but Henry put a hand to my shoulder. 'We can keep our peace today, Will. They tell me . . .' He leaned over at his seat at the table. I sat on a lesser chair near him in his private chamber, populated by a few men and pretty women, including that Boleyn woman, who eyed me suspiciously. 'They tell me you found the man . . . the corpse. Are you well?'

I thought to make a quip of it, thinking it might be expected, but by the look in his eye, I saw that it was all right, that I *could* simply be Will, not Will the Fool. 'Yes, sire,' I said softly. 'I did. And I am well. But . . .' I shook my head. 'I've never seen a dead man like that.'

He patted my head like he would a dog, but I wasn't offended. His touch was calming. Now he rested his hand on the back of my head, as he would a son. 'Now, now, Will. Don't think of it again. I shall offer a prayer for you as well as the dead man. You offered a prayer for him, too, didn't you? I was told . . .'

'I did, sire. There isn't a lonelier man in all the world than a murdered one. I suppose the prayer of a fool is better than no prayer at all.'

'You mustn't say that. I'm certain that God looks down kindly on you, Somers. I think He always has.'

'Thank you, Harry. God bless you, sir. Do you desire that I play for a while? I have a gentle song I have learned. I'll not need to sing.'

'Today is not a day for singing. But yes. Play, Will.'

I shifted my chair back, gave him a bow, and snatched my lute from my basket of trickery. We were in Henry's privy chamber. I settled in the window alcove, partly shielded by the curtains, with my back warmed by the sun in the window-panes, and plucked out my solemn tune.

I could tell Henry was pleased, because he nodded with the rhythm for a moment before he refilled his cup. Lady Nan served him tidbits of food, and poured more wine into his cup when he emptied it.

I played a long while, listening to the men talk, even as the women were finally shooed away. They talked of various politics, of this fund and that, of this project and that, until I nearly dozed. Playing was second nature, and I could pull a tune from my lute even without paying attention.

'Will?'

I thrummed gently on the strings as I looked toward the king. 'Uncle?'

'Leave that for now. I will talk with these men alone.'

I hadn't noticed when Thomas Cranmer – a quiet, thoughtful

cleric with a calm manner and a gentle voice that often soothed Henry – entered the room, followed by Wolsey and his man Cromwell.

'I shall go to see the queen,' I said, draping the lute by its strap over my shoulder. Mention of her caused the men to glare at me. Henry studiously looked away, but his lips were pursed.

Wolsey sneered me out the door. That he should trouble himself with the likes of a fool didn't speak well for him. *Besides*, I thought, *he'd best see to himself.* For he was in more trouble than me.

But when I traveled down the corridor to get to the queen's chamber, I was turned away by the guards and a courtier I did not recognize. When I insisted, the guard threatened me, finally smacking my rump with the flat of the spear shaft.

I took the hint.

So that was the way of it, eh? The king wanted a divorce from her, but how was that possible when he'd received a special dispensation from the pope to be allowed to *marry* his brother's widow in the first place?

Of course, Henry's own sister Mary had divorced, and *her* husband Suffolk did so twice! There is nothing so irksome as the Scriptures when it disagrees with the expediency of politics. Oh, it was the fond game of the nobility when for financial or progenitive reasons the Scriptures are set aside, or changed. Move this lord to this square and move this lady to that square until out pops an heir. There are games and games at court. But this sport of divorce . . . is too hurtful. My poor lady queen. She was robust once. But now she was weary and sick at heart that her husband of some twenty years had abandoned her because of a bit of misread Scripture.

I took m'self to the serving hall to eat with the servants – alas, Wednesday was a fish day, so sayeth the Church – but they only wanted me to talk of the murder. I took my plate and wandered away, thinking to bring some scraps for Nosewise. I'd have to let him out at any rate, unless I wanted a shit-covered floor.

I found an alcove in the hall to eat alone, but where I could watch the doings of the court: the more furtive Spanish retinue as they talked in corners with one another; the occasional flock of clerics winding down corridors, trying to appear important; lesser courtiers discussing what was on everyone's mind, that of the king's Great Matter of trying to divorce his lawful wife, the queen . . . and the Lady Nan circling, always circling, like some great dark vulture. What was I to do about her? I wanted to mock her, of course, but that was a delicate thing. For Henry was plainly besotted, more than he ever had been on his other many mistresses, and a misstep by me could lay me low, as low as Gonzalo.

But surely the king would not get his divorce. In which case, the Lady Nan might be the mother of another of the king's bastards. Just like her sister. But alas, her sister Mary had bedded the king and it was the king's custom to lose interest in his women once they had his babes. The king had not acknowledged her children.

Yet, if the Lady Nan birthed a boy, then that was a spare beside Henry Fitzroy, his other acknowledged bastard.

It made me think of Marion. She had so little in dowry, but at least she had that much. The daughter of a much beloved mistress, she was fortunate. Other mistresses who bore the children of courtiers could not say that fortune had smiled upon them.

It was then that I became aware of someone nigh me, in the manner of my neck hair standing up. When I turned, I saw one of Lady Nan's maids of honor, Lady Jane Perwick. She wasn't exactly staring at me, but she was toying with a long gold chain hanging from her neck and trying *not* to look at me. I decided to take the bait she so freely flung my way.

'My lady,' I said, putting my plate aside and bowing. The bells on my coat tinkled.

'Master Somers,' she said with one of those coy smiles.

'Is there . . . something a poor jester can do for you?'

'Hmm,' she said distractedly. Her gray-eyed gaze drifted down the corridor, not spying what she wished to see, and only the blessed saints knew what *that* was.

I did a little dance, switching feet and gracefully, artfully extending my arms. 'If you will not say I cannot do.'

'If you cannot do . . . then what is for me to say?'

'I . . . er . . .'

'Never fear, Master Somers. I need nothing from you.'

'But I would gladly sing you a song . . .'

'I need no songs. I am currently . . . satisfied.'

'Oh. Then I . . .'

But cuds-me, she turned away then and, blithe as you please, took herself down the corridor away from me. But not before she turned her head once, almost-but-not-quite looking back at me.

What in the world . . . But there were no answers. Only her oddness sitting sourly on my belly.

I stuffed a few scraps for the dog into my basket, and wiped my hands on a kerchief. Picking up my lute and my basket, I noticed a bit of folded paper I had not put there. I set down all again to pluck out the paper and unfold it. A note in a hand I did not recognize.

I know what you and the Spaniard got up to. And if you don't wish for the king to know, you will meet me at midnight in the Great Garden. There is much we need to know of the king and his doings. Be there, or it won't lie well with you.

THREE

I dropped the paper. My hand trembled too dearly to pick it up again, but pick it up I knew I must. I stooped and crumpled it in my hand, holding it fast, and searching about. No, I was quite alone. When had that note been put there? By whom? It could have happened anywhere. In the corridor between my chamber and Henry's; in Henry's chamber; in the serving hall; down this very corridor?

Just now by Lady Perwick?

But no. She had not been close enough to the basket for such foolery. Had she?

I shivered. They knew what I was. Was I to be extorted in order to spy on my king? What to do?

You're in the thick of it now, Will. You thought you'd done it the first time you came to court and called the king 'Uncle', but that doesn't compare to this. No, I was in trouble right good this time.

I stumbled back to my chamber and distractedly fed the dog. I took him out for a walk without the leash, for he needed to learn to go about without it. But even as we walked the corridors of Greenwich, I studied each face I passed. *Was it you?* I wondered. *Or you?*

I did my duty. I entertained and belittled the king . . . but my heart wasn't in it. Later in the afternoon, I sought out Marion in her rooms and told her all.

She was fortunate to have her own rooms, not too far from her father's, who spent more time with courtiers, trying to find his way into the echelons of the mighty though never quite achieving it, than with her. Perhaps he had thought better of acknowledging his mistress's progeny. But sentimentality can do that to a man. The mistress died in childbed, and his lady wife – dead these many years – had produced no living heirs. Maybe he thought Marion was the best he could do. And it was best to marry her off to some swain either at court or out of it, though, faith! Were there any left in England who were *not* at court?

So far, his plan hadn't worked, for Marion refused many of these gallants. I think her heart was set on me. *I* was landed. Well . . . at least once my father passed in God's mercy. And though I am no knight, I have good income and a pension to boot. Still, he hoped to better himself through an alliance. Such is life at court.

Marion's rooms were homely and warm. The curtains were cast wide and sunlight streamed in from her windows. Comfortable with tapestries, cushions, and lovely embroidery by her own hand. The embroidery frame stood by the diamond-paned windows, the little chair she used to work at her sewing before it, the worn coffer she had inherited from her mother with its scuffed, golden tones, the always pleasant scent of lavender and thyme that soothed, and a table with her writing things, paper scattered and smudged, the candle on its brass holder, leaning from a legion of drips on one side.

She made some of her own income by doing embroidery work for other ladies at court who spent more time scheming than sewing. Sometimes she did her work alone, in these rooms, but at other times, she was in the company of other minor noble ladies at court, even with the maids of honor and ladies-in-waiting, absorbing the gossip that seemed to be part of the currency of court life.

I loved to come to Marion's rooms. I spent many a happy hour in her bed with her, in fact.

But now was not the time for laying myself down, but for laying plots.

She stared at me aghast during the whole of my telling the tale and finally lowered her hands from her mouth.

'Will Somers, you do know how to step in it.'

'I do. I surely do.'

'If you tell the king, then he will know your . . . proclivities . . . and sack you.'

'He would.'

'But if you don't tell him . . . you could be hanged for treason.'

'You see the predicament.'

'All too well.' She looked up at me, the paper forgotten. 'We need to think on this. Who could it be? And who would want to spy on the king?'

'Anyone. Everyone.'

'But who *now*? And why kill this aid to the imperial ambassador? And why Spain? They could have simply blackmailed you without the murder.'

Her words came upon me like a balm. Marion was a sensible woman. I knew she'd have sensible things to say. 'You're right. Why kill *him* in particular?'

'Well . . . to make his threat viable, for one. So that you would believe it.'

'I would believe it in any case, for dead or alive, a witness to me and Gonzalo was still a threat.'

'True. But if we could find this man who threatens you and expose him as a murderer, then you'd be safe. For he could tell his tale all he likes and no one would believe him.'

'They might. And the whisper of that rumor could still reach Henry's ears.'

'You'll have to take that chance. Or you might as well head back to Shropshire now.'

'To my father's farm?' Oh, what a bleak prospect was that! For I made far more gold here at court from my royal patron than I ever could as a farmer. Even a farmer with tenants as we were. I couldn't go back to pigsties and shoveling cow shit and worrying over this tax or that one. I was my own man here, with my own apartments, my clothes, my . . . freedom. I *couldn't* give that up, even if it meant my life.

'I can't go back. I won't.'

She smoothed the brocade of her bodice, head tilted, brow furrowed, thinking. That was my Marion. Determined. Clever. She looked like a huntress, like a Diana. 'Then we shall have to find this churl.'

'Yes. And we can begin tonight. Shadow me. Hide in the shrubbery and spy on us.'

'Then I could be a witness.'

'And if I'm murdered you can raise the hue and cry.'

'You won't be murdered. Not if I can help it.'

I grabbed her arms, pulled her in, and kissed her soundly. 'Oh, Marion! You're my better half.'

She gave me a shy look for only a moment, before she bestirred herself and pushed me back. 'Of *course*. But none of that now. We have work to do.'

'Yes, I was thinking that very thing. I should like to find out what Don Gonzalo did all of Tuesday, before his . . . his demise that night, and in whose company he kept, who he supped with, and all.'

'How do we discover that?'

'You forget. *I* can go anywhere in the palace. There is no place that I am not welcomed. Well . . . or at least, there is no suspicion as to why I am there.'

'You would make a good spy,' she said thoughtfully.

'I would. I *am*. For how else am I to be a buffoon if I don't know what the court is doing? Henry loves gossip.'

'It's a good thing you are Henry's man.'

'I'd have my head lopped off long before this if I weren't. But, er . . .' I touched my neck over my collar. 'Let us not speak of that. The first logical place to go is the Spanish wing in the palace. And it won't be suspicious, because it was *I* who found his body, after all.'

'Be careful, Will. His murderer might be there.'

'I'm counting on it. Don't forget. Midnight, in the Great Garden.'

I made my way to the inner courtyard, to the apartments of the Spanish. These were the finest apartments besides the king's own, because our queen is Spanish and naturally England's close ally. But because of Henry's putting her aside and talk of divorce, the only time we at court have seen them of late was stalking about with angry treads, discussing with this cleric and that lawyer in secret circles. Could you blame them for their anger?

And the more I thought on it, the more the idea of a *Spanish* man murdered seemed to connect, somehow, to the king's Great Matter. It was too coincidental. Maybe Gonzalo knew of a plot to hurt the king and he had to be done away with. Oh, it was too horrible to contemplate. And yet, it made much sense.

I carried my lute by its neck, striding with purpose, as if I had been called to entertain some dignitary. I sought the lower courtiers, those that traveled and worked with the ambassador's retinue, but whose names were not important, whose persons would not be present except as clerks and stewards. Higher than servants, lower than lords . . . like my Marion.

And there was my quarry through an open door. A handsome youth with a Greek nose and shiny brown hair. He cut an elegant form, sitting at his writing table in the Spanish quarters, clarifying his notes, no doubt. I passed through the door without being remarked, and made m'self comfortable in the window seat. I slung the strap over my shoulder and began carefully and gently picking out a tune. That's when he looked up.

'You there! Who are you?' His accent was thick, but I well understood him.

'Oh, I'm no one, *señor*. Just the king's fool.'

'Well . . . what are you doing here?'

'I am like the squirrel, scampering all over the palace . . . looking for nuts. But today, I do not gather, but offer. Because your people are in mourning, I thought I'd come to add some comfort.'

He seemed to consider this for a moment. 'Oh. Then . . . I suppose that is all well.'

'I won't disturb your work, will I?'

He looked down at his papers. 'No.'

I set the instrument aside and came up to his table, glancing at his papers. 'Is it dull work?'

He smiled slightly, still not looking up. 'A little.'

'But a clerk is honest labor at least.'

'I am training to be a lawyer.'

'Well now you've foiled it. Lawyers!' I gave a shiver.

'You are unfair, *señor*,' he said good-naturedly, playing along.

'I have seen far too many layers of lawyers these days for my taste. But you are still studying?'

'Yes. In Barcelona. I hope to go back there soon.'

'You don't like our English court.'

'I don't like your English weather.'

I laughed. 'You see, the sun likes to winter in Spain, and summer in England, though the latter, not too well. You can't have it both ways.'

'That is true.'

'I'm Will. And you are . . .?'

He smiled while looking at his papers. 'I am Francis de Aguilar.'

Since we had made friends, I decided to make my move. I sighed, lowering my face. 'I'm sorry about your countryman. A dreadful thing.' I crossed myself. 'God rest him. What do you suppose happened?'

He glanced over his shoulder, looking for spies, for any ears. 'We aren't supposed to discuss it.'

'Oh, I know. But he seemed like such a merry fellow. Did you know him?'

'*Sí*. I mean yes. He liked England. He planned to stay in Ambassador Chapuys company, but . . . alas.'

'Alas. What was he doing all day Tuesday? The day of his . . . well. Surely not work.'

'Don Gonzalo de Yscar was diligent and always at his work.'

'What *was* his work?'

He narrowed his eyes slightly. 'I do not discuss it.'

'Of course not. Forgive me. I am naturally a curious fellow. I merely wondered if he had vexed anyone, angered them, irritated.'

'I don't know, because I don't know his work, but there was a . . . a woman.'

'Ah! There is always a woman.' I don't know why I was surprised. Perhaps we are all cony-catchers in the end.

'*Sí*. And she is very saddened.'

'A Spanish lady or English?'

'You ask many questions . . . for a fool.'

'A man who asks *no* questions is more a fool than me. But as I said, I am a curious fellow.'

'So you are. I thought I saw *you* talking to Don Gonzalo Monday night at King Henry's entertainments.'

My heart stuttered, shattering its well-worn pattern. I looked this man over, this *boy*. Was it him? Could he have killed

Gonzalo in such a vile way and threatened me? I donned my mask of a smile. I don't know how I kept my hands from trembling. 'He asked me about a song I played earlier. Perhaps he wanted to play it for this lady you spoke of.'

That seemed to satisfy him. 'The lady is Ursula Marbury.'

'Oh? English then. I don't wish to grieve her, but I would like to give my personal condolences. And perhaps play the tune for her that Don Gonzalo would have played.'

'Whatever contents you, sir.'

'But where can I find such a worthy?'

His nose twitched just that much. 'In the Lady Anne's household.'

FOUR

Aye, marry. Just the place I did not wish to go. To the Bullens. God mend me.

I wandered about in the Spanish men's lodgings, poking here and there, before I was tossed out by a large man who spoke no English, though his expression translated well.

I wondered about my seeking justice for Gonzalo . . . and myself. Would the king's coroner investigate as diligently? Would they be speaking to this lady as well? Was I on the right path at all? Well, at the moment, it was the only path I knew.

The watching chamber door was closed and, just as I got to it, thinking what to do, that young musician Mark Smeaton pushed it open from the inside. When he nearly ran into me the startled look on his face was almost comical.

'What are *you* doing here?' he said none-too-politely.

'Why not here?' I answered, as glib as a be-belled man could be.

He didn't bother stopping. He merely pressed his own lute close to his body as he glared at mine. 'They want no music here,' he muttered, and it was then I could hear shouting. A woman. And I suspected who, as Smeaton cringed and hurried away.

I caught the door before it closed and slipped inside, past the dining chamber and into the withdrawing room. It was likely Lady Nan having her usual cat-fit.

Her rooms – every one of them – were resplendent, almost as those of the king. Walls of wood paneling, tapestries, tables, coffers, chairs with embroidered cushions, wide fireplaces, large windows, delicate side tables, and chandlers with plenty of candles not yet lit until the evening, for the windows flooded the chamber with light and the room was big enough to accommodate the many maids of honor and ladies-in-waiting. Blind me, she had more than the queen ever did.

Ladies were seated all around her as she paced, hands fisted. She wore long ruffles with black embroidery at her wrists that led to a rumor that she had six fingers on each hand, the more to do her grasping, so they said. This wasn't true. About the number of fingers, that is. As for the grasping, well. Lady Nan was a fisher of men. But only the biggest fish. Her sister Mary had given it up to Henry, but Lady Nan was much more calculating than that. She had a commodity to bargain with and would not trade it until the final sale was struck. And *would* it be? Though I didn't believe it at first, I have since come to the conclusion – given the whispering and nodding of Cardinal Wolsey and scholar Cranmer and the other lick-spittles who want to keep in the good graces of the king without a care to what the Holy Scriptures say – that Henry will have his way.

Oh, I used to be a son of the Church, like any other lad. I knew of this priest or that whose indulgence could be bought, or which village maiden they were swiving at the time, but I never knew, until coming to court, how bishops and cardinals could be so swayed by a little power or gold or both. It has made me a cynic in my religion. How even Henry, once touted as 'Defender of the Faith' by Pope Leo X, could twist the words of Scripture to his will.

I knew not whether it was lawyers, Wolsey, or Henry himself who had come to it, but Henry insisted that God was punishing him for marrying his brother's widow. He had got a dispensation from the pope, right enough. In time to wed her, but he reasoned it must have been invalid somehow, because Catherine could not have been a virgin as she had avowed. And this was why Henry could not beget sons, or so he thought. He twisted the Scriptures. He claimed Leviticus said: 'Thou shalt not uncover the nakedness of thy brother's wife, it is an unclean thing . . . they shall be childless.' Now, my Latin isn't as good as Henry's, but he insisted that 'Liberis' – 'children' – was mistranslated from the Greek and should have read 'Filiis' – 'sons'. That seems to be very thin parchment to me. Especially if you ask his bastard Henry Fitzroy. But . . . I am not a learned man like a cardinal or a lawyer. Just a simple fool.

Did Henry truly believe it? I think in the repeating, he does now. It's more's the pity for his immortal soul. *Oh, Henry. How the devil can I ever help you?*

Scanning the withdrawing room, I thought I knew most of the ladies who served the Lady Nan. There were the maids of honor, those who were unmarried, and the ladies-in-waiting – those who *were* married, noble ladies all who served at court. There was Anne Gainsford and Mary Zouche. Bess Holland, Margery Horsman, Nan Cobham, Jane Perwick . . . and many more. Such a garden of beauties. And several more sitting farther away from that inner circle whom I didn't know. Perhaps one of these was this Lady Ursula that I sought.

Nan was ranting about . . . well. Who else? And how slow these councillors were and these clerics and why did it have to take so long and God's death, what the devil was Will Somers doing here . . . Oh!

I found myself the center of attention. Again. Not in a way I preferred, for when I called attention to myself, it was to make sport and *I* was king. But now, I'd rather have been an invisible servant.

Nevertheless, I postured. I stuck my foot forward beauteously, and bowed most eloquently. 'My lady,' I said.

'Get out,' she spat.

'But my dear, dear Lady Nan . . .'

'I said get out!'

Some of the ladies rose. I was certain they could jostle me out through the door as a gaggle of geese surrounded a fox. I took a step back and pleaded again. 'My dearest Lady Nan. I am not here to make sport.'

'Are you not, sirrah? For I have had my fill of your sour wine.'

'Never, lady.'

'Ha! You lie.'

'I would not lie with you, my lady, for that place is for another.'

Some of the ladies covered their mouths and tried to look as if they had not tittered behind their fingers. Suddenly, as Lady Nan swept her scowl over them, their embroidery was the most fascinating thing in the world.

'Jackanape!'

'I beg your mercy, my lady. It's a slip of the tongue. I slip my tongue most when in the intimate company of ladies.' I took in all their faces. Some laughed outright this time.

'But I digress. I am here to deliver a message.'

She turned her glare back on me, raising her chin and staring down her nose. 'A message?'

'Oh yes. A message.'

'Well? From whom?'

I again glanced deliberately over the many faces looking back at me. 'From . . . a personage who wishes to remain anonymous. In company.'

She put a hand to her bodice, directly below the neckline. A brooch hung there, encrusted with pearls and given to her by Henry. 'You wish to convey this message in private?'

'It would be most convenient that way, lady.'

Since everyone knew I'd only deliver a message from the king, there was a thickened air of expectation in the room.

And surely the expectation was greatest in me, for I had no idea what message I was going to concoct to give to her.

She took a deep breath, bosom heaving over the tight bodice. She said nothing, only flicked her head like a brood mare. It meant for me to follow.

I dogged her steps into her dining chamber and closed the door after me when she stopped in the middle of the room. She touched the brooch again before settling her hands in front of her, decidedly *five* fingers over the other *five*.

It occurred to me suddenly that I could ease my poor queen's soul by committing murder. I was alone with the Lady Nan. I could do it. Me and my little dagger, I could. But what of Will Somers then? I'd be drawn and quartered, my ugly head on a pike on London Bridge, that's what. And it wouldn't do Queen Catherine any good when – in the end – Henry would simply find another wife. But worst of all would be the look of betrayal on my king's face. He trusted me. With all his intimacies. He trusted me, and damn me but I could not break that trust.

And I couldn't even blame Henry for his lust. Anne Boleyn was dark-haired and small with a mysterious and seductive look to her eyes. She had a secret smile she shared with few and a full-bodied laugh when entertained. A fiery spirit, one would say, and a woman who was not so great a beauty but an intriguing one. She would be a fine match to any man who enjoyed a good fight. She was the opposite in almost every way from our lady queen. I wonder if that's what intrigued Henry the most.

That and her youth.

'Well?' she said again, impatiently. 'What is the message?'

Yes, Will, what IS the message? Think!

Like an angel's kiss, a thought occurred. I reached into my doublet and pulled out an old, discarded kerchief from Henry. He'd given it to me some time ago. It was stained and worn, but still had the embroidered aitch on it, with crown and rose. It was even stained with my sweat, and all the better.

'My lady,' I said, brandishing the cloth, allowing her to see the aitch on the corner of it. 'The admirer who does not wish to say his name has told me to bring this old and discarded token to you. You see, it is well used, well worn. But it has his tears upon it, for he weeps that he cannot be with you.'

I held it out but not at arm's length. Close enough that she would have to approach to take it.

Yet, she hesitated.

'Why should I want an old kerchief?'

'The personage from whom this kerchief came wanted you to think of him as ragged and lost . . . without you.'

Ah, that hit the mark. Her face, so taut with frustration, suddenly softened.

'This is what he said?'

'Oh, yes, my lady.' And may God forgive me for my lies. 'He wanted that you should have it . . .' But as she reached for it, I snatched it back. 'And yet, he feared to give it to you, this old, stained token, sensing that you would think ill of him for it, perhaps misinterpreting the sort of message it told.'

She drew her hand back and frowned, but only slightly. 'No gift from this . . . personage . . . would ever make me think so.'

'Ah, that's what *I* told him.'

More hesitantly and like a child, she said, 'You did?'

In that instant I saw her for what she truly was: a young

woman cast into the raging sea of politics, perhaps thrown in by her father, her sister-in-law Lady Rochford, and the many, many voices of men who would use a woman for their own power. Was Lady Nan as much of a shrew as we sometimes saw her at court? Or just a pawn on another man's chessboard?

The moment was fleeting. She raised her chin again and looked down her nose at me, the mask of innocence falling away.

I bowed slightly. 'I did.' When I straightened, I gave her as sincere a face as I could muster. 'I am not your enemy, lady. But I am the king's mastiff.'

'Mastiff? Ah, yes. I see. You may not carry a pike but your tongue is just as deadly.'

I nodded. 'You do see, then.'

'It appears I'm more fool than you are, Will Somers. Thinking there was only the jester in you.' She held out her hand downward, but not to take the kerchief.

I stepped forward, took her hand, and kissed the back of it. For the first time, she smiled at me.

'This doesn't mean I won't continue my japes.'

She laughed. 'I know you will. It's to please the king.'

Dear, dear. Was I beginning to like Lady Nan?

I bowed again, and handed her the kerchief. She took it, sniffed it, and tucked it into a slash of her sleeve. 'Very well, Somers. You may go.'

'There is one thing more, my sweet lady. I wish to talk with Lady Ursula Marbury. Is she there amongst your ladies?'

'Why should you want to talk to her?'

'I have a message for her, too. Oh, not from this unnamed personage, but from another. Today, I am a herald, delivering all my messages abroad. Will you direct me?'

'Since we are friends now, I see no reason not to.' She moved to the door, opened it, and called softly, 'Lady Ursula.'

A dark-haired woman, with a heart-shaped face and large dark eyes, turned and rose. She came towards Lady Nan and curtseyed.

'Somers has a message for you.'

I bowed again to Lady Nan, who dismissed me by turning away, and holding Henry's discarded kerchief to her cheek.

I closed the door to the dining chamber behind me and faced Lady Ursula, who was looking at me expectantly. I gently took her arm and directed her to the farthest corner of the withdrawing room, and even though they strained their ears, I did not think the others would be able to hear our soft discourse.

'Lady Ursula, allow me to extend my condolences for the death of Don Gonzalo.'

She was clearly shocked at the mention of his name and gasped. Her eyes filled with tears and she stifled a sob. I put my arm around her to console, but mostly to conceal our conversation. 'Please, lady. Can you tell me if he had any enemies? What did he do all day, the day he died?'

She sniffled into her own kerchief she kept up her sleeve and dabbed at her nose. 'Why should *you* want to know?'

'Because it was I who found him. And . . . because he was kind to me.'

'Aye,' she said softly between sniffles. 'He was that. He had few enemies that I could tell. But like all the Spanish in their company, they were angered at the king.'

'Because of the . . . Great Matter?'

She glanced back at the others. 'Yes. But unlike the others, he hid his posturing. To all the court, he appeared neutral on the subject. I know that caused resistance amongst his fellows.'

'*Was* he neutral?'

She shook her head. 'I do not know. He wanted always what was best for Spain. But he was coming to like England.'

I smiled congenially. 'Because of someone *in* England, I think.' I chucked her chin.

She blushed and looked down. Helen of Troy likely had such a look to send armies to war. I felt a twitch in my own cod at the sweet look of her. I wondered if Gonzalo had loved her. If he were like me. Or was he like so many others I encountered, and simply did his duty to wives and lovers so that no one would suspect?

'Did you know of any argument that day? Any conflict with his fellows or those of the court?'

'I know he had an argument with a cleric. I am not certain of his name, but he is English. They argued over the . . . the

Great Matter.' She only mouthed the last, considering the company we were keeping.

'Against, I should think.'

She said nothing, as any good lady of Anne Boleyn would.

'But you say you do not know this priest?'

'He is one of Wolsey's company. He has a beard. Kendrick, I think, is the name.'

'I see. Is there anything I can do for you, Lady Ursula?'

'There is nothing,' she said, lowering her head. She had a rosary of precious stones on her girdle and she clutched it. 'There is nothing to be done now.'

I bowed, leaving her in peace. I glanced at the others, who were trying hard to pretend not to be listening to us, and made my hasty exit.

'Father Kendrick,' I muttered as I moved through the passages, my lute slung over my shoulder. 'How shall I find you?'

I had to return to my chambers to feed and walk Nosewise, when I encountered Edward, the house servant. The one with whom I often frolicked in the bedclothes. He was a handsome devil. All dark-haired and dark-eyed. He immediately rushed up and slammed the door, caging me in his arms. 'Will Somers, you rogue.' He kissed me soundly and pressed me against the door. His kisses were always hard and bruising, possibly trying to prove something to me. I whipped my head away.

'You make it hard to breathe, varlet.'

'I want you to breathe only me.'

'But the palace is full of so many . . .'

He pushed away from the door, away from me, combing his fingers through his hair. I liked pulling that hair m'self. Especially when he was on his knees. 'Why have you not sought me out?' he complained.

So that was it. Never had my time been so valuable. Had it been as much back in Shropshire, I never would have left it.

'I can't seek you out *all* the time, Edward. My time belongs to the king.'

'And Marion.'

'You mustn't be jealous of Marion. I do love her.'

'You told *me* as much.'

'And I do. I love lots of people.'

He flounced onto a stool with a whoosh of expressed breath. 'Damn you, Will.'

'Oh, so many wish to do so. You must get into the queue.' I patted my chest and Nosewise jumped up into my arms as he was trained to do. I mussed the wiry hair on his pate.

'Do you take nothing seriously?'

'Of course I don't. I'm a fool by profession . . . and by my person, as it happens.'

He looked so downtrodden, I released the pup and put my arm around his shoulders. 'Edward, you know how it is with me. We'll share a bed again soon. Don't I always return to you?'

'Even if you marry Marion?'

'The wench has even given me permission.'

He looked taken aback by that. His mind went in all directions. I could see it in his eyes.

'In the meantime, I must walk and feed this little fellow.'

'I will do it.'

'You will?'

'Surely. I don't mind doing things for you.' But there was more meaning to that than his words had said. I smiled and kissed him quickly. 'I am in a hurry. It would be most appreciated.'

'I can't stay cross at you.' His cheeks warmed in embarrassment. He tried not to be jealous. It was no good when one was the king's man and he well knew it. I could never be Edward's completely. Not at court.

I exchanged my lute for my basket of nonsense, including the bladder on a stick, a noisemaker, a puppet, and small pipe for making rude noises. I had my job to do, after all.

I waved to Edward as he cuddled Nosewise to his chest while I sought out Henry. He might need me and he was my first duty, though I found myself watching the time, and listening to the chime of the bells that marked the day. Midnight I was to meet this blackmailer. I could kill him, I suppose, but how many more conspirators were there? And . . . well. To be perfectly honest, I have never killed a man and dreaded the thought of it.

Henry was with his counsellors and even Wolsey was there, but I could tell Henry was sick unto death of him and his failures. Time for me to prance in and make a proper fool of myself.

Wolsey had been Henry's advisor almost from the beginning, or so I was told. He was Bishop of Durham, Archbishop of York, the papal legate, cardinal, and Lord Chancellor. To say he was ambitious is to play coy with the very meaning of the word.

He was clean-shaven, as many clerics were, but he was fat, for he loved to indulge in good food, better wine, adornments of jewelry, houses to entertain his many followers – and to keep his many enemies at bay. Indeed, it was said he was building a grand house, as big as a palace – even bigger than Greenwich – not too far away along the Thames in Surrey.

But for all his faults, he was also a statesman of some repute, for no man could remain in power if he were not competent at some things. And so it was with Wolsey, one of the many courtiers whose opinions were easily swayed along the lines of the opinion of the king's. Wolsey worked hard as papal legate to engage the pope in this divorce. Henry was assured that Wolsey's powers of persuasion would work on the pontiff to Henry's benefit. But that had not proven to be the case.

Hmm. Houses. I recalled that he had houses . . . to entertain his mistress. Or was it mistress*es*? So it was this last that I had decided to play with.

'Harry, do you remember when we passed by the house in London where I told you our fair cardinal here had him a mistress?'

As expected, Wolsey harrumphed and sputtered. But Henry was now grinning.

'Rhyme me what you saw,' I said, 'and I'll rhyme you back.'

'Sire, do we have time for this . . .' said one of the many men – perhaps a lawyer.

Henry scowled at him. 'We have the time when I say we have the time.' He looked back at me and grinned again. 'Very well, Will. Try this:

'Within the tower,

'There is fair flower,

'That hath my heart . . .'

I thought for a moment, letting the rhyme come to me.

'Within this hour,

'She pissed full sour,

'And let a fart.'

He laughed and slapped his leg. He loved to trade quips with me. I was one of the few who could return quip for quip as quick as *he* could.

'A rod in the school,' he said,

'And a whip for a fool

'Is always in season.'

I thought for only a heartbeat.

'I prance and I preen,' I said,

'But who shall be queen,

'Against all right and reason?'

Henry's laughter stopped and he eyed me with a warning.

'You've done it now, Jester,' muttered that lawyer again. I noticed Cromwell stood in the corner, eyeing me but not with the usual disdain.

'Oh, I've done it, right enough,' said I. 'Harry must think on what I said, as he always does. But does he remember at all what *you* say?'

The lawyer would have drawn his blade had he not been in the king's presence. Any time a courtier did so, they usually pulled it halfway from their scabbard before realizing they were drawing their sword on a fool. And then *they* felt foolish, especially when the court laughed at them. My foolishness was my armor, my motley my shield. Few realized it, but I was the safest man in all of England. And, because of that, perhaps the most dangerous.

In any case, it was Henry's Royal Secretary, William Knight, who put a hand on the lawyer's shoulder to stop whatever it was he would have said. For William Knight was most trusted by the king, more so than Wolsey these days.

I prattled a little, interrupting the king's discussions before he had enough of me and sent me away. I pulled out my little pipe, and made farting noises with it as I left the room, pulling it quickly from my lips when the door closed. Finally!

Father Kendrick had not been in that meeting, so perhaps I could find him somewhere else. Henry was going to eat in his chambers and that meant that the court would be supping in their own halls. I rounded a corner swiftly and ran straight into a courtier, almost bowling him over. 'Pray mercy, my lord. I . . .'

It was Lord Robert Heyward. Marion's father. Were it any other man I would have rolled upon the floor and made a proper arse of m'self. Before my king, I could harass and bully and call the royal person a churl to his face and know that I'd be spared. Though there was always the possibility that he would send me either away or to prison, I didn't fear either of those prospects.

But under Lord Heyward's dour scrutiny, I froze as I always seemed to do before him, my knees knocking.

He brushed at his doublet and long coat, studiously looking away from me. 'No harm done, Somers.'

'But I do apologize, Lord Robert . . .'

'No need.' He looked me over once more – as if he hadn't seen me hundreds of times before – and strode away. And I, the coward, did not try to stop him. To tell him how much I loved his daughter. Truly loved her. And that we would make each other happy.

But even though I had the ear of the king, what manner of man wanted his daughter to marry a fool?

I ate very little that afternoon. My belly was dancing a caper and I had no stomach for food. A little cheese to keep me and some wine, but that was all. I spent the hours carefully cutting the bells off all my clothes. I had been slowly weaning the court off my silly wardrobe. Daily I had stripped the bells bit by bit from all my doublets and coats. I had been leaving fewer to announce my arrival. I had hoped to take them all off, and now I had. As long as Henry didn't notice. Perhaps he'd take me more seriously without my motley and fool's hood.

And speaking of bells, I listened carefully each time the bell tower chimed. Ten of the clock. Eleven of the clock. It was time to make my way to the Great Garden between the

Donjon towers and the queen's lodgings. The gate was locked but I had no doubt the murderer could find a way in. He had to be clever. He had to be close to power to be able to spy on us. But in such a busy court, that left too many to name.

I knew that Marion would have a key because she, too, was clever.

I left early to go to the garden. I wanted to be there before this murdering blackmailer arrived and situate Marion where she would be hidden and safe.

The corridors and passages were dark and empty. There were so many people at court, stuffed to the rafters we were, that it was like a little village. About fifteen hundred people, all told. But for now, I saw only the shadows of guards as they walked the passageways, halberds leaning on their shoulders. And what a devilish shadow it made, stretching across the floor and up the walls, all sharp points and danger.

I emerged through a doorway and to a colonnade, and before me, the gate. There was a shadow. My heart beat like a tabor until I recognized Marion's shape. I embraced her tight, took comfort from her familiar scent.

'Let us go in,' she whispered. 'Should we leave it unlocked?'

Should we? Perhaps that was what the murderer wanted all along. But if we *were* to meet with him, we'd best do so.

I nodded and we went in together. We stopped just inside the wall and paused, listening to the sounds of the night. The birds were silent but the sounds of crickets and frogs served to calm me. Marion gestured toward the dark shadows of the trees to the right. 'I'll wait there,' she said softly. 'Tell me if you see me.' She trotted on the tips of her toes across the gravel and then the lawns, suddenly disappearing into the black shadows. My eyes had adjusted well, but I could not see her.

'Marion!' I hissed. 'Are you there? Are you well?'

'Yes!' came the answer from her invisible person. 'Now be quiet.'

I fell silent and stood like a ninny in the moonlight. I was restless and afraid. I paced. First along the gravel walkway. But my feet seemed to make a din, crunching and crackling over the stones. So I made my way over the wet lawn, found a bench, and sat, my fingers curled over the edge of the seat, my back straight as a rod, my ears pricked like a fawn in a meadow.

The clock tower chimed twelve strikes and I held my breath, staring at the gate we had left ajar. Maybe I should have brought Edward, or any of those brawny fellows from the kitchens that I sometimes dallied with. They could have protected me. Why did I put Marion in such a dangerous position? Was I a coward after all for not taking this on myself?

Time dragged on. I waited for those footfalls I was sure to hear. I waited longer than any lover did under their paramour's balcony, waiting for the husband to depart. I waited and waited.

The crickets stopped.

I stood. My eyes searched the dim garden, each leaf painted black by moonlight.

Was that a shadow? Was it moving? I waited several more heartbeats without breathing, until I finally *had* to draw breath. I stared until the impression of the gate was burned on my eyes.

And then I waited still more. But no one ever came.

FIVE

When the clock struck one, Marion crept from the shadows and hissed to me across the lawn. 'Will! I'm numb with cold.'

I stared at my sodden shoes. 'Me too.'

'No one is coming. Could we have missed them?'

I shook my head. She met me at the bench. I put my arm around her shivering shoulders. 'They either discovered you and it scared them off . . . or they changed their mind.'

'What will we do?'

'I don't know. Come to my chamber, Marion. Warm yourself.'

'In your bed?'

'I would like that.'

And so we two, damp with dew and shivering in our clothes, locked the gate, trod lightly through the palace and found our companionship in my bed. It seemed like a long time since we had spent our company thus, and it was a relief to me.

I loved the grate of a man's beard under my fingertips, but I marveled with a special kind of awe when grazing the soft, *smooth* contours of a woman's skin. I traced her cheek, her chin, her lips swollen with our kisses, and couldn't resist kissing them yet again. Her breasts were small, young, and I pressed my palms full to them, liking how they pooled in my hands.

She smiled at me. I could see her face in the firelight, all brightness in her eyes and cheeks round in her pleasure. I could not resist those two mounds of her bosom again, and indulged myself.

She chuckled and lay back her head, watching me with drowsy lids. 'I can scarce believe you like bedding men when you are so bewitched by a woman's mams.'

'What can I say, Marion? I am a man of many interests.'

She cocked her head at me, simply gazing until she said, 'What . . . is different . . . with a man?'

I sensed the seriousness of her question and made no obvious quips back at her about it. Pushing her hair off her face with my fingers, I gazed at her. She seemed to glow in an amber mist in the candlelight, almost like a saint painted on a church wall. Well . . . almost. Her nakedness would never be appropriate there as it was here.

'Men . . . are stronger, more sure of themselves. Not that you, dear Marion, are not a proud and headstrong woman. But there is more force behind the kisses of men. And that is appealing in its way.'

'But you have never been forceful with me. Too forceful.'

My hand fell away from her face and hair. 'Because you do not expect it, or want it. We rise to meet the expectations of our partners.'

She lowered her lashes and said softly, 'Will you be forceful with me?'

I stilled. 'Do you want me to be?'

She gave a little nod. This was a delicate thing. I did not wish to frighten her, but then again, she had asked. She wanted to know.

I sat up and grasped her shoulders harder than I ever did and pressed her deep into the bed. She grunted her discomfort, but instead of my moving in with care in my kissing, I leaned in and took her lips hard, forcing them open wide and moving my tongue where I wanted.

She tried to keep pace with me, even as I reached quickly under the sheets and with my fingers, I plunged . . .

Hands pushed hard at me and she squirmed up and away. She wiped the back of her hand across her mouth.

'Is *that* how it is, Master Somers? Is that what you crave?' Her voice was strained and taut. Frightened.

'Not from you, Marion. But you asked what men offered me. I suspected you wouldn't like it. I have learned that women, being weaker, need more softness, more careful caressing. Even the ones who claim they want it rougher. That is why I am as tender as I am with you, my love.' I watched her carefully for signs of a fight as I slid gently toward her and reached for her face. Cupping her jaw, I leaned in and gently kissed her cheek, her chin, and lastly her lips with delicate pressure. I pulled back slowly and smiled. 'I won't be rough with you. Not ever. Not unless you want it so.'

Her expression was growing more mollified with the gentleness of my caressing. It couldn't have been easy for her to have asked.

'You've seen young boys wrestle with one another,' I said. 'They are rough and tumble and don't mind a bruise or two. And so it is in the bedchamber with grown-up boys. We . . . er, wrestle, too.'

She shook her head. 'I had no idea.'

I embraced her and pulled her close, dropping a kiss to her head. 'And why should you? Content yourself that you are a soft woman, for it is what I love about you. Truly.'

And soon, her soft cries told me I pleased her and that she was, indeed, content to be mine. Softly. Tenderly. As we had done.

'Marion,' I murmured into her breast after a while of soft breathing and gentle kisses. 'When will your father relent? I ran into him in the corridor hours ago, quite literally, and he barely looked at me.'

She sighed as she stroked my hair. 'I fear he never shall.'

'If he doesn't, then you must promise me. Marry another.'

'No.'

'Marion . . .'

'No!' She slid up to the top of the bed and settled herself at the pillows, dragging the covers to her chin. Farewell, lovely breasts.

'Marion, you must. You want children, don't you?'

'Not bastards.'

'And so you should not. You should have a proper husband, one who can keep you well.'

'I don't love them. I love *you*.'

'And I love you. But . . . I love you enough to let you go.'

'What sort of damned fool thing is that to say?'

'It's the noble thing to say. I would not have you suffer for my sake. Who knows how long I can be the knave I am? Henry could kick my arse out tomorrow for some slight. What sort of life is that?'

Her lower lip jutted in a pout. Such a luscious pout. But I do not think she would thank me for kissing it just then.

'And you and your men,' she said softly.

'Is that the crux of it? You would not have me swive my way through the livery? I won't. I'll give it up now.' I got up on my knees, the blankets falling away from my privities, and I raised my hand to Heaven. 'I will not bed any more men. I swear it.'

She leaned forward, and shoved my shoulder, pushing me over. Raking me with her eyes, she sighed again. 'I will not make you swear it. You know I won't. I would not have you lie to the Almighty.'

'That's why you are perfect for me. For I *can* swear I will not lay with any woman but you.'

We were content with one another, as a man and a woman . . . or a man and a man could be. But in the morning, we still had the puzzle. My blackmailer had not shown and now I was on tenterhooks wondering when he would approach me again. In fact, even attending the king, I was nervous, and he noticed.

'What's amiss today, Will?' he asked me.

I seemed to have been in my own thoughts, for I had entirely forgot I was in the king's presence. That would never do.

'Oh . . . nothing, sire. I was merely thinking of the next rhyme for you.'

'Bollocks. You were dreaming. And I can plainly see a worry line across your forehead. Tell me. Is it a woman?'

Christ save me. Getting advice on women from Henry! 'Oh, no, my lord. I-it's nothing like that.'

'Aye, marry, Will. I can tell.' He looked around his watching chamber, as if examining it to see if any were listening. And of course, they *all* were, but perhaps too far away and too preoccupied to care about what *I* had to say.

'Harry, Harry. You do care, don't you?'

'As I care about all my subjects. But perhaps . . . a little more for you, my little coxcomb. Come. Sit beside me. Have some wine.'

A servant moved forward to pour but Henry waved him off impatiently. He wanted to be the solicitous uncle all on his own. I suppose I should have been flattered. And I was. His tender care of me was singular throughout the kingdom. Sometimes I marveled where I lay my head.

'Here is wine. Drink up. There now. You tell me what ails you.'

I couldn't tell him. But something else was now presented to me. Oh, I knew I had the king's ear, but if I told him outright about my wanting to marry Marion, he'd wave his hand like a sorcerer and it would be done. By the mass, he would. And my mouth was poised to open on it . . . until I halted. Henry didn't want to hear that. As much as he wished to be my solicitous uncle, this he did not want to truly be. So instead I smiled and said, 'Is there nothing that you can imagine more valiant than the collar of a gentleman's shirt?'

'Eh? What's that you said? Are you spouting nonsense again? What *of* a gentleman's shirt?'

I turned to take in the courtiers at the outer edge of our semi-private circle. 'Marry, because every morning it has a thief by the neck.'

Henry looked at me questioningly for only a moment, before he burst into laughter. He grabbed me and dragged me into an embrace. 'You perfect little fool. Even when *you* are the one who is down, you perk *me* up.'

'It is the very pleasure of my life, Harry.'

'And the pleasure of mine.' He gazed at me ever so fondly and with tenderness. Softly, just for our ears, he spoke, 'But if you ever need my help, you know I am yours.' He patted his chest, over his heart. 'You are here.'

I smiled. 'I know. You bejeweled great bladder of a man.'

He cuffed me and I fell over, feet quivering in the air.

I was dismissed for most of the day. He had his matters to discuss with sour-faced clergy and, though I had sat in many of these meetings, he made it plain he did not want me nigh today. That was all well. I had other matters myself to deal with.

There was nothing for it but to go back to the Spanish men's apartments and see if I could discern whom it might be, this blackmailer, for I was certain that the culprit must be there. Who else would wish to scheme against King Henry, for I was certain that Henry's wish to put aside his Spanish queen was making enemies of them.

Back in my apartments, I grabbed my cittern and slung the strap over my shoulder. I walked through the corridors, plucking a tune composed by Henry. I hummed along with it, my steps walking in rhythm to the tune. Henry was a fine composer. Sometimes his music had something of a melancholy air about it. I don't know why. He was ever a merry fellow, but the agonies of the state must confound him and his heart shewed itself in the notes. Aye me. I prattle. For I don't know Henry's heart as much as I thought I did. But it still seems to me that there is something sad that weighs on him. Perhaps it is the male heir he so desires, that he *must* have. And yet it might be even more than that.

I walked and plucked, plucked and walked. When I passed courtiers, they gave me a polite nod, standing away from me. Always, they stood away, as expected.

When a lady or two strolled by, I made it my business to particularly serenade them, following them until they yielded and stood, blushing, waiting for me to move on. I'd bow to them and stroll again, but when I looked back over my shoulder, one or two seemed intrigued. Who would not be so? I was the king's ear, his eyes, his mouth, his song. I bore his secrets, his woes, his merriness. Aye faith! I was his very conscience. And much work I had ahead for me, to be sure, if he intended to do this thing, to put aside the good queen for Lady Nan. And there were too many scheming men around him to encourage it, and none to tell him nay. That was *my* job, I supposed. A voice crying out in the wilderness. Would Henry listen? Not if it did not suit him, and protestations to the contrary, he would not even listen to me when his mind was set on a course.

I thought all these things as my fingers picked at the strings. Playing was second nature to me. I did not have to think on the playing. Not anymore. I learned the playing at my father's house. It was something to pass the time between my lessons or my chores. I never learnt the notation, but I could follow it easily enough. When you hear a thing, it is easier to play it, to embellish. Henry liked that about me and my fellow musicians, though I never accounted myself among that lot. Peter van Wilder and Giles Duwes were among Henry's favorites. When one of them appeared, I'd put away my instrument, for I could not hope to match them in quality. I was a sometimes musician. More often than not I styled my tunes to make fun of someone or something. But there were times when Henry liked me to play softly, liking my company and my strings. He preferred my lute, because its voice was softer and soothing. But the cittern was easier to carry. And so I wandered, like a minstrel, but instead of traveling from town to town for my meat, I traveled from corridor to hall to alcove . . . and thence to the apartments of the Spaniards.

And then . . . that little tingle at the back of my neck caused a shiver to travel down my spine, and, on instinct, I twirled round to look what might be after me.

There she was again. Lady Jane Perwick, twisting her long chain between her fingers. She stopped when I stopped. Or . . . *had* she already been there and I had not noticed that I had passed her? No. I was certain she had not been there.

I bowed, strummed a chord, and smiled. 'Are you following me, lady?'

'Following *you*? Who but a fool follows a fool?'

'Well . . . indeed. Do you need anything of me, Lady Jane?'

'So you know me.'

'Aye. I know nearly everyone at court.'

'So they say,' she said into her shoulder.

It was a remark I would usually pass over. But suddenly, everyone was suspect. What had she meant by that? And that sly expression. It was the sort of thing someone might wear when they knew something that they were certain *you* did not.

I girded m'self and took a step closer. 'Aye. I know many things and many people. But I don't know why you dog my steps or haunt this corridor.'

Her coy expression faded and a frown creased her brow. 'I'm not following you, Jester.'

'And yet, when I look, there you are.'

'You imagine things.' She turned away with a sweep of her skirts, but she stopped just as abruptly and turned back. 'I'd watch my own step, Jester, if I were you. You never know just who you are making into an enemy.' With a final bristling look, she turned again and hurried away.

God mend me. What was that? Another threat? For there was little reason for her to be in this particular corridor . . . except to follow me. But not artfully either, for surely she could have stayed well back and I might not have noticed her at all. No, she *wanted* me to notice her . . . to even admonish her?

Could she have something to do with Gonzalo's murder?

But how do I even imagine it? Could a woman cut a man's throat? Rush forward and slash it? Would they not get blood all over themselves? For I have helped butcher hogs and blood was aplenty if you did not do it right. The throat squirts it – but I did not want to think it, not about Gonzalo. I pressed my hand to my own throat. A gown would be covered in blood, and how would you explain it to your servants? And your servants would not keep quiet on it, that was a certainty.

You could stand behind the victim, I supposed, but would a woman be tall enough to reach?

But there was a bench! If he were sitting and she stood behind . . .

God's teeth! Anyone could have done it.

I swallowed, eased my breath. I had to comport myself. Lady Jane bore watching, aye. For her actions and words were suspicious. I did not like their tenor. But I had come to the Spanish wing to do my investigating and that I would do!

I was myself again. Clear-eyed, sharp-eared, ready to spy. I hoped.

As I neared a hall, I was witness to the strident tones of an argument in full throat, and it was English they were shouting, one with a decidedly Spanish accent and the other with the circuitous tones of an English lawyer or cleric.

I plastered myself against the wall and carefully peered past the edge of the doorway. Cleric, then. One Father John Kendrick himself, I believe. His face was painted with a cultured beard with its thin lines cropped close and precisely along his jawline, with two thin barbs of a mustache on either side of his pinched mouth, joining the beard. His brows seemed just as sculpted, and arched with their own mind on the matter, as punctuation to each of his carefully pronounced words.

'I tell you, *señor*,' said Kendrick, 'the king is anointed by God, and therefore his pronouncements must also be so.'

'This is the purview of His Holiness the Pope,' argued the Spanish gentleman, whom I knew by sight but not by name. 'It is only the pope who may speak for God in his capacity as the descendant of Peter.'

And so they went, back and forth like a tennis game. Kendrick drew breath to reply, no doubt lengthily and biliously. But thank Christ the Spanish courtier lifted his hand to stop him. 'There is too much at stake on both sides of the argument, my lord priest, and so let us not prolong that which will not give either of us the outcome we seek. But I do wish to discover what you might have heard regarding our dearly departed Don Gonzalo.'

Aha! I pressed tightly to the wall, making a mural of myself; *The Fool on a Somers Day Cavorting Amongst the Ladies*, it might have been called, had I been paint and plaster. I breathed slow and quiet in order to drink of every drop offered by cleric and lord.

'Nothing,' said Kendrick. 'It has fallen to as much silence as his corpse.'

My heart juddered. To talk so casually about someone I had so recently called my lover

. . . It was a sore thing indeed.

'I seem to have heard,' said the Spanish gentleman, 'that Don Gonzalo had been negotiating terms for the queen to return to Spain.'

'Ah,' Kendrick said, nodding, his lids falling low over his eyes. 'And so he *was* on the king's side.'

'He was on the side of Spain . . . as well he should be. Another shall be appointed to make certain that the queen's humiliation should be minimized, and that she shall leave for Spain with all dignity.'

'What makes you think she will leave England? If she leaves, she must leave the Princess Mary behind.'

'So the king would disown her, but would still leave a pawn on the board?'

'He has no legal heir. There is only Bessie Blount's bastard.'

'And that boy will never see a crown.'

'Would that be a threat from Spain?'

The Spanish gentleman paused, took a step back, and bowed most courteously. 'Not at all. It is merely an observation. The king is set for the Lady Anne and she is young and healthy.'

'Indeed. But was there not some *other* mischief your Don Gonzalo was about?'

'Whatever would you mean, my lord?'

'Was he not—'

But damn me. My foot slipped, making but a soft sound, yet enough for both their heads to turn and see my face peering around the doorway. The Spanish gentleman drew his sword. 'Sirrah!' he called, his steel gleaming in the candlelight. 'Come forth and show yourself!'

I gulped my heart back into my chest, plucked hard on the cittern likened to some Spanish tune, and stepped into view. 'My lords.' I bowed. ''Tis only the king's fool.'

Kendrick breathed a sigh of relief, but the Spanish gentleman narrowed his eyes and it was a long time until he sheathed his sword. 'The king's fool indeed! Why do you spy on innocent conversations?'

'Why sir, I *only* spy on *innocent* conversations. For that is the meat of the court and I would feed the court, sir, so that it does not starve.'

'I see,' he sneered. He reached for his purse hanging from his belt. 'How much?'

'My lord, you insult me. I am paid good and heartily by the king to fool about in court. I need not take coins from his courtiers. Or those courtiers that are *not* his. But . . .' I said hastily, before he drew his hand away from his purse, 'a groat or two for the poor box. Aye, that I can carry all on my own, being a strong soul.'

He scowled, but now he did not seem to be as suspicious of me. He dug out the coins and tossed them to me. I caught them expertly. 'Bless you, my lord. The Church thanks you.'

His lip twisted sourly and there was nothing for it but for me to take my leave. Had either of those gentlemen schemed to blackmail me? What other thing was Don Gonzalo at that I had missed with my untimely disruption?

'Incautious foot,' I scolded my appendage. 'Why so chatty at so inconvenient a time?' I stomped it on the floor, but if punishment I sought, it would have been mine as well. As it was, I limped on through the corridors, thinking about their conversation.

And so, Don Gonzalo was looking to ease the queen's pain by offering a dignified exit from court. But they did not know our queen. She would never leave Henry, nor their daughter. England had welcomed her all those years ago and she loved it as her own kin. And further, *they* loved *her*. I wonder if Henry truly understood that, that they would never accept Lady Nan as queen for usurping the place of Queen Catherine. Henry could devise all the Scripture he wanted to serve his cause, but what would the people care for that?

Oh, Gonzalo. Could you have been murdered for more than your dallying with me? Could this letter of blackmail have only been a ruse? After all, the blackmailer had not come to the garden, nor sent me another missive with further instructions.

I scoured about me, at the benign faces, the blank expressions, the crafty ones, the obvious ones . . . and decided that the court was full of dragons, lounging lazily on their hoard until they felt threatened and poised themselves to strike at just the right time.

Which dragons must I slay to protect Henry? And which to protect myself?

SIX

Marion was in my chamber mid-afternoon, begging for further details. I had little to offer, except for what I had overheard earlier from Father Kendrick and the Spanish man.

She held Nosewise in her arms, scratching his head as he licked at her face. 'Will, you must find out what other thing Don Gonzalo was about that the priest worried over.'

'And how can I do that? Who would tell *me*?'

'You can't just ask people. You must make them *wish* to tell you.'

'You think me a sorcerer rather than a jester?'

'Oh, come now. I've seen you plenty of times beguile someone into telling you something they did not wish to divulge. You did it to me when first we met.'

'Did I?'

She set Nosewise down and brushed the dog hair from her gown. 'You don't remember? I was sitting at the edge of one of the king's great gatherings. And you were trotting about like Nosewise, making a jackass of yourself as usual when you spotted me. I was terrified as to what you would say.'

'You were?' I softened and took her hand. 'Oh, Marion.'

'Terrified. You have no idea, Will Somers, how frightening a loud pronouncement from you was to a courtier. And there I was, all alone and quite timid.'

I laughed at the last.

'At the time,' she assured. 'And so, instead of some loud insult at my expense, you were kind and sweet and spoke low to me, asking if I were well and enjoying myself. And the more you talked in that soft way, the more relaxed I became and talked and talked to you. I never talked so much to anyone at court up till then. There is magic in your speech.'

'Honesty, Marion. It was honesty. No wonder you didn't recognize the language of it spoken at court.'

'You were probably trying to get me into your bed.'

'I was. But not in that instant. And we are so close now.'

'And so you must find someone close to Don Gonzalo.'

'Ursula?'

'Someone Spanish, perhaps.'

'He must have a clerk. Or a groom!' That was an excellent idea. And I told her so, kissing her at the same time. I thanked her and headed out the door, thinking how I was to pass through the gates of the Spaniard's chambers, when she stopped me.

'But what of Lady Jane?' Aye, I had told her of that, too, and she frowned with a finger laid to the side of her jaw. 'Is it merely your fancy, or was she up to naught good?'

'I'm of two minds on it, Marion, dependent upon the hour. On the one hand, it could be entirely coincidental, and I was making more of it than there was, being suddenly suspicious of everyone. But, on the other hand . . . there she was. Twice.'

'Well,' she said carefully. 'If it is thrice, it shall bear some thinking. Meantime, get you to the Spaniards.'

I bowed to her and set off. Hurrying through the corridors, a dark shape emerged from the shadows and startled me like the Devil himself rising out of the smoky pits. But it wasn't the Devil. Only his apprentice, Cromwell.

'Master Crumbled-Well,' I said, posturing.

'Keep your caustic words to yourself, Somers. I have a proposition for you.'

God's beard. Cromwell must want something dear if he were trying to make friends with me. I thought to make a quip, but my throat went dry and I could not have wrenched the words from my mouth even if called upon by God Himself. Instead, I waited, nose high, ears acute.

'You think I don't like you, don't you, Somers? Because you call me names and point a finger at my doings. But I am not afraid of your words or their barbs. And it is not because I am invulnerable. Oh no. Every man has their vulnerabilities.'

I narrowed my eyes just that much. No. It couldn't be him, could it? Did Cromwell want me to spy on the king for him? To what end? He already had his ear. Was he intimating that he knew more about me than I would have liked? Or was it his best weapon to make men *think* he knew more and was merely holding his tongue? Oh, wicked Master Cromwell. You played a tune whilst the Devil did his dance.

He did not wait for me to speak, but went on. 'Please don't take that as any sort of threat, Master Somers.' *Master* Somers was it now? And his assurances only seemed to pile upon the mistrust I had of him. I could do naught but listen. 'It isn't. As children of God Almighty, we are all vulnerable and unto Him must we subjugate ourselves, as we must to our masters. To the king. For he is master of us all. *Both* of us, Will.'

'Well, *Thomas* – since we are using our Christian names – you speak the truth of it. The king is my master and I am his man. All of court know this.'

'Of course they do. Would it surprise you to know that I admire you?'

'Very much so.'

'But I do.'

I almost expected him to approach me and throw his arm about me, but thank Christ he did not.

'I do admire you, Will. That is why I have this proposal.'

At last. What great boon would he ask of me? What thing would it be to cause the king to pull my limbs apart and set my poor, ugly head upon a pike to stare endlessly and sense-lessly from the ramparts of London Bridge?

'My proposal is . . . to continue to do what you do. To advise the king to move wisely in this course on his Great Matter. To advise him to caution and to do what is best for the kingdom.'

A knife-sharp rejoinder was ready on my tongue. Until I reckoned what it was he said. 'What?'

'You are the soul of the king. I have not failed to notice it. Tell him what his soul should hear.'

'My Lord Cromwell, what makes you think that my mind follows your reasoning where this Great Matter is concerned? Though I am but a poor uneducated man, it is my sense that the kingdom would greatly benefit from the king keeping Catherine by his side. And though I bow to the king's command, it would be my fervent prayer to send Lady Nan on her way. Why would you wish for me to undermine the very thing you are persisting in teaching him?'

He smiled. Would the crocodiles in the Nile recognize a brother in that smile? 'I only want what's good for the kingdom, Will. As do you. And for the king, of course. And the king needs a male heir.'

'But how could what I say help that cause?'

'I said I admire you. Your counsel is wise. And the king hears the words of many counselors. Yours might be a little more . . . strident . . . than the rest.'

'But . . .'

'It is simplicity itself, Will. Do as you are doing. Counsel the king. We both will save his soul.' He nodded once to me, and walked sedately away.

Cuds-me. What had happened? Was Cromwell agreeing with me . . . or I with him?

In a manor house, and as a servant of such, one had only to maneuver around the gossip and romantic entanglements, and the worst thing that could happen was to get a bruised chin from a fist or get sacked and set adrift along the road. But at court, it was a viper's nest of intrigue where a man's life hung in the balance from some jealous courtier, or if one said the wrong thing to the wrong man. Was I really suited to this life? Was I able to tread carefully over the river stones and make it safe to the other side, or would I plunge into the churning waters bestirred by men such as Cromwell?

I blinked for a time, just thinking, weighing . . . until I brushed thoughts of Cromwell aside. I had to. After all, I had a killer to find. I considered. *Best start at the best place, Will*, I told myself. *Who benefits from Gonzalo's death?* I couldn't answer that, for I did not know what Gonzalo was about.

I made my way back through the corridors, back to the Spanish chambers with their guards who eyed me with the utmost suspicion. But I raised my cittern and plucked the strings. I had learned a Spanish song some years ago from the queen and I played it now, humming, for I could not pronounce the words.

One of the guards relaxed from his stiff posture, and I strummed and moved closer until the other succumbed too.

Of course, I didn't know how to proceed. What if they didn't speak English? How would I make them understand?

And then the door opened a crack. A Spanish lady was standing near the door, receiving orders in that speeding language, tripping over itself to get to the next word, when out of nowhere came running a small creature behind me. And it was only when it slipped between the doors and the tail disappeared that I realized it was Nosewise! How had he got loose?

I dived for the door, calling the dog's name. A woman rushed out of the doors, the guards got entangled with her, and I slipped in, running after that naughty dog who seemed to have saved the day.

'Nosewise!' I hissed, scouring the corners and alcoves for the little cur. Behind me, I heard the sound of running feet. I spotted the creature behind a curtain, whereupon I snatched him up, held him against my chest, and ducked behind said curtain as the guards rumbled past. I kissed the side of his snout. 'Good boy,' I whispered. 'Now. Stay close to me, eh?'

I peeked behind the drapery and saw no one in the corridor. I moved carefully forward toward Gonzalo's chamber. When I reached it, I held the dog close and knocked.

I didn't know what I expected but it certainly wasn't Father John Kendrick. And yet, here he was.

He answered the door and stared at me a good long time. He obviously didn't expect me either and I could very well see the cogwheels behind his eyes moving into place.

'Somers? What are you doing here?'

'My lord,' I said, bowing. 'I've come looking for Don Gonzalo's groom.'

'Why?'

'Well . . . truly. I don't think everything must be confessed to a priest, sir.'

He narrowed his eyes. 'He's not here.'

'Oh? Might you be acquainted with where he's got to?' I tried to look past him with keen eyes, but could discern no one else lurking in the shadows. I turned Nosewise this way and that like a puppet, in search.

'I'm not your servant, Somers. Go away.' And he slammed the door in my face.

And so. Father Kendrick. Again. What was he doing in Gonzalo's quarters? Searching his papers? Why was he being allowed to do so? An English priest in a Spanish embassy?

There was nothing for it but to continue my search. If only these men here spoke English. If only I spoke even a smattering of Spanish. I could try Latin, but I didn't know enough and who could be certain about these gentlemen . . . although they were strong in their religion and likely knew their Latin well enough.

And there, coming from the other direction, was the clerk I had met earlier, Francis de Aguilar. I bowed to him, and he stopped. 'Oh,' he said. 'You're the fool.'

'Indeed, sir. Could you do me the service of directing me to the groom of Don Gonzalo?'

'Groom? I do not know this word.'

I reached into my mind for the proper Latin. 'A . . . *kalator*?'

'Ah. *Sí*. Rodrigo Muñoz. The poor man. He is in mourning.'

'And where would that be?'

'In the Church of the Observant Friars.'

'I thank you, *señor*.' I bowed again, and held the dog under my arm as I rushed back down the corridor and headed for the church.

The friary church was adjoined to the palace. Henry and Catherine were married there. The Princess Mary was christened there. It was Henry's church more than Westminster ever was, but it was also Catherine's, for they supported her against this divorce. It was too bad. They were pious men in this friary, where there were so few on this island of ours, and I feared for them.

I released Nosewise and sent him on his way before I stepped into the cool, dark interior. I saw friars moving about, like ghosts in their gray habits, but I think I was looking for the man kneeling at the rood screen.

Thank Christ I was wearing no more bells, for I did not want the sounds to ring out in the desperately quiet silence as I made my way down the nave.

I got as close as I dared to whisper, 'Señor Muñoz?'

A face of a carven statue. Perfect features and bright

though saddened eyes of hazel. Dark hair curled just so behind his ears. A noble nose, noble lips. A handsome creature this, made for a tumble.

God's beard, Will. This is a church! A man's eye will wander even in a church, I feared.

He got to his feet and looked at me. 'You are the fool.' His accent was thick enough to cut with a knife, but thank God he spoke English.

I bowed. 'Will Somers. And you are . . . were . . . the groom to Don Gonzalo?'

'I do not know this word . . . groom.'

'You were his man, his attendant *personalem*.'

His eyes filled with tears again and I put my arm around him to steer him out of the church before the friars noticed us.

In the courtyard under a pleasant autumn sky, he broke down, weeping on my shoulder. I patted him whilst searching for anyone watching us. Finally, he drew back.

'Er . . . your attendance upon him was . . .' I searched for the words. 'I know it was very sad. Were you with him a good many years?'

He sniffed. 'Not so many years. He was a good master. Good to me.' A sob broke through again, and I patted him on the back condolingly.

'There was once an older man kind to me. He, er, taught me much about life. And . . . other things.'

Muñoz's face rose, tear streaks etched on his cheeks. 'Taught you about life?'

'Took me in hand . . . if you will.' *Christ's toes, Will. What were you confessing to this man?* A servant can have deep feelings for his master without any poking under the sheets. Except that I was as broken as Muñoz when my older patron passed from this world. I took a breath, and tried, 'Was he more . . . *personalem* . . . than anyone might have thought?' I asked quietly.

He stared at me in fear. I knew that look. 'Ease your mind, *señor*. I, too, was . . . erm . . . *personalem* with Gonzalo.'

Now his eyes scoured me, running higly-pigly over my features, no doubt trying to discern the truthfulness of my admission. I shrugged, holding out my arms, for I could not be called a handsome man. My beauty was in my character. Or so I liked to think.

'I was with him last, I think. I . . . I also found him.'

'Oh.' It was a sigh, an expression of shared grief. 'I knew he was meeting someone. We . . . we were *amantes*. Lovers. Sometimes. He was my *señor*, my master, mostly.'

'I'm sorry.'

He wiped his nose with his finger.

'Why would anyone wish to kill Gonzalo?' I asked.

He shook his head. 'I have been thinking on this myself. He . . . he was an important man.'

'Aye. Anyone belonging to the imperial ambassador's retinue must be important. Do you know what he was about . . . what he was entrusted to do? Was it about . . . King Henry's divorce?'

He looked around again. We were quite alone. Unless the trees themselves were spies.

'*Sí*. It was the most important business.'

'But why kill *him* particularly? Do you see my meaning? Surely there were others who were *more* important to this business.'

'I do not know, Señor Somers.'

Señor Somers. I rather liked the sound of that. But I said, instead, 'Will. Call me Will. And I shall call you . . . Rodrigo, eh?'

He nodded, even tried to smile amid his sadness.

'And so, Rodrigo, my handsome friend . . .' He smiled shyly, cheeks blooming with color. Ah, such a sweet visage. 'It is important to me to know who killed our friend. Can you spare some time to talk to me of this?'

Nosewise took that moment to run up to us and leap into Rodrigo's arms. The poor man was so startled he let out a little yelp. But that most precious of dogs began licking his face, and Rodrigo could no longer be startled or sad.

'Who is this creature?' he asked, giving him a grateful smile.

'I must confess that he is mine. His name is Nosewise because, as you see, he pokes his nose into everything. Much like his master.'

Rodrigo did not relieve himself of the dog, but found comfort in holding him. I let him. Without more words spoken, we retreated to my rooms, and it was there that he finally let the dog down. Nosewise sniffed his way all around Rodrigo's shoes, hose and coat and, when he was satisfied, he found his basket, circled within it, and settled in.

'He is an affable dog,' said my guest. And then he raised his eyes to me. 'Like his master.'

He fell upon me, his mouth on mine. The rough feel of his cheek with its stubble always aroused, and I kissed him heartily back before I got hold of myself. I whipped my face away from him.

'We cannot do this here in the mid of the day. But I would be agreeable this evening.'

'I'm sorry,' he said, flushing with embarrassment.

'Oh, never fear that. We are the sort of men who must rush in when we can when we find an available and willing partner. It is I who am sorry about Gonzalo.'

'*Sí.*' He nodded. 'I fear my feelings were stronger for him than his was for me. Of course, my status is lower. We were . . . the English word? . . . *convenient* . . . for one another.'

As Marion was convenient to me when I lusted for the taste of Woman. As I was to her to get the love of a man.

'I'm afraid, my good sir, that we are the kind of men who live between the shadows of such convenience. Aye me. I am sad for the both of us. Not for this life, but for the one so carelessly wasted. The one we both mourn.'

He sniffed. '*Sí.* Wasted.'

I got in closer and he raised his face to me. I glanced once at those lips and looked away. 'You see, my dear Rodrigo, I am looking for a reason why he was killed. So I can find the cur who did it.'

'You are looking for the murderer? How can I help you?'

Could I trust him? I was going to. 'My friend, not long after his death, I received a missive, extorting me. Telling me that they would make known my relationship with Gonzalo if I did not spy on the king for them.'

'Oh!' He jumped to his feet. 'This is horrific!'

'Yes. And I was to meet them in a certain garden at midnight two days after I was with your master to discuss what they wanted.'

'What happened? Who was it?'

I shook my head. 'They did not arrive. I have heard no more from them. I wonder if they, too, are dead.'

Slowly, he sat again, his mouth agape. He crossed himself and murmured a prayer. 'That is strange.'

'Yes, it is. I can think of no other reason why my blackmailer should have stopped sending me messages . . . or even meeting me. Though I know they could see me at any time. I am nearly more visible than the king himself.'

He stared at me. And now I could see it all in his eyes. 'What the hell was I doing with a jester?' he must be thinking. A man so visible, so envied *and* feared. I measured the man. Would he excuse himself, run in fear? Would he disappear never to be seen more? Either made sense.

I waited.

He ran his hand over his face and dropped that hand to his lap. 'This is difficult.'

'Yes, I know it is. It's all right, Rodrigo. If you must flee from me, I will understand.'

He blinked. 'Flee from you? Why should I do that? Do you want me to go?'

'No, of course not.'

'I thought you wanted my help.'

'By Christ, I do.'

'Then . . . what can I do?'

'What can you do? Why . . . be my spy.'

SEVEN

Rodrigo said, before I could mention it, 'You should come to my lord's apartments. You should see for yourself. We can see together.'

Yes. I wanted to see for myself. To look one last time and to touch the things Gonzalo had touched. Perhaps I was not through with the memory of him any more than Rodrigo was.

'Can you steal me in there?'

'I . . .' He faltered. '*I* can go. But how to bring you? How should we explain it?'

'Aye, that is a problem.' I looked about, trying to discern the answer from the very stones of the palace walls. 'You will simply take me in. And if we encounter anyone, there is a piece of music you know that Lord de Yscar wished for me to have . . . since he and I were discussing music.'

'Will that be enough?'

'With God's grace it will suffice.'

But I sent up an additional prayer anyway.

We walked down the corridor, side by side. At first, we were silent, filled with nerves as we were, but it suddenly seemed absurd to observe me, the jester, silent. And so I engaged Rodrigo in nonsense conversation, telling him to laugh occasionally, for I could not think of any of the usual prattle I do.

I still had my cittern over my shoulder, and I brought it round to the front so that I could pluck and walk. After all, the guards seemed used to me doing so.

We came to the Spanish apartments, and though the guards glanced at me, they were familiar enough now with my few brief moments here, so I was allowed through. We had worried for naught.

I urged Rodrigo to enter Gonzalo's apartment first . . . just in case Father Kendrick was still skulking about. With a whispered word from Rodrigo, I entered and closed the door behind me. 'Where are his papers and such?' I asked.

'Well . . .' He cast about; the room had been gone over fairly thoroughly. His coffers had been opened and clothes and other things hanging from them. His desk had been ransacked and his writing things disturbed. Even the mattress of his bed and its bolster had been turned over.

'What disgrace is here?' I cried.

'They were looking for his secret papers.'

'That Father Kendrick!'

'The English priest? *Sí*, he has been here often in talks with my master. But I was always sent away when he met with him.'

'Then all is lost.'

Rodrigo smiled grimly. 'Not so.' He strode to one of the coffers and knelt beside it. Carefully, lovingly, he folded the linen shirts and nightshirts that had belonged to our mutual lover. I came to stand beside him and ran my hand over the pieces. I had only had the one night with Gonzalo. But Rodrigo, being in love with the fellow, felt the loss that much more keenly. Poor Rodrigo. I dropped my hand to his shoulder and squeezed it in sympathy.

After he had carefully repacked the coffer, he closed the lid, pressed his fingers to the carvings on the side of it, and a click sounded before a small drawer slid out.

'Rodrigo . . .' I breathed.

He reached into the tiny compartment and pulled out some folded papers. He unfolded one and flattened it out on his thigh. It was scratched out in Latin. Rodrigo's eyes widened. 'This was dated only a few days ago. Listen to this part,' he said quietly, reading it haltingly:

> *Both the king and his lady, I am assured, look upon their future marriage as certain, as if that of the queen had actually been dissolved. Preparations are being made for the wedding . . .*

'This was written by Eustace Chapuys . . . and addressed to the Holy Roman Emperor.'

'God's teeth,' I muttered. 'What else?'

'This is a paper written by my master. See here.'

I implore Your Majesty to use all the cunning at your disposal. I shall contact the spy to send word back to you of plots from this English king to put aside his Good Queen, and we shall put a stop to it by any means necessary . . .

Rodrigo dropped the letter to his thighs. 'What does he mean? What "means" should he deem necessary? Oh, Holy Mother! What has my poor master plotted?'

'And more importantly, who is this spy?'

He shook his head, still staring at the paper. 'I do not know.'

'Is Henry's life in danger? I must warn him if it is. But how to do so and not implicate m'self? Cuds-me.'

'I do not know. What are we to do?'

'I'll think on it. What's that next letter?'

Rodrigo unfolded it but it was torn in half. He read only what was there. 'It says something about the Princess Mary. Something about Spain and a ship.' He shook his head. Because most of it is torn away, I cannot make sense of it.'

'A sarding shame is what that is.'

He stuffed them into the opening of his doublet, and we both hurriedly searched into all the hidden places Rodrigo was privy to, but we found naught else.

Finally, we gave up. Rodrigo wanted to clean the room, and so I helped him put back all the objects so carelessly thrown about. After an hour – and I worried that every passing moment would find us discovered – he deemed the room repaired to his satisfaction. After all, the truckle bed, under the four-poster, was where he usually laid his head.

We moved toward the door to leave at last when a figure appeared in the doorway.

'What are you doing here?' Kendrick!

Rodrigo stiffened and raised his chin. 'I live here.'

'You were told to stay away.'

'And what was I to do? My things are here. My clothes. And very disturbed they have been.'

He stood his ground and Kendrick could do nothing but fidget and sneer. Until he cast his eye upon me. 'Somers. *You* don't live here.'

'But all the palace is mine. Uncle Harry has said so.'

'You disgust me, Somers. Your useless prattling, your vile indiscretions, your mockery. There is no place for you in a godly court.'

'If I ever find one, Father, then I shall assuredly *not* go there.'

'You think your cleverness will save you from the Fires? I know your kind, Somers.'

'Fore God! Did he know about me? Oh, I had been far too free with m'self. I had to tread with better care.

'Fires to warm me,' I said, rubbing my hands together. And then I turned, bending over and facing my bum toward him and rubbing those cheeks. 'And to warm me all over, my lord.'

'If I had a switch, I'd show *you*.'

'What would you switch, my lord priest? Your nose for your knob? Or your ear for your arse? That would make for a mass to behold.'

'Infidel! Begone!'

'That's what we're trying to do, but some talkative cleric is in our way.'

We moved forward until Kendrick stopped us once more. 'What is that? Give me that paper.'

The letters Rodrigo had stuffed into his doublet hadn't stayed stuffed and were peeking out.

Kendrick lunged for it and managed to grasp a letter. He unfolded and started to read when a streak of white flashed before us and snatched the letter right out of his grasping hand.

I blinked. Was it a ghost? A spirit?

The growl and the rattle of his collar gave him away. Nosewise! You wonderful, scrappy, escaping little cur!

Nosewise shook it as if it were a rat, and Kendrick dived for him, trying to wrest it from his jaws. But the little dog proved he was the better, and dodged the priest, thinking it a game.

Picking up a candlestick, Kendrick raised it to hurl at the

dog. I leapt and grabbed his arm, dragging it down, and his projectile missed the mark.

'Damn you, Somers.'

'Oh, not yet, sir.'

'That's your mongrel, isn't it? I want that paper!'

Nosewise had already torn from the room, heading back to mine, I hoped. 'And you can have it, my lord. Just as soon as the hound is done with it. Though, by the time it passes through him, I doubt it will be very legible. I'll be sure to save it, though, just for you.'

Kendrick wore as foul an expression as ever a man could wear. He got in close to me, and nearly growled like a dog himself. 'I've got my eye on you, *Jester*. Make no mistake, if I decide to rid the court of you, not even the king can save you.'

'It would be amusing seeing you try.'

'Mark me. Your days are numbered.'

'I should hope so. Else how can we tell which day from the next?'

He moved in even closer and said in a dark voice, 'I know about you, Somers. I know . . . things.'

It startled me to silence again. I said nothing in reply, but raised my chin as Rodrigo had done, for in truth, my voice caught in my throat.

His eyes narrowed as he glared and, finally, he jerked away before he squared on Rodrigo. He pointed to his doublet. 'You have papers that don't belong to you.'

Rodrigo slapped his chest, covering the letters with his hand. 'And they don't belong to you.'

'These are matters for the English court.'

'I think not. Rather, they belong to the Spanish ambassador.'

Oh, such a wretched visage Kendrick offered. For he could not argue that. Rodrigo kept his hand over his chest and we sidled out of the room like crabs. Then, once free, we ran like the Devil were after us down the corridor.

Once we got outside, we stopped in a courtyard, gulping in air.

Rodrigo turned a worried face to me. 'He threatened you. Are you not afraid?'

'I've been threatened by better men than him. It has always come to naught.'

But even as we got to the serving hall to get us something to eat, I began to think on Father Kendrick. What was his meaning? *Did* he know about me? Was he the one who had killed Gonzalo and threatened me?

Was *he* the spy?

I was not myself as we supped in the servants' hall on bread and cheese. Edward was there, and he tried to beguile me with some cold chicken, but gave up after he saw I wasn't interested in the meat or in him for the nonce.

Rodrigo was silent as well, measuring my mood. After I washed my hands in the basin, I looked to him. 'I must find the king and attend to him.'

'I will make enquiries,' he said thoughtfully. 'About the . . . the spy,' he said, mouthing the last instead of speaking it aloud. Yes, he could go about the Spanish men and find any that might have had association with Gonzalo. He could talk to the other servants. Servants always knew.

'Before you go,' I said quietly, 'know you anything of a woman, a Lady Jane?'

Rodrigo blinked, thinking. 'I *think* this lady – a pretty one with light hair? She came to see my master on the day he died.'

I breathed hard. 'What was her business?'

'It was strange.' But then his eyes widened and his jaw fell open. He crossed himself. '*Madre de Dios!*'

'What is it?' I got in close, scanning about for listening ears.

'I thought nothing of it at the time, but now . . .' He grabbed my arm. 'Will . . . she asked . . . about *you*.'

EIGHT

*J*esu. About *me*? Something was not right. Something was clearly not right. But I had little time to ponder it, for the next day, Friday, was the day of Gonzalo's memorial, and I could think of naught else. The court dressed in black. Bells in the Church of the Observant Friars tolled. Eustace Chapuys, the imperial ambassador, wore his usual stern face, but all the Spanish contingent was there.

I couldn't recall the last time I had felt so sad. Our encounter had been brief, Gonzalo's and mine, but he'd left a mark on my soul. He seemed genuinely to be a kind man, a thoughtful man. I would have liked to have spent more time with him, just drinking wine, playing chess perhaps, talking. I would have liked him to speak more of Spain, his lands, what his household was like.

I remember when Queen Catherine spoke of Spain with fondness and with a streak of sadness for never being able to see it again, of her parents King Ferdinand and Queen Isabella. I imagined them as great royal personages, dignified, regal.

Oh, Henry could be regal, and he could even be called upon to be dignified. But once you've seen a man on his close stool, well . . .

In Queen Catherine's eyes, I saw that she knew her duty to her lord husband and her God meant that she must sacrifice the life she had known. After all, it was the duty of all princesses to be bargained with and be sent away to unite countries and keep the peace. What great responsibilities we laid upon the laps of these young girls. Did they know? Could they have imagined?

And now Gonzalo was to return to the land of his birth.

There were great benedictions from Cardinal Wolsey in the courtyard. He in his mitre raised his hands to all of us and shouted out his Latin prayers. The Spaniards, stoic but with wet faces, raised their eyes to God. For the question still remained. Who had killed him? What English hand had done it and when would the culprit be found?

I, too, wondered that.

There were hours of prayers and today of all days was hot with a yellow sun above us. Should not a memorial be shrouded in dark clouds and rain? It seemed that all English funerals were thus remembered. But I suppose, for a Spaniard, sunshine was more to God's taste.

And anyway, it was not a funeral, but a memorial. Dear Gonzalo was to travel by barge down the Thames to a seaport, where he would sail to Spain and be laid to rest there. Ambassador Chapuys was insistent that he not be buried on English soil. This caused a bit of an uproar in Henry's chambers, but in the end, it was decided that the Spanish in this case must be allowed to do what they liked.

I dreaded the thought of what they did to Gonzalo's poor corpse, for this traveling would be days, and to preserve a body was to desecrate it; eviscerate, stuff it, drape herbs about it, cover it in lead. Pour soul. Poor lovely man.

And then I looked about for any sign of the queen, and my heart boiled with anger that she was not even allowed this little thing, to bid a fellow countryman Godspeed. I wondered vaguely if Henry had wanted to allow it, but his lawyers and clerics had advised against it. Curse them.

After a mass was held in the Church of the Observant Friars, there was much ceremony carrying the draped body in its coffin to the barge.

Farewell, Gonzalo. May you rest eternally in God's grace. You didn't deserve this. And I give my oath to you that I will find the culprit and give you your justice.

Only I and the Spanish contingent had remained at the wharf and watched until his barge disappeared around a bend of the river.

The clouds moved in then, and the proper English weather with it. It rained at last.

I was glad that the court had not gathered as usual. For I was in mourning for my friend. I knew that the English court didn't care if a Spaniard died. They didn't know him. But at least they were somewhat respectful.

I stayed in Henry's company because he wished it. But after a time, he shooed his men away, and he offered me a game of chess in his withdrawing chamber. Only occasionally did an usher enter to see to the fire, to fill our goblets. We drank ale, for neither of us wished to get drunk.

I knew Henry would have rather ridden today, been out of doors, even in the rain. He liked to move about, did Henry, a man who loved his exercise. But he somehow sensed my mood as well. Perhaps all of our minds were on Spain, as Queen Catherine, our own Spanish princess who had become the English queen, languished behind closed doors.

'I've taken your knight, Will,' he said.

'By the mass, Uncle. I am not paying attention.'

'You can't play a decent game, Somers, if you don't pay attention to the board.'

I picked up my black queen, examining the exquisite carving of the thing. A mere playing piece, and here it was, the finest object of the artisan's hand. 'Do you ever wonder, Harry?'

'Wonder what? Are you playing that piece?'

I rolled the queen betwixt my fingers. 'Do you ever wonder about God's Providence? We are each a piece on His chessboard.'

'We have free will.'

'Do we? It seems a foolish thing to give something so precious to the likes of Man. We are all too much of an idiot to know what to do with it. Wouldn't it rather be better if God simply laid out His plan to us and we were to follow it, like a garden path?'

He shook his head indulgently. 'Well, Somers, as someone who has spent a great deal of his time in the study of God's plan and His words, I can tell you that it is a complicated thing. Like architecture,' and he raised his hands to the ceiling. 'Observe, if you will, the art of Man, given through God's gifts, the ability to create . . . this.'

I looked up as he did at the wooden ceiling with its fan-vaulted roof and carved pendants. 'It is amazing, Harry.'

'It is. Not only decorative, but it keeps out the weather.

Masons and carpenters worked all their lives to learn this craft of beauty and practicality. This was God's plan for them.'

'As it was that it was His plan I come to court.'

'Truly, and I have thanked Him most prodigiously for that.'

I put my hand to my heart, which burned with sudden tenderness for Henry. 'I'm touched, Harry.'

'I pray for all my subjects. But for some, those prayers are more fervent.' He smiled. 'The point is, none of us can know the Almighty's plan that He has set out for us ever before our birth, but it is up to us to say "yes", to have the free will to take the first steps in His mighty course. Yours was to be a court jester – and so he gave you wit and verve. And mine was to be king. Though that was never *my* thought on the matter. And least when I was a boy.'

I set the chess piece down and leaned on the table with both arms crossed. 'I wish I'd known you as a young boy, Harry.'

'Why is that?'

'Oh . . . I think we would have been fast friends.'

'Do you truly think so?'

'Though . . . sadly, I would not have been allowed to play with you. But I do play with you now.'

He stared at the board, but I sensed rather that he was looking beyond it with that wistful look in his eyes. 'I wish there had been more playing when I was a boy.'

'You didn't get to play? Oh, poor little Prince Harry. Always at his books and tutelage.'

'You don't know how right you are, Will.'

I gazed at the man. And I pictured him as a lonely little boy with only adults as company. Not even allowed to play with his older brother, who had his own army of tutors, for he was to be king. King Arthur. Would he have had his Round Table? I wondered. Would he have served his Camelot with fairness and courage? He had married Queen Catherine . . . and then he died. And then poor Prince Harry had become the heir, and then king before his time.

I glanced down at the chessboard and thought of all the manipulations there were. From God first, then kings, then lords. Aye, we were all likened to these pieces. Some could

move most anywhere they liked, but others had strange directions they *had* to take. For a man born a fool could never be
a king, while a man born a king could most certainly be a
fool.

NINE

Rodrigo had left the letters with me and the next day, Saturday, I scoured them all, trying to make sense of them. But especially the partial letter about Princess Mary. My Latin was not good. And so I made neither head nor tail of it. Something about a ship and the King of Spain . . . who was also the Holy Roman Emperor.

But then there was the problem of Lady Jane. Why did she want to know about me? And why ask Gonzalo, of all people? The only conclusion I could draw was that she knew. She knew about him and me. And since no one at court could simply come out with the truth, she had played her coy games with Gonzalo. And perhaps he dismissed her, was rude to her, or worse, *ignored* her. And she, in her anger, had killed him and sworn to blackmail me. It made sense.

And yet . . . I was unsatisfied with it. Perhaps some of it was true, but to know which part made my head ache. It was the notion of a woman doing the murdering that fouled my mind on it, a woman of nobility. How could this be? Yet, thinking of someone like Lady Nan, she had the anger to do it . . . but *would* she? It seems that a noble lady would . . . get a servant to do her bidding. But would a servant kill a lord?

This is not what a jester should be spending his time on.

I looked in on Henry after a few hours, but he was as sour as he had been before. After a time, I feared not my quips, my rhymes, nor my music stirred the furrow from his brow, and so, before I got a kick for it, I left his company. How I longed to comfort the queen and Princess Mary, but I was not allowed.

I wondered if I should harry Lady Nan . . . until it occurred to me instead to enquire of one of her ladies, Ursula to be precise, what I might have neglected to talk to her about before. And so, with cittern in my hands, I plucked a tune here and there, making my way to the chambers of Lady Nan.

She was not there, but I was directed to the Great Garden. She was surrounded by her attendants, and they were making amusements on the lawn, playing hoodman's blind.

She was not participating, but instead, sitting on a chair under shade, watching them distractedly. I tried to stealthily bypass her, but her eye caught mine and she called out, 'Somers!'

Cods. I presented myself before m'lady and bowed low, the perfect courtier.

'Dear Lady Nan.' Her smile was perfunctory. And even though I had begrudged her only moments ago, my resolve began to wither when in her presence, for she was just a woman, after all. 'What vexes you, m'lady?'

She sighed, watching her carefree ladies cavort, while her cavorting days were behind her. At least . . . with other lads. 'I am passing sad today, Somers.'

'But my lady, you have your high place at court, your jewels . . . the love of the highest head in the land.'

She motioned to the stool beside her and I lowered myself to the cushion.

'But what will come of it? Will I ever be married, Somers?'

'You can call me Will.'

'That's right.' She wore a genuine smile and leaned over her chair toward me. 'For you are my friend now.'

'Of course, m'lady. Whomsoever is loved by the king, is so loved by me.'

She chuckled ironically. 'That is a two-edged blade. I know well your meaning.'

I lowered my face. I did not wish to lie. For I also loved my lady queen.

'So you know me as well.'

She shook her head. 'I do not begrudge you, Will. But know this. The king wants a son. And I can give it to him.'

I nodded. 'I know, my lady.'

'But surely you are not here to see to me.'

'You have reckoned that as well. I am here to see Lady Ursula again.'

'Why so interested in that particular lady? I have heard that you are besotted with another lady, one who works in the shadows of court.'

'Know you that? It is a sacred love I have. For it is one of the king's lambs, a lovely woolly creature, so lighthearted. But alas. She is smitten by clover.'

She swatted me on the shoulder. 'Stop being such a silly arse, Will. Very well, we will not speak of this. But why so enamored of Lady Ursula?'

I turned to her and studied her features. A charming face. And young. Softly I said, as seriously as any jester could be, 'Because I found the body of her young man, Don Gonzalo de Yscar, and I want to discover who murdered him.'

She stared at me quizzically . . . as well she should. Was there ever a stranger sheriff? But she did not laugh. She knew me suddenly, so it seemed, and leaned over the chair arm to talk confidentially to me. 'It's an outlandish occupation for a fool. But why not? God keep you on your quest, Master Somers. Shall I call her over?'

'If you would, m'lady. And God keep *you* for understanding.'

Lady Nan talked to the maid standing beside her, and she ran to fetch Lady Ursula. The lady in question looked up sharply toward me, seemed to steel herself, and trotted forward. She curtseyed to Lady Nan, and kept her eyes strictly on her lady.

'Lady Marbury, Master Somers here wishes to speak with you. Privily.'

I rose and bowed, gesturing to a place with a bench under a tree in the shade. Silently, she followed and when I asked her to sit, I sat beside her.

October had its chill, rainy days, and also its sunny days, and one never knew which it would be. But the weather was good today except for a chilling breeze. Some of the leaves, in their autumn array, clung fast to the trees, while others had given in to their rest.

'The season turns,' I remarked.

She scarce took note. 'What do you wish to speak to me about, Master Somers?'

'Well, you see, I can't seem to get Lord de Yscar from my thoughts.'

She looked down at her hands. Rings she had, but not the one she had desired. 'Nor is he far from mine.'

'Of course, lady. Do forgive me. But I seem to be the only one doing anything about it.'

'What is your meaning, sir?'

'I mean that I am investigating his death. And so I must ask you, lady—'

'What are you saying? *You* are investigating?'

'I know it is quite unusual. But since I found him . . .' I shook my head. 'It is hard to explain.'

'No. I understand you. Were I a man, I should be going about the court demanding to know who did the deed in such stealth and ill-regard.'

'And so. There are questions I must ask you. Are you prepared to answer them?'

'If it will help.'

She was a dark lady, but her heart-shaped face framed by pearl biliments on her French hood made it all the more enticing. There was the merest pink to her cheeks. Most charming in aspect.

'When was the last time you saw him? Perhaps this could help me identify whom he might have met.'

She bit her lip, making it redder, and thought. 'You mustn't think ill of me, Master Somers. And this mustn't go any farther . . . not used for any of your antics in the court. You must promise me.'

'Oh, no, m'lady. On my oath. There is a time for nonsense and a time to put away nonsense.'

She nodded, keeping her face angled downward. 'The night before my lord was . . . was taken . . . Monday night, I was with him.'

'*With* him, m'lady?'

Her cheeks colored and she fiddled with her rings. 'Aye, Master Somers. With him. In . . . in his bedchamber. All night.'

My heart gave a lurch as if prodded with a hot poker. I looked at her face, her downcast eyes, her coy demeanor.

As faint as she was about admitting such an indiscretion

to the lowly court jester, I knew her pronouncement to be false.

For after all, *I* was the one spending that night with Gonzalo, and I think I would have noticed the presence of his mistress.

She was lying.

TEN

I wiped the astonishment from my face. I could not naysay her, for if I admitted that I knew her statement to be false, how could I explain it? Perhaps she was saying so because *she* was with another on that fateful night. O unfaithful heart! If that were so, then she was saying so to deflect any attention from her lover! By my troth, how was I to untangle all the knotted threads of this?

I licked my lips and pulled my doublet taut. 'Let us put that aside for now. Can you tell me, were you privy to where Lord de Yscar was on Tuesday, during the *day* of his death, whom he met, and so forth?'

'I spend my days with Lady Anne, as you know. But I did see him on occasion in the company of Eustace Chapuys and his attendants.'

Eustace Chapuys. The imperial ambassador. Ambassador to the Holy Roman Emperor Charles V, who was also the King of Spain. And Queen Catherine was aunt to Emperor and King Charles V. 'Was this the work he was engaged in most of the day?'

'I believe so. This was why he was here, in England, after all.'

'And did you happen to notice him engaged with any you were not familiar with? Any unusual person.'

'I don't understand.'

'Lord de Yscar was in conversation with many men from the ambassador's retinue, but his groom, Rodrigo Muñoz, intimated that he might be in the company of a man *not* of the ambassador's retinue. I, er, cannot say more.'

She bit that lip again. 'Well . . . if I understand you aright, then I have seen him with Father Stephen Kendrick and others. I think they were Wolsey's men.'

'But no one else that you can recall? No one not part of such worthy company?'

'Not that I can recall.'

I nodded, trying to reckon a way to put my thoughts into words. 'Are you certain, my lady, that you spent *Monday* night in Lord de Yscar's company? Might it have been the night before? Sunday?'

'I assure you I know what I am talking about.' She rose abruptly. 'And now, Master Somers, I must go back to attending my lady.' She curtseyed to me, and whirled away in satin and rustling linens.

But I do not know what you are talking about. Why was she lying? Now, it seems, I must discover who the lady *was* sleeping with.

It was then that I cast a casual glance at the other attendants, when my gaze suddenly landed upon Lady Jane Perwick. All the other ladies were watching the entertainments and laughing and clapping.

But Lady Jane fixed her eyes on me and never looked away.

I got a distinct chill when thinking about Lady Jane. Just as soon as I was satisfied with what I could learn about Lady Ursula's lovers, I would attend to her. But for now, I needed to satisfy myself on who Lady Ursula's attendants were. Surely they would know where she was the night *I* was with Gonzalo. *I'll wager Marion would know.* I trotted through the corridors on my way to Marion's chamber when a servant called out to me. God's bones, Edward. I didn't have time for him.

'I must be on my way, Edward,' I threw off as I hurried by.

'But the king is in want of you, Will.'

My heels dug into the tiles. *That* is another matter. 'Where is he now, Edward?'

'The garden beside that of Lady Anne's.'

Of course it would be. He spied on her often enough. 'I will get myself there. Thanks for that, Edward.'

'You know how you can reward me.'

I stepped forward and laid my hand against his cheek. 'Anon,' I told him. And when he turned away, I grabbed a handful of his arse and squeezed. He smiled at me over his shoulder.

I rushed back to my chambers and looked for some tricks to put into my basket, and then thought of Nosewise and where that damned dog had got to. He turned up in the corridors as I was scurrying off to attend to the king. I gestured for him to follow me and admonished him to behave, as I wasn't certain if Henry liked little dogs.

And there was Henry himself, in his garden, listening to music played by one of his favorite musicians, Giles Duwes, and surrounded – as Henry always was – by some of his groomsmen. There was Sir John Giffard and Sir Edward Neville, serious men when required, jovial when required, silent when required. In other words, the perfection of courtiers. I didn't know if they liked me or liked me not. Such men are adept at not making their opinions on trivial matters known so that they may sway with the wind.

'Somers!' bellowed the king. 'Where the devil have you got yourself these days? Always when I turn around, you aren't there.'

'Then Uncle, don't turn round so much. Anyway, I am here now.' I set Nosewise down and allowed him to wander.

'Sit at me feet, then. Tell me the news.'

I was the king's gossip-monger, for there was never a fellow who could move in and out of the high and the low of court as the king's fool. I told him tales of the wenches at the nearby dairy, of the laundresses, and varlets of the kitchens – which always seemed to interest him the most, for he fancied himself just another Englishman who could be a country farmer if he liked and blend in with them. Nothing was further from the truth, but he liked to think so. Then I hinted at other things going on between lords of No Name and ladies of No Name, for I would not like to be a carry-tale or slanderer, even if some of it were true.

Then Henry got to talking to Giffard and discussing dealings they had both had with city merchants, and they began to argue as to who was the most plain-dealing. Harry turned to me. 'Will, who is the most plain-dealing: nobility, gentry, city merchants, tradesmen, rustic or countrymen?'

I thought a moment. 'No, none of those. It is the bath and hothouse keepers.'

'What inanity is that, Will?' he said with a smile.

'Why sir, for they who come to the baths are given equal heat and warmth to all, without any difference or least partiality.'

Harry laughed. His grooms did alike.

'I tell you,' he roared, 'there is not a man more honest in the entire kingdom than a fool.'

And like it or not, that was the truth of it. For there was no man *able* to be as honest as the king's fool.

As I watched the king relax and make merry, my heart gave a sudden jerk in my chest. For I feared for him. I feared that I was unwittingly involved in some mischief to hurt him or slay him. And *that* I could not have. Not just for my job, for that would be gone the moment Henry was gone. But because . . . well. Henry was mine own now. I don't know if I were like his son or his pardoner, but he was mine and I was his. And never should a thing as silly as that ever be spoken aloud, but it was truth nonetheless. I wanted no harm to come to him. And I wondered how I could protect him. And why I was to spy on him.

I put my hand on his knee. 'Harry,' I said in soft tones. He leaned toward me and oh! What a handsome varlet he was. Ginger hair and beard ablaze in fiery red, cheeks ruddy from the sun, eyes sparkling with light. And as fine a figure as ever there was in a man. This was a man one was proud to call one's king.

'Harry, if . . . if something were amiss . . .' But I did not know how to finish such a statement.

Henry leaned further and looked me in the eye. 'Are you troubled, Will?' His voice was soft, so soft the others couldn't hear. 'Is there something that vexes your heart?'

I wished I could tell him. Speak it straight out. But I also wished to tell him to set aside that Bullen woman and take up again his good wife the queen. Yet this was the one thing I could not tell him outright, for it was the matter of the kingdom itself, and I could jest and poke and prod that bear-of-a-matter, but I could not come straight out and say it. It would be like walking upon the thin ice of a pond to plunge forever into its icy and forbidden depths.

A fool had to know when he could speak and when he could not.

I shook my head and made a silly face. 'It's a custard, Harry. All thick and eggy that I cannot see within it. Should I eat it anyway?'

He shook his head in amusement and sat back up against his chair. 'You speak such utter nonsense that I cannot fathom it.'

'Indeed. Utter nonsense.'

Or was it? While I played the fool, always in the back of my mind were these things, this nonsense playing over and over, like follow the leader. Why was Kendrick allowed into Gonzalo's room? What were these Spaniards plotting with the Princess Mary? Who was the spy? And who in God's name killed Gonzalo and blackmailed me . . . and why had they not courted me since that first time?

Henry let me go after some hours when he had to meet again with Cromwell and pointedly ignore Wolsey, for there was a game afoot. Wolsey could not accomplish what he wanted and so Wolsey was all the more vexed that Henry would not give him the time of day. It would have been more amusing if it hadn't been such serious matters.

I went a-capering throughout the corridors, playing the silly arse so as to not arouse suspicion, when I ran straight into the clerk, Francis de Aguilar.

'Oh, *señor*, my apologies!'

'No need to apologize, Master Somers.'

'Are we not friends, Francis? For I have a *Will* to be *Frank* with you.'

His English wasn't so good that he could understand my wordplay, but he smiled politely even so.

'What I mean is,' and I caught up with him as he began to walk, 'may I ask a question?'

'Of course.'

'The other day, I noticed Father Kendrick – the English priest – alone in Don Gonzalo's chambers. What on earth was such a man doing there?'

Francis's brows frowned ever so slightly. 'I have not heard

this. I . . . do not know. Perhaps he was asked to by Don
Gonzalo's groom . . .'

'Oh, but you see I was with Don Gonzalo's groom – Rodrigo
Muñoz – and he did not know what that worthy was doing
there either. In fact, he had booted poor Rodrigo out of that
same room in which he lived. Can you imagine such?'

Francis stroked his close-cropped beard. 'No, I cannot
imagine . . .' Then he seemed to awaken from his musing
and looked at me. 'You seem to care about matters not accustomed to one for your station.'

'All matters are fodder for a fool.'

A corner of his mouth drew up. 'Of course. I will . . . look
into the matter.'

'And tell me?'

He stopped, and now his eyes were hooded when he turned
them on me. 'Forgive me, Master Somers. But the doings of
the Spanish court are not your doings.'

'Forgive *me*, Master Aguilar,' I said with a bow. 'But it
seems, these days, that the Spanish court has much to do with
the English court.' I bowed again, and seemed to spy the least
little crack in the veneer of his face.

Dear me. I *had* struck home. It seemed that all the Spanish
retinue knew full well what was happening with the Great
Matter and were equally determined to stop it.

ELEVEN

Methinks that spying was not my best side. I seemed to speak too much, give away too much with my silly face, and suspicion grew around me like a garden of weeds. What is a fool to do?

The king ate in the banqueting hall, and most of the courtiers were there, including dancers and musicians. I sat in front of him at the high table on my stool and took meat from his plate before he could slap my hand away. I performed a puppet antic about scandalous priests – which Harry liked very much – and then another about maids at court who wanted to be queen – which Harry did not like – and then I recited a bawdy bit of poetry.

And then a joke. 'Harry,' I said, 'what hangs at a man's thigh and wants to poke the hole that it's often poked before?'

The king cracked a smile. 'As if I didn't know, you knave.'

'Why, you *do* know it well, sire,' I said with a leer, and all the men chuckled while the ladies hid their smiles coyly behind their hands. 'It's . . . a key.'

Harry laughed loudly and slapped his thigh. He reached into his purse and tossed me a gold coin, which I caught expertly (I am more expert in catching gold than any other denomination).

Soon other merriments caught his attention, and I was again free to roam. I used my little pipe to simulate farts when I found a woman and a man in close conversation, which made the ones around them laugh, until I was free to fade into the background.

Father Kendrick was there with Cromwell and I sidled over to them. As soon as Kendrick noticed me, he made a face of contempt. But I noted how Cromwell studied the priest with narrow-eyed interest, perhaps savoring the man's expression as something *he* could use at a later time.

'Gentlemen,' I said, sitting on their table and shoving aside their broken meat plates with my arse. 'How goes the marriage business? There must be some money in it, else you'd have given it up for another vocation by now.'

Kendrick's face reddened and he raised his fist. 'Why, you jackanape . . .'

Cromwell reached over and grabbed his arm, forcing it down. 'Now, *Father*, is that the way of peace that you preach?'

'Not for this boil.'

I snatched up his goblet and drank from it. 'Aye, Kendrick, what sort of example are you setting? Why, what would the Spanish ambassador think of such a display? Or the *imperial ambassador*? They'd no longer share information with you.'

Cromwell's eyes followed mine and then he looked at Kendrick . . . and sat back away from him in a very deliberate fashion.

Kendrick was absolutely beet-like. 'You bench-whistler, you slanderer! Bring-a-waste!'

'Tut tut, Kendrick. The Spanish court can't use that sort of language. It isn't translatable.'

He shot to his feet, looked furiously around, and then stomped off. Those nearby who had not heard our exchange laughed anyway, likely supposing Will Somers had said something off-color and snippy to the priest.

Cromwell sat like a toad on a leaf. He watched after Kendrick as he left, and then he turned his gaze on me. Slowly, he reached into his pouch and pulled out a coin. He placed it on the table and, with one finger, slid it toward me on the cloth. 'I would be anxious to hear, Master Somers, what you have heard about our Father Kendrick.'

'Oh, that was mere nonsense, Master Crumbled-Well.'

'There is more intelligence in your nonsense than from the brightest at court.' He slid the coin closer to me. 'Take it. You'll earn it.'

'I cannot take a coin from you, sir. I would not have the court think I am *your* fool and not the king's.'

Cromwell paused with his index finger on the coin. His face

seemed to show him considering before he shrugged, scooped it up, and returned it to his pouch.

'Then . . . will you freely share what you seem to know about Kendrick?'

I snatched up a crust of bread, tore off a piece, and dipped it in a dish of sweet sauce. I popped it in my mouth and chewed. 'My lord, it is only that I witnessed Father Kendrick looking about in the poor late Don Gonzalo de Yscar's chambers. And strangely, allowed to gather papers. Was this not at your behest?'

'Strangely, no. Was he not stopped or questioned?'

'Strangely, no.'

'And might you know what he was after?'

'I don't. But I know he did not get what he sought.'

'Interesting. How would you know that?'

I smiled and wiped the crumbs from my doublet. 'My lord, there are just some things one knows, if one is careful enough and sly enough and sharp enough. As you are.'

'And as you are. But why, my dear Jester, do you care so much?'

'Well, for one, I care about King Harry. And for another . . . for another . . .' I slumped and lost my foolish face. 'It is for to find a murderer.'

His voice fell to a hush just between us. 'The murderer of Don Gonzalo?'

'Yes.'

'And why so keen?'

'Because 'twas I who found him. Have *you* ever seen a dead man?'

'I've seen many a dead man.'

'And does it not move you to act, sir?'

'I am . . . moved.'

'Well. So am I.'

'If that is so, I shall do my best to help you on your course, Will Somers. And perhaps you can find the time to help me. In mine.'

Make a deal with the Devil? I think not. But I said, 'I will do what I can, on that course, Master Crumbled-Well.'

He nodded as I leapt off the table and bowed low to him before I scampered off.

Odd bedfellows did murder make.

Lady Nan sat near the king and Henry would send special dishes from his place at the table to hers, thinking no one would notice.

Lady Jane Perwick was also there. She tore her manchet into tiny strips and fed them to herself one at a time. And every time my gaze fell on her, she was looking at me with hooded eyes.

This could not go on. I meant to talk to her as soon as I might. For I needed to know if she was a murderess or a spy . . . or both.

I lingered at the festivities until Lady Nan and her attendants excused themselves from the king with curtsies and backward glances. I promptly jumped up and followed, using a puppet of Wolsey to utter nonsense polemics: 'All good Christians should wear cheese upon their heads,' I said in the dry tones of the cardinal. 'The rule shall be that maids swing fleeces before sitting in chapel . . .'

They laughed, for my Wolsey impression was good.

But I capered near to Lady Jane and said quietly for her ears alone, 'A word, my lady?'

Lady Nan noticed – as she seemed to notice all at court – and she tilted her head in enquiry. 'Somers, you wish to speak to one of my ladies? Again?'

'Forgive me, Lady Nan. It is to you I must ask permission. I forget myself.'

She inclined her head, acknowledging my words, before she looked on at Lady Jane. 'The jester would have a word with you. Wait without. Join us when you are done.'

And so Lady Nan assisted me by withdrawing with the others and leaving me with a stiff Lady Jane in the corridor.

The woman seemed furious. She clutched her hands together as they trembled with repressed rage.

'It seems we are moving at cross-purposes, my lady.' I gave her room, for I did not wish to be too close. Aye, faith. I was worried she'd grab me, truth be told. 'I understand you wish to know about me. Well! I'm here to answer you.'

She blinked slowly. 'I don't understand.'

'Dear me. I feel foolish now if it is not true. That you've been asking about me.' I smoothed my short hair and preened, making it look as if I was primping myself for a suitor, hiding behind my foolery.

'There is little I care to know about a jester,' she said coolly.

'I am struck!' I clutched at my heart. 'For I believed you were enamored of me. And though I have this silly face, I've been told I caper on the bed very nicely.'

She scoffed. 'You have misheard. I might have asked how intimate you were with the king. Simple curiosity.'

'Is that all? I am disappointed, for you are such a lovely lady. But as to your question, of course I am the king's intimate. I can even flit in and out of his bedchamber. Do you?'

Her lip twisted in an angry snarl. 'Sirrah, you had best watch your tongue.'

'Oh, I do! Especially in the bedchamber.'

She grabbed my shoulder painfully, digging in with her nails. It was then I noticed she was as tall as me, with a strong grip. Strong enough to slash a throat? 'I know more about you than you think,' she said in a tight voice. 'You keep your mouth shut about me and I shall keep mine about you.' She gave me one last glare before she shoved me aside and stalked after Lady Nan, letting the guards shut the doors behind her.

Keep my mouth shut . . . what about exactly?

I rubbed at my neck and then the guards sent me on my way.

I girded myself and brought Nosewise back to those remaining in the hall and showed the court the tricks I'd taught him. He could rise on his hind legs and twirl now, and paddle his paws in the air for scraps. He earned the treats they threw to him.

It was late when we finally made it back to my chambers. I was exhausted. I opened the door to darkness. The hearth had some glowing coals, so I set the dog down and grabbed a straw from the shelf and lit it from the embers so that I could light some candles.

I startled good when a voice from my bed bade me greetings. At first, I thought it was Edward, and a sound boxing to his head I had planned to give him. But in the next moment I realized it wasn't him.

'You are late, Señor Somers,' said Rodrigo.

I dropped to the end of the bed. 'And what are you doing here?'

'You promised me.'

I leaned closer on my elbow. 'Did I?'

'You did.' He leaned over and I could see that he was not wearing a shirt. What other surprises awaited beneath the bedclothes?

Before I could further think on it, he grabbed me by my doublet and pulled me up against him, capturing my mouth with his. Ah, his lips, his forcefulness, the scent of him . . . I was undone before I was even fully unclothed.

He was a spirited lover, full of verve and hot blood, and I must say, he well-sated me. I hope I did the same for him.

We lay together afterwards, me toying with his hair as his cheek lay on my chest; he toying with the wisps of my chest hair.

'I did not note before that your back is crooked, though only a little.'

The matter-of-fact way he put it stung for a mere moment, and I shrugged said crooked back. 'It is one of the many interesting things about me.'

'It makes no matter to me.'

'And it makes no matter to me most of the time. Only when someone mentions it.'

'Oh.' He sat up and looked at me. 'I should not have said.'

I pulled him back down against me where it was most comfortable. 'Don't be absurd. It would have been strange had you not mentioned it. And because it does not trouble me, it should not trouble you.'

'It doesn't,' he said, kissing my chest.

All at once, the door flung open, a figure rushed in, and then stopped at the foot of the bed and shrieked, 'Who is *this*?'

Rodrigo dived under the bedclothes.

I huffed. 'Marion? By the mass, you frightened me out of my wits. And poor Rodrigo here.'

Marion hadn't moved. She knew well about me, of course, but she had never seen it first-hand. I have to admit that I was a bit chagrined by her witnessing me with a male companion. I got out of bed, slipped on my nightshirt, and took her in my arms. 'I'm sorry,' I whispered.

She shrugged me off. 'You don't have to apologize. I know your sinful ways.'

'But nevertheless, I am sorry . . . that it troubles you.'

'Well . . . who is this Rodrigo scoundrel? Hold . . . that is a Spanish name . . .'

'Yes. He was the groom of Don Gonzalo.'

She turned to gaze upon the bed and slowly, Rodrigo pulled the sheets away from his face.

'Rodrigo, this is Marion Greene. My, er . . .'

He blinked. 'My lady,' he mumbled, blankets still in his face. His eyes darted between Marion and me.

'It is a long tale, my friend, but she is well aware of my . . . well, as she so aptly put it, my sins.'

Gradually, he came out of the blankets and sheets and sat up in the bed, keeping the bedclothes wadded in his lap. His eyes were still as wide as cups.

Marion glared at him for a moment more before she sank to the edge of the bed. She dropped her face into her hands. 'It has been a very long day.'

I sat beside her. 'I'm sorry. What troubles you?'

'Only my father. He wants me to leave court.'

'No! I don't want you to leave.' I swung my arm around her, completely forgetting Rodrigo's presence.

'And I don't wish to, but he does not think it fitting for me to stay. He . . . he . . . cannot find an appropriate suitor for me. And by this he means he has been turned down when he has asked.'

'But . . . you're *my* betrothed . . .'

'He refuses to acknowledge it.'

I heard a rustle behind me and Rodrigo had pulled up his braies. 'Where are *you* going?'

He gestured toward Marion and shook his head.

'Don't be silly. Sit down.'

Marion wiped her eyes and twisted to look at Rodrigo . . . who was quite a sight bare-chested in his braies. 'As always,' she said, a gleam in her eye, 'you have good taste in men.'

'And that is why you are my beloved,' I said, taking up her hand and kissing it.

Rodrigo had not lost the frightened aspect to his eyes.

'Be at ease, Master Rodrigo,' said Marion. 'I will not chase you away. For I can see it is not my night to take my comfort in Will's arms.'

'Oh, but Marion . . .'

'Will Somers! What are you proposing?'

Cuds-me, what *was* I proposing? And then images cavorted in my mind. Marion must have sensed the glitter in my eye and stood. 'I think it time for me to leave.'

'Wait, Marion.' I dragged her back down to the edge of the bed. But she seemed ready to spring up at the least provocation. 'Rodrigo and I discovered some secret papers in Gonzalo's chamber. Something Father Kendrick was looking for. Let me show you.'

She rubbed her arms. 'Kendrick, that detestable man!'

'Indeed.' I rummaged through my things in a coffer and pulled out the folded letters, even the torn one. Her Latin was better than mine and she reckoned right away what they all said, including the scrap.

She shook it at me. 'Do you see what this says? It looks as if the Holy Roman Emperor was after abducting Princess Mary secretly by ship to Spain to use as a bargaining chit. Either to force King Henry to keep Queen Catherine, or to marry the princess to one of their own.'

I took the scrap and turned it this way and that. 'Is that what it said?'

'Yes. And this other. They threaten the king's life. Is that what your Lord de Yscar was all about?' she accused, swinging back to stare at Rodrigo.

'My master would never have plotted this. It could be that he uncovered the scheme. And the spies . . .'

'Maybe not so much spies,' I said, thinking, 'as . . . assassins?'

Rodrigo clutched his head with his hands. 'Oh, my poor master!' His face was suddenly flooded with tears. I glanced at Marion to commiserate and she, with a heart as big as the ocean, seemed to feel for my companion. She shot up from the bed and rushed to the other side of it, enclosing him in her arms.

'Master Rodrigo, I'm certain if your lord was as good as you knew him to be, then it couldn't be possible that he had plotted murder. Never fear.'

His face was partly muffled by her bosom pressed against it. 'And my master was killed for it.'

'Oh dear.'

What was to be done?

'Will,' she said, still cradling Rodrigo, who looked as if he didn't know how to get out of it. 'You must warn the king.'

'And how to do that without compromising myself?' As I looked about my room, I saw two of my lovers together . . . and then poor Will, standing alone. Speaking of compromising . . .

'You must write him a letter. Simply warning of the Spanish plot. His men will know what to do.'

I looked to Rodrigo. 'What do you think?'

'As much as I hate this Great Matter, I cannot abide murder. Or abduction.'

'Then I will do it.' I flung myself from the bed and, in only my nightshirt, sat at my writing table. I tore a sheet of paper in half, took up quill, dipped it, and paused. 'What should I say?'

Marion paced behind me. 'Say this: Your Majesty, God and His Angels deliver you. It has come to my attention that—'

'God 'a mercy, Marion! *You* write it.' I slipped from the chair and steered her to it. She sat, I handed her the quill, and she set to.

I paced behind her, gnawing on a cuticle. She seemed to be taking an interminable amount of time, but by the look of the candle, it had only been a few minutes.

'There!' She dusted it with sand and then held it up to look.

I snatched it from her hand and read. Yes, she was concise, and the few words conveyed the urgency we sought.

'This is perfect, Marion. You are a wonder.' I kissed the top of her head, folded the paper, and stuffed it in my nightshirt. 'I'll put this under Harry's pillow tomorrow when all are occupied elsewhere. And then you, my dear Rodrigo, you must studiously set to spying to discover just what Don Gonzalo did all the day before he was killed. And you, Marion, sweeting, you must discover if Lady Ursula had a lover, someone she could not let the others discover.'

'What? Why? She doesn't know me.'

'The why is that she claims she was with Gonzalo the night . . . well. The night *I* was with him. She must have another lover, and might *he* have murder in mind? And what lady of court does not know your skill with the needle? You are the second most necessary person at court.'

'And the king is naturally the first.'

'God, no. It's *me*. Now, get you to your bed and I will get back to mine.' I slid my gaze to a blushing Rodrigo . . . before I turned toward Marion. 'Unless . . . you'd *like* to stay . . .'

'Will Somers! Why God loves your senseless face I shall never know.'

'But He does love me . . . like you do, my dove. To bed with you, then.'

She looked me over like a mother to her unrepentant child, kissed my cheek, and left.

'She is your betrothed?' said a meek voice from the bed. 'And . . . she knows about you?'

'Of course. And I love her for that and much more. I am not like you, Rodrigo. I love women just as much.'

He shook his head. 'Would that I could.'

I blew out the candles and threw back the bedclothes. Carefully, I took Marion's letter out of my braies – which I shook off of me – and stuffed it under my own pillow. 'Well, since you can't, Rodrigo, you'll just have to make do with me.'

The next day after mass, I was sore attentive to Henry, frolicking here and there around him, spinning him bawdy verse, singing raucous songs, mercilessly haranguing his courtiers, just making certain Henry was not bound for his rooms. I can't believe I cheered when his councillors bid him go elsewhere.

At last!

With the privy chamber *and* the withdrawing chamber wide open, I headed through to his bedchamber, whereupon a Yeoman of the Guard stopped me. His face was one I hadn't seen before.

'Hold, man. This is the king's bedchamber. None may pass.'

I recognized well that Shropshire accent and I let mine grow deep as grass. 'Hold y'self! You're a Shropshire lad, same as me.'

His eyes brightened and he lowered his spear a might. 'It's good to hear the tones of me home.'

'Oh, aye. I've only been at court four years on. You must be new not to know Will Somers, the king's fool.'

'You're Somers?' His spear lay relaxed in his elbow as he gestured. 'I thought a jester wore bells and a hood. I never knew you were Shropshire born.'

'Aye. But . . . I'm a proper courtier now. It won't take you long neither.'

He gestured to the door behind him. 'Why'd you want to go in there when the king isn't in?'

'I always go in there. I like to leave things for His Majesty to make him laugh. It's my vocation, lad.'

'You do this often?'

'Sometimes I await him with my cittern. He likes his music, does Harry. Come, lad. Don't make me have to get another guard who knows me.'

The man looked about, wondering what he should do . . . when of all the things, *Cromwell* poked his head through. He stopped and glanced at the guard, then at me. The guard came to attention, and at that, Cromwell sauntered forward.

'Ah, Thomas,' I said, slipping my arm in his. 'Tell this lad, here, that I am free to come and go to the king's chamber whether he abides there or not.'

Wide-eyed, the guard looked from me to Cromwell and to my arm in Cromwell's crook.

Cromwell, too, looked down at my arm in his and gently shook me loose. 'I'm afraid the fool is correct. He does have leave to go whither he wishes. And now, Somers, if you will excuse me . . .'

I bowed low to him. 'I will give you every excuse you wish, Thomas.'

He barely restrained from shaking his head before he moved back into the privy chamber, grabbed his leather satchel from the table, and exited to the king's dining chamber.

The guard smiled. 'That's good enough for me, Master Somers.'

'Bless thee!' I saluted, and entered. And when I closed the door, I rested against it, catching my breath. The last thing I wanted was for a witness to say I left something in Henry's room. But maybe I could still be unknown. Especially if I left him a silly note on his writing table. For then it would be in another hand. After all, Marion had written the note I was even now about to place under Henry's pillow.

I approached the huge bed, with its tester above and curtains pushed back and tied to each post. It had been made beautifully, which meant it was ready for his weary body when night fell. I smoothed my hand over the soft linen of the pillow with its embroidered H, filled with the down of goose and swan, and marveled again how privileged I was to even be in such a room, to touch the royal pillow that cradled the royal head. Who was Will Somers of Shropshire to be able to do such? Only a crook-back fool of a lad, that's who.

I lifted the pillow, took the scrap of paper from out of my doublet, and slid it there, carefully replacing the pillow and smoothing it out, like any groomsman or usher.

Then, I sat m'self down at his writing table, took a quill, and penned a naughty few lines to make him laugh. He'd know it was from me, even if I didn't sign it.

I chuckled to myself about that, glanced once more hastily to the pillow, and made my way out again. Simple as that.

I spent some time with Nosewise, teaching him more tricks, and never was there a more malleable cur than him. I fashioned a little hat for him to match my own, and he willingly wore it, so as I walked through the passages playing a pipe, he trotted along behind me, garnering laughter at the little dog that looked like the jester.

And when a servant came to fetch me to attend to the king, I was prepared and went forth. He was in one of his chambers playing cards with Lady Nan. Nan's ladies, some of them, were there, and some of Henry's men, and it made for a bright little gathering, where the grooms trifled with the maids with their eyes, and the maids trifled back.

But it was Lady Nan who started it, started talking about the Spanish influence at the English court and why were they allowed such latitude, and Henry grew more cross as she talked. I interjected with a bawdy song, but it did not ease his brow. As talk moved across the room, Henry finally shot to his feet, hurling down his cards. 'No more of this! I shall order *all* the Spanish in this court to be killed if there is even a whiff of conspiracy, from the noblest man down to his faithful groom. Make no mistake, I shall not tolerate any form of intrigue in my court!'

We had all fallen to silence. I swallowed hard. God's body! If any conspiracy was told to him, he'd kill *all* the Spanish? Even Rodrigo! What had I done?

'Will?' cried Henry, grabbing my arm painfully. 'What's amiss? You look as white as a winding sheet. Here! Thomas, get him some wine.'

Nosewise whined at my feet, gazing solicitously up at me with his wide round eyes.

'It's naught, sire. I merely felt a bit faint. I was so busy teaching this little dog that I forgot to eat.'

'Bring the man some meat,' said Henry, and it was brought. And the dear man fed me himself, taking each scrap and holding it forth, until, like a baby bird, I opened my mouth to receive it.

Oh, Henry. If you only knew. I secreted that letter for *you*, to warn *you* of Spanish plots. But now I had to steal it back before you saw it.

And how the devil was I ever to do that?

TWELVE

I hovered by Henry's inner sanctum door, which wasn't suspicious in itself, for Will Somers could always be counted on to abide near the king wherever he was at court, even at his close stool. There was many a time I helped along the king's regularity by spouting some nonsense, and he shat himself right good laughing in the best place for it.

But on my oath, I felt as guilty as any sinner, felt it could be read right off my silly face. For I desperately needed to steal back that letter!

Why had I been so stupid as to think that Henry did not know of plots threatening him? Surely Cromwell and the many courtiers of the privy council knew of these plots and had already made them known to him. Or kept it from him so he would not erupt like a volcano. And here I was, bumbling Will Somers, tossing fuel into the eruption.

I needed to leave the conspiracies to the men who knew what to do about them, and stick to foolery. For I didn't want to get poor Rodrigo killed on my account.

Still . . . should that also be left to the investigators? And who might they be?

'First things first,' I admonished myself. 'Get that letter.'

I had no chance to get in there, for Henry was in one or other of his rooms all day and it looked as if he'd be there into the evening, gaming, plotting . . .

Maybe I could lure him out with other entertainments. Yet if I was with him, how would I get back to the chamber?

But then, like an answered prayer, here she was, my excuse, my savior. Simply strolling the corridors without her ladies.

I bowed low. 'Lady Nan.'

'Will Somers, you vexation.'

'Indeed, my lady. What are your plans this fine evening?'

'My plans are none of your affair.'

'Oh, but they are.' I took her arm, and though she resisted

at first, she relaxed when she reckoned the only thing I had in mind was to hold her close, like siblings. 'But you are not here with your ladies. What would the court think of this!'

'You prating fool.'

I forced a laugh. 'No, my lady. What do you think of this suggestion? Take Harry out to the gardens and walk with him.'

'What? Why should I bother to do that?'

'Because it is a fitting thing to do while the king is still married.' Her body stiffened and she pressed her lips together. Aye, when she went about in the city or into towns, the people called out to her most viciously, calling her a whore and a sorceress. And in the same breath hailed our queen. She knew it all well.

More softly, I said, 'Henry loves the outdoors. He'd sleep out there if he could. Take him for a lovely walk and amuse yourselves in the privacy of the gardens. A lovely place to woo and be wooed.'

Cods! She was actually considering it. 'He'd like that?'

'Anything *you'd* suggest, dear lady.'

She had decided. She had probably thought it before I made the suggestion, for what was she doing so near his chambers without her escorts? Coming to the king's chamber alone was folly at this point, but a walk in the gardens, that was accept-able. 'Go on, Will. You tell the king I await without.'

I bowed, and sent up a prayer of thanks to God who would care for the small neck of His greatest fool.

I pushed the door open to the watching chamber, getting only a glance from the guards. Then I stalked through the presence chamber past two other chambers to the withdrawing room – passing more guards as I went – where I finally found Henry reading some papers in his bedchamber with a frown creasing his brow.

'Uncle!' I slapped his shoulder and he twisted in surprise to look upon me.

'Oh, it's only you.'

'*Only* me?' I pressed my hand to my breast as if an arrow had struck me there, and I fell to the ground, legs shaking. 'You wound me, sire. It is *only* Will Somers. I die. I *die*!'

'Get up, you pillicock.'

I sprang to my feet and leaned on him, looking over his shoulder at his papers. 'These papers seem to make you into a foul thundercloud.'

'It is all these lawyers!'

'Alas. But . . . if you are very good to me, I will make a suggestion to ease your brow.'

'Eh? What's that?'

'What you need, my liege, is a good walk in the garden.'

'I haven't time for that. I have issues of state to consider.'

'Issues of state can wait. You need good English exercise. Up with you, man.'

He pushed me away. 'Leave it, Will.'

'Oh, but Uncle, did I say you'd be alone? Silly me for my forgetfulness.'

He cocked his head toward me. 'What devilry is here?'

'No devilry, Uncle. Just . . . a lady. Who seeks good exercise with you. She awaits without.'

He rose. 'Is there a lady outside my chamber?' he whispered.

'Why yes, Harry. A goodly lady, a dark lady, a mysterious lady . . . who likes taking walks with you. The Lady Nan, in case you wondered.'

'Why didn't you say so, you cur?'

'Because I delight in surprising you.' I grinned.

Henry already looked happier.

He didn't even glance back at his papers and pushed past me, as I rubbed my hands together, edging my way to the royal bed.

Henry was out the door, and I thrust my hand under his pillow and found . . . nothing!

'What the devil?' I dived my head under the pillow to inspect just as Cromwell and his secretary, Ralph Sadler, strode in. He was fair of face, brown-haired, with a soft beard and mustache. He might be comely, but he had in his eye the same fervency as his master, that of ambition, and be damned who he trod upon. I have noticed, in my time at court, that such things were common, but never ended well.

I scrambled out from under the pillow just in time to sit cross-legged on the center of the bed.

They had not noticed me when they began talking.

But Cromwell here in the king's private chambers when the king wasn't here, I wondered mightily what was afoot.

'The king took his leave with the Lady Anne once again,' said Sadler.

'It is good for the king to be seen with the Lady Anne,' said Cromwell. 'Is this not true?'

'Your supposition is that if they are seen together often enough, the court will forget that the king still has a wife?'

'Not so much that, Ralph. But that they will become *accustomed* to seeing her on the king's arm. And soon forget Spanish influence at the English court.'

Sadler nodded. 'Is that the idea of His Grace the Cardinal?'

'Wolsey encourages his assistants to do the groundwork for him. I am merely a paver.'

'Our cardinal seems more of a furrier, seeking to wrap the king in comfort with his words, rather than his actions.'

'The actions are left to me. And to you.' Perhaps that was a reminder to the secretary not to speak so freely.

I began casually picking at my nails with my knife. It was this little sound that soon awakened the notice of Cromwell. He turned and Sadler followed, about to open his mouth, when Cromwell laid his hand on his arm. 'Master Somers. What keeps you nigh the king's bedchamber?'

'Oh, Thomas, I am always here, in some capacity or other.'

Sadler gave his master a wide-eyed question, but Cromwell silently admonished him before he turned back to me. 'It is obvious that you could not help but to hear our conversation.'

'I heard. It matters little to me.' I concentrated on my nails as I never had before. 'I already reckoned what each of you did in court. It is up to me to discover this and make fun of it.' I looked up with a grin.

Sadler couldn't hold his tongue any longer. 'Is it quite proper for you to sit on the king's bed?'

'Very proper, Ralph. May I call you so?'

'You may *not*.'

'That's not fair. Master Cromwell lets *me* call *him* so. Well, it is no matter.' I sheathed my knife again. 'I think the better question is, what are the two of *you* doing in the king's bedchamber when he is not present?'

Sadler flushed as red as Wolsey's cloak. He looked to Cromwell to cobble that answer. Cromwell, as expected, offered a perfunctory smile. 'We are here on the king's business.'

'Even when the king is not here?'

'We are always on the king's business.'

'On the close stool, in the laundresses's bed, playing dice . . . so many places to be at the king's business where the king is not.'

'Why you . . .' Sadler began, but Cromwell merely shook his head at him.

'Why berate the fool when he is in the midst of fooling? That is *his* business.'

I nodded. 'Indeed, it is.'

'But now it is time for you to depart, Master Somers. For we cannot complete his business with a fool for an audience.'

'That's where you're wrong, Thomas. There is no more perfect audience for you. I keep the king's business always in my heart. And I would see not anything untoward as concerns it.'

Cromwell never dropped his smile. He bowed slightly to me. 'I concede it, Master Somers. Come, Sadler. Our business can be conducted anywhere. Even in the light of day.'

'Let us hope so, my lords.' I waved my hand regally as Henry would do to send away any low-ranked courtier.

They left through the many opened doors and doorways, and I sat still for but a moment before scrambling back under the pillow, looking for that damned missive.

The door opened again. Was this London Bridge, with all-comers doing their business here? I sat cross-legged once again, arms folded over my chest.

Groomsmen moved in as one . . . until they saw me. 'Will Somers,' said one of them. 'What are you doing here?' One of the grooms retreated to the guard outside and questioned him.

'Merely sitting here.'

'He's plotting some devilry,' said another.

I smiled back at him with a chuckle. 'Of course.'

They shook their heads and took away the plates and cups and crusts and other detritus, not touching the papers and other documents that might be strewn about. And then they shuffled out just as quickly as they came. I noticed no guard coming to fetch me, so he must have told them what to do with their worries.

The door closed again and under the pillow I went. Perhaps under the other pillow? I dived there and . . . alleluia! My fingers closed over the missive, and no sooner had I pulled my head out than Thomas Giffard, Gentleman Usher in Ordinary, swanned in, no doubt sent to rush me forth.

'What have you got there, Somers?'

'This?' I held up the missive. God knows how I kept my hand from shaking. 'This is a bit of nonsense I was leaving for the king . . . but thought better of it. I left a better one on his writing table.'

He strode toward said table, leaned over, and read. And then he laughed. 'Gracious Christ, Somers. How your mind works.'

I stuffed the missive in my doublet. 'How indeed,' I said as I slid off the bed. 'Like the blacksmith at the forge, I must strike while the iron is hot or I forget it. God keep you, Master Giffard.' And with that, I was able to escape the king's bedchamber at last!

I found a fire and tossed the paper in it, watching to make sure it was good and burnt to ash. And after, I wandered. And then I pondered if I should seek out Rodrigo and see if he was successful in his spying. Who had Gonzalo seen that day? And what had spurred that attack? Enemies abounded at court, but was he an enemy to his own countrymen for foiling plots they had laid? And what about that blackmail note to me? Was I still in danger? Cuds-me, of course I was. For the knave who threatened me and had killed Gonzalo was still at court, wasn't he? And though he had not immediately gone after me, he still could at any time. What was he waiting for?

The face of Jane Perwick rose up in my mind. She wanted to know how close I was to the king. Didn't all know that I was? And then the unpleasant visage of Father Kendrick rose up too. He was a scheming whoreson if ever there was one. Would *he* hesitate to use this information against me? It didn't seem likely . . . and yet. When a man finds a groat, does he spend it all at once or does he wait for the best opportunity to make the most of his windfall? I did not know enough about Kendrick. He might bide his time. But . . . would he – a priest – kill a man such as Gonzalo?

I leaned against a wall and absently glanced out the window, at the sun shimmering on the grass and gleaming the gold of the foliage around it. Now, *Cromwell* would not kill a man with his own hands. He was not such a one as that. He would plot and make certain that the man was killed but by other, more devious means. That was the sort of man *he* was. Never sully his own hands yet make certain the job was done.

Cromwell wasn't my man, this I knew. But Kendrick . . . or Lady Jane . . .

I needed to clear my head so I returned to my rooms to fetch Nosewise and we made our way outside to the gardens.

It was a pleasant evening. I wished I had someone by my side to enjoy it besides a dog. Marion or Rodrigo or . . . Gonzalo. But that could never be again. And besides, he wouldn't have been caught dead with a fool. Oh. Caught dead. But that was precisely what caught him dead . . . No, no! I refused to entertain the idea that it was my fault. They wouldn't have killed him for that. They would have taken greater pleasure in publicly accusing him and making him suffer. That was the way of the coward. Or the one who himself felt the stirrings in his cod for his fellow man. Dissemblers were the worst . . . and the most desperate of lovers.

Now I wish they *had* confronted me in that garden at midnight. At least I could have known and found a way to stop them.

Nosewise trotted ahead of me, running about and sensing his freedom to do as he pleased. His cheerful brashness cheered me. But suddenly he pulled up short, tail up, ears back. His nose began to twitch and cautiously he stepped forward.

What has he got into now? I wondered. But even as I neared, a chill of remembrance shuddered through me. Hadn't he done that very thing when he found Gonzalo? *Please God Almighty, make it not so.*

Nosewise was as good as his name. Alone, on the grass, lay a man. I ran forward. God help me! I slid to the ground before him and grabbed his hand. Not again!

'Rodrigo?'

THIRTEEN

His hand was warm . . . and a pulse throbbed under my fingers. He was alive!

'Help! Help! Guards!'

My cry was taken up by unseen servants or courtiers and I heard the running of guards from somewhere.

I smoothed back the hair from Rodrigo's face and he moaned and turned his head.

'Don't try to speak, Rodrigo. It is I, Will Somers. Help is coming.'

With the guards, crowds arrived. Everyone wished to look because it is human nature to want to see. When I looked up, I noted Kendrick in the mix, and the whoreson never bothered to offer prayers or kindness. He looked him over, sneered, and made haste away.

What's amiss, Kendrick? Disappointed he's still alive? Aye, that's when I began to rightfully consider that this priest was priest in name only, and willing to murder. I had to find out more about him, but not for the moment. I held Rodrigo's hand instead, muttering a prayer.

A guard ran off to fetch a physician, but one of the friars arrived first. He commanded we carry him to the infirmary in the Church of the Observant Friars, and I and others carried him thence.

Once he was laid gently onto a cot the friar dismissed them all but bid me stay.

'Master Somers, you seem to know this man.'

'Aye, Brother. He is Rodrigo Muñoz, from the Spaniards' men.'

He wrung out a cloth in a basin and gently wiped at the wound to his head. 'What happened?'

'I don't know. My dog found him.' *Just like he found Gonzalo*, I mused with a tingle of warning rushing over my skin.

The friar bent over the man, pushing his hair aside as Rodrigo squirmed. 'This man was coshed on the head. A little blood, a little bruising, but I don't think it will be a great matter. I will keep an eye on him tonight to make certain of it.'

'I am grateful to you for that, Brother . . . Brother . . .?'

'Fulke. I will make him a potion to drink to ease the pain and possible fever. You can help me, Somers.'

'Anything, Brother.'

I chopped the leaves of a plant as directed, and then Brother Fulke, with his stubby, calloused, and scratched fingers scooped it up and put it in the small cooking pot on a trivet before the fire. He stirred it about, added honey, and then poured the brew into a cup. He brought it to the cot and sat at the head, gently cradling Rodrigo and hefting him up so that he could drink it. The patient made a face, but when he'd drunk nearly all of it, Brother Fulke seemed satisfied and laid him down again. He examined his head, decided he didn't need a bandage, and gestured for me to come with him to the far side of the room.

'You are his friend?'

'Oh aye.'

'Then you will come to check on him, eh?'

'I will. Whatever you say.'

He patted my shoulder. 'Some take you for only a fool, Will Somers, but you are much more than that.'

'May I sit with him now?'

'If you are quiet. He needs to rest. But someone does need to attend to him the rest of the night. To listen to make certain he is only sleeping.'

'I can do that. But I must know, Brother. Did someone try to kill him?'

He looked back at the man in the bed and sighed. 'If so, they didn't do a good job of it. Striking a man to kill takes a good, solid blow. He was blessed that it did not crack his skull. So I would say that the blow was not hard enough.'

'Or he's got a hard head.'

He smiled. 'Even so. God has watched over and protected him.'

'Then . . . if you or I would have coshed him, we would have fouled it. Is that what you are saying?'

The friar was about ten years my senior, with hazel eyes and brown hair, where it wasn't shorn for his tonsure. And though he shaved his face, his beard was stubborn and left a shadow on his cheeks and chin. 'That is the gist of it. It was an inexpert hand, I should say.'

'Then . . . not an assassin.'

'Assassin? What notions you have.'

'He is in the imperial ambassador's retinue. And his master, Don Gonzalo de Yscar, was murdered nearly a week ago.'

He looked back at Rodrigo, chest rising and falling in his troubled rest. 'That is very interesting.'

'Aye, it is.'

His eyes roved over me. 'It is rumored you found the body of his master.'

'It is true, Brother. And I have been troubled ever since. I have been trying to ascertain who could have killed him. And now they are trying to kill his groom. Something is very amiss.'

'*You* have been?'

'It was a terrible thing that happened to Don Gonzalo. And in King Henry's court! And now this. I need to know that they will both find justice.'

'Well . . . then sit with him a while. When he is better, you can ask him if he saw anyone. It was to the back of his head. He may not have seen the assailant. Or he may not remember. The blow to the head . . . it does things to the mind.'

'Oh. That is a fearful thing.'

'Pray on it, Somers.'

'I will. I beg you to help in that, Brother.'

'And so I shall.'

I found a stool and brought it to his bed and sat myself upon it. Sometime in the evening, Nosewise wandered in and jumped onto the cot to lay beside him, and by that I knew that the pup was saddened as I was saddened. I felt that Rodrigo would be eased by the dog's soft presence. And I sat watching him most of the night . . . until I dozed off.

* * *

'You are no great watchdog,' said a rough voice as I climbed up to wakefulness.

'Rodrigo!' I nearly shouted. I scooted to the edge of the stool and grabbed his hand. It was morn, with a hazy sun streaming in through the shutter ajar. He looked fine and flushed with good health. Nosewise sat up and panted a smile. 'How are you?'

'My head rings like a bell, but not as badly as last night.'

'You poor, poor thing. But God is good and has preserved you.'

'He has.'

'What happened? Do you know?'

He slowly shook his head. 'I barely recall it. I was following an idea I had, and walking through the garden to get to another part of the palace when I felt this hard pain in the back of my head. I don't know what happened after that. I must have fallen. I remember you there . . . and then many hands carrying me here. Where *is* here?'

'We are in the infirmary of the Church of the Observant Friars.'

He nodded before he stopped himself with a hand to his forehead. 'Ow.'

'Lie still. I will fetch Brother Fulke. He nursed you.'

I left Nosewise in his care and went in search of our friar apothecary. Their liturgy of the hours had finished, and Brother Fulke met me at the door with a tray of food. 'How is our patient?'

'He awakens.'

'Good. I hope he has an appetite.'

I hurried ahead of him and stood beside the bed. Rodrigo was sitting up and petting Nosewise. 'Bless you, Brother,' he said.

Brother Fulke set down his tray and sat in the stool by the bed. He cupped Rodrigo's face and turned his head gently this way and that. 'And how are you feeling today?'

'Much like someone who has been hit on the head.'

Fulke held up a finger. 'Do you see one, or two?'

'One.'

'God is good. I don't think you will suffer any ill-effects, except for an aching head. I urge you to have some gruel.'

'I will eat it, Brother, whatever it is.'

Fulke handed Rodrigo the wooden bowl, spoon and cup. 'Water will slack your thirst. Take a little wine today – only a little, mind – to aid the blood that was lost.'

'Thank you, Brother.' He scooped a spoonful and shoved it in his mouth.

When Fulke moved off, I sat in his place. 'Did you see who attacked you?'

'Alas, no. I do not even remember such a thing happening. One moment I was investigating, the next awakening here.'

'What was it you were going to investigate?'

'I had an idea about Kendrick. But now . . . I don't remember what it was.'

'Oh, that poor head of yours. Did you find out anything else about your master's doings?'

Rodrigo gingerly scooped up more gruel from his bowl and seemed to enjoy it. 'I found more letters . . .' He snatched a glance to where the friar had disappeared, reached into his shirt, and pulled out some folded papers. 'You see.'

'I don't read Spanish, my friend.'

He set his bowl down and, as soon as he did, Nosewise had his face in it, lapping it up.

'Nosewise! You little beggar.' I grabbed him away, but Rodrigo waved his hand.

'Let him eat. I've had enough.'

I set the dog back down and he was back in the bowl again.

Rodrigo wiped his hand on the blanket and unfolded the paper. He sighed and shook his head. 'I wish what I found would have been good news, but it was not. It seems my master was promising Queen Catherine one thing – help from Spain to stop this divorce – but also promising Henry something else; help *with* the divorce. Oh Will. Why was my master doing this?'

'He said this, did he?'

'*Sí*. Plainly.' He rested the paper on his lap.

'Aye me. Your master was a diplomat. His task was to walk a very fine line between two sides. To what end? Well . . . we cannot guess. Was he a friend of Cardinal Wolsey?'

'He had occasion to discuss certain things with him. Once,

the cardinal was in his chambers, but mostly, he went to the cardinal's and I did not accompany him.'

'What was said when you were nigh?'

He sighed again. 'Something about making it easier for both Spain and England. But each time I tried to hear more, they would dismiss me from the room. The rooms are built very solidly and, alas, I could hear no more.'

'Was Wolsey alone?'

'Never. He was always with Cromwell and Kendrick.'

Kendrick again. But of course he was always with Wolsey. And Kendrick was the one looking for papers in Gonzalo's room.

'I am tired,' said Rodrigo, lying back against his pillow.

'Shall I take the letter for safekeeping?'

He handed it to me without another word. I took the bowl away and set the cup of water at his bedside. Should I leave him? I thought Brother Fulke would look after him, so I sought him out to tell him I had to depart.

What would Henry think of his absent jester? I was not there to soothe his brow whilst he went to his bed after his stroll with the Lady Nan . . . alone. Unfulfilled. Poor Henry. A lusty man like him would surely not wait for a divorce and a new wedding. Would he find another more willing? I wish I had the time to find out who kept the king warm at night, but I had other things on my mind. I was beginning to suspect that Kendrick had something to do with this, so that was my next pursuit. After the king tired of me, that is.

Kendrick was not as difficult to find as I thought he might be. He had a perpetual snarl to his face. One wonders how any poor soul would pour out their hearts in confession to such a one as he. But that gave me an idea.

I had my bladder on a stick as I cavorted through the crowds at court and found his clutch of crows in their dark corners and whispers. I tapped him on the back of his head with my bladder stick. He whirled about, ready to take me to task when I announced, 'Father Kendrick, I wish to make my confession!'

'Who has the time for that many hours?' he snarled.

They laughed. *I* laughed, for it *was* a good jest. But I was not in a jesting mood, but in a more bodkin sort of mood. 'For shame, Father. Making light of the sacraments? Well, I'm certain Wolsey would be displeased. I'm certain *Henry* would be displeased.'

The laughter fell suddenly away.

Kendrick stalked toward me. 'It was not I who made light of the sacraments, but you, you jackanape.'

'You wound me, sir. For I do wish to confess. I confess . . .' All held their breath listening. I yanked at my hose. 'I confess . . . that my breeches are too tight.' I waddled about, grabbing my cod while the others laughed. Kendrick did not.

'Ah, that *was* a jest in truth, Kendrick. But I have other business with you, if you will find another dark corner to talk. I will shoo the spiders away for us.'

'I have nothing to say to you, fool.'

'But *the king's* jester has plenty to say to *you*.' I emphasized 'the king' just that much, and his brows ticked upward. Men such as these cannot take a step without thinking of their ambitions, and here was a man – Wolsey's man – who gave great thoughts to his ambitions. That ladder again. It was a wobbly thing, that ladder, pegged together with greed and evil against their fellow man. It would never support such a weight for too long. Indeed, Wolsey was on the downward rung. Perhaps Cromwell thought to take his place in Henry's esteem.

He led the way, saying naught, and I followed him to an alcove far from the others. 'What is it you want, Somers? You are like a piece of meat stuck betwixt my teeth and no straw will flick it out.'

'Ha! That's good, Kendrick. Very vivid. No. I merely wondered something. About your association with the Spanish.'

He stalked forward and I suddenly found myself backed against the wall. He had murder in his eyes. 'Harken, Somers,' he said in a low growl. 'Your games have got me in trouble with Wolsey. I've been working for years to be in His Grace's company. One flippant remark from you has undone it. Be certain that I have not forgot it, fool. And I will find a way to make you pay.'

It was like all the air was sucked out of my lungs. I had not been in peril of m'life before. Oh, once or twice from the king, but he didn't mean it. But this man certainly did. I am ashamed to say that my knees knocked as I tried to make m'self smaller into that corner.

And yet I still piped up with, 'You can pay me by any coin of the realm, Kendrick.'

I felt his hand, then. He swatted me good with his open palm across my cheek. It burned but, when others turned to look, he paled and skulked away. Kendrick's star was a falling one and I felt no guilt at all if I had aught to do with it.

I shrugged to the others in the corridor and flattened the bladder to make a farting sound. They laughed. Aye, all was merry in their lives again. So what if the fool is slapped by a priest? So what if that fool's knees knocked in fear of his life? It was just another day at court, wasn't it? *Will, you forget your place too often. One of these days, one of these fine courtiers you insult is going to slip a bodkin right between your ribs, and it might take days for your poor corpse to be found.*

At least Marion would come looking for me.

I decided I was hungry, and headed for the kitchens.

Edward was there, giving me his smoldering looks. *I don't have the time, lad,* said my look back at him.

'Who's gone and smote you, Will?' said John Bricket, Master Cook.

'What?' My hand went to my cheek. It still felt hot. 'Oh, it was a blessing from a priest. And a pious hand he has.'

'You no doubt deserved it,' said the French cook, Pero Doux, the privy kitchen cook with the exalted title of Yeoman Cook for the King's Mouth.

Laughter followed the remark even as Bricket gathered his cooks and gave them orders.

I adjusted my doublet and retied one of the points that had come loose when I yanked at my hose. 'Is that any way to treat the king's fool?'

'What are you doing here, Will?' Bricket said, adjusting his apron.

'I'm hungry.'

'Breakfast is over, my lad.'

'But I was tending to a sick friend. Should *I* suffer after doing God's own work?'

Bricket sighed and opened the buttons of his coat under his white linen apron. The kitchens were never idle, and he was fixing to get the dinner ready for its presentation hours away. It was hot work. 'Walter,' he called to one of his kitchen serjeants, 'get this varlet a bit of cold capon.'

'Oh, bless you, sir. And bless you, Walter.'

'You'll eat in the serving hall,' said Bricket over his shoulder as he hurried to the doorway to the many smaller kitchens. 'On a wooden trencher,' was the last order he gave before he disappeared.

'With bread, eh, Walter?' I called.

Walter was an obliging lad and he set my meal down at a long board table and served me ale from a leather jug into a wooden cup. But none of that vexed me. A Shropshire lad making airs above his station? I was grateful to eat at all. I did thank him, for it was more trouble to clean up after me as late as I was.

I ate quickly after crossing myself with a prayer of thanks. I swallowed just enough to satisfy my hunger. I wolfed down the small manchet and then wiped my hands on the napkin that I had perched on my shoulder. I took that off, wiped my mouth, and told the scullions I was done. Now. On to serving the king.

I went in search of him and found he was still busy with his privy councillors, but not too far off – in a withdrawing chamber with an open door – was Lady Nan and her ladies. There was one lingering in the doorway and, cuds-me, it was Lady Jane.

I made as if I didn't notice her until she was forced to call out.

'Jester!' she said.

I stopped in a comical turn and slowly faced her. 'Do *you* call out to me, fair lady?'

She demurred by bending her head in a slight bow. She wore a kennel headdress with a green velvet veil. Her neckline was daringly low and I couldn't help sweeping over it with my eyes.

'Is it entertainment you seek?' Her air was different today. Less obscure, more playful . . . as a cat plays with a mouse.

'I saw you with Father Kendrick earlier.'

'Oh?' Was she here to mock me, then? How I deserved the slap, perhaps?

She stepped closer. 'I do not like that priest. He is cruel. And he was cruel to you. It is your vocation to mock, to make merry.'

I stepped ever closer to her. 'As I try to make others understand,' I said cautiously. 'At least you, dear lady, do. I thank you for your kindness.'

'It's just that . . . I know something about that priest. Another lady told me so.'

'Ah. And what little tidbit did she tell you?'

She moved still closer so that we could speak in whispers if we desired, and it seemed that she so desired, looking both ways down the corridor to see if anyone was nigh, but I thought, somehow, that it was a mummery. 'Yes. She told me something quite interesting. Did you know that Kendrick's mother . . . was Spanish?'

Faith! Aloud, I said, 'And why should that be of import?'

'Oh, come now, Master Somers. Surely you are cleverer than that.'

I was. And this was news indeed. Just where *did* Kendrick's loyalties lie? My first thoughts were to tell Marion.

'I thank ye, my lady. For there is some foolery I can make of that.'

Just as I tried to reckon Lady Jane's motives in telling me such – was it murder, was it blackmail, was it to help or to hinder a spy? – she leaned in close to me and said, 'You know, it is dangerous work, this poking and prodding you do. Someone at court will not like it. They might . . . well, try to do you harm. Or . . . try to do harm to those you favor. It is said that there is a particular lady you—'

I grabbed her wrist tight and scowled. 'Threaten me all you like with whatever scheme you can devise. But leave those I love out of it.'

'My arm, Jester. You are hurting it.'

'I don't know what you plot, lady, but I will fight you.'

'Plot? Me? Surely you mistake me.'

'How can I know when you will not speak plain?'

'You are still holding my wrist.'

I looked down at it and finally let it go. She rubbed it, lifted her chin, and left me, only looking back once when she had traveled some yards down the corridor.

I sighed, watching her until she turned a corner. I could not fathom her. The blackmail note that I had long ago burned said something of my spying on the king. Why did she wish this?

It was time I headed toward Marion's chambers.

The corridor was fairly empty. There were always stragglers and servants and the occasional guard, but I could move unmolested and that was a boon, but as I approached her apartments, I saw the door open and heard shouting. *What is amiss?* I wondered.

I peered into the doorway of her withdrawing chamber, and there was Marion's father, yelling and pointing a finger at . . . Rodrigo.

FOURTEEN

The gist of his shouting seemed to be that he had found Marion in a compromising position with Rodrigo, which had me staring at the Spaniard with some questing brows.

Suddenly, Lord Robert spun and bore down on me. 'You're supposed to be looking after her.'

I sputtered. 'What? Me?'

'Yes, you, Somers.'

'And I have, sir.'

'Yet you let this . . . this *foreigner* ruin her.'

I stared at Marion, asking with open palms.

'As I tried to explain to Lord Heyward,' she began tersely, 'I was helping our poor injured friend. He had made his way unaided from the monastery's infirmary, but when I found him, he was pale and sickly, so I naturally brought him here since it was closer than the Spanish quarters, and I was trying to help him to my bed when he came of a sudden into a faint. And that's when my . . . when Lord Robert arrived.'

'Oh, I see.' I made myself look humble and truthful. I don't think he believed it. 'Lord Robert, Rodrigo Muñoz is a friend of mine from the Spaniards' men. And he was hurt only yesterday. The kind brothers of the Observant Friars nursed him through the night, as indeed, did I. I didn't know you were well enough to leave,' I said accusingly to Rodrigo. He merely kept his head down and swayed a little as he stood before the lord. 'And look, my lord. He is still ill.' I rushed to him and sat him down on a chair before he fell. 'He's in no fit state to be walking about. And definitely no state to . . . to do what you suggest, my lord.'

'Nevertheless. I will speak to the Spanish ambassador and see what can be done. This man must marry my daughter.'

My lungs seized. For a brief moment, I thought *I* might faint. No, not my Marion! The only woman in all this world who would understand me. I loved her! She was mine own as I was hers.

And still, I did not speak.

Lord Heyward stalked from the room and the three of us stood mute. Until Rodrigo softly said, '*Mi señorita*, I am sorry for bringing this upon you.'

'Don't be absurd, Master Muñoz. My father is headstrong. I . . . I can talk him out of it.'

'I'm not so certain, Marion.' I wrung the pleated hem of my coat. 'He looked determined.'

'He's been looking for an excuse to send me away.'

'And now he's got one.'

'No one else has asked to marry me that I would accept.'

That barb hit direct. For it was true that, coward that I am, I had not actually formally asked him. He certainly knew about our courtship, but that was as far as it went. I glanced up at her with a wince. 'I should have asked long ago. Will he agree to it now, do you think?'

She threw up her hands and paced.

'Should I . . . should I go after him now . . . or wait?'

'Wait for what, Will?' she hissed, exasperated. 'The Second Coming?'

Would that it *was* here! I crumpled my hem again. 'Will you be well, Rodrigo?'

'I would feel better if I didn't have to marry the lady.'

'Oh. Then I'll go to Heyward. Now.'

I left her rooms, looking both ways down the corridor. I didn't see him, but I supposed the best way was in the direction of his apartments. I imagine that those in the corridors weren't used to a solemn-faced jester, but today was a different day.

I almost passed him, so occupied were my thoughts on reaching his lodgings. He was talking to some gentlemen of the bedchamber, for he was part of the king's retinue – as were we all.

I stopped myself and doubled back, waiting impatiently behind him as he concluded his business. Then he turned to me with as stern a countenance as a stone gargoyle. 'What do you want, Somers?'

'My lord, I crave a private conversation with you.'

'I haven't the time now.'

'You must make the time!' I insisted. The lion had come to the fore . . . and then just as quickly devolved into a mouse. For his visage had turned storm-black. He looked me over as a fishmonger examines yesterday's fish. Finally, he turned his face away and jerked his head for me to follow.

Follow I did, a few paces behind him. I knew what I had to say but, cuds-me, I couldn't remember how to say it.

His groom was there when we entered the withdrawing room and Heyward waved him off, dismissing him. He settled himself in a large chair by the fire, didn't offer me one, and looked up expectantly.

It's a simple question, Will. Just ask it!

By the mass my mouth went suddenly dry! I swallowed and placed my hand upon my heart. 'My lord, you know I've been a good friend to your daughter since I came to court . . .'

'So I've been told,' he said. He wore a severe aspect to his face.

'But . . . but w-what you may not be aware of was that this friendship became something . . . dearer. Sir, I know I should have come to you sooner, but me, being the king's fool, well . . . Not that it isn't an honorable profession, if a somewhat foolish one. But my wage is good, my lord. Very good. And I have drawn the favor of the king over and over, so I have every reason to expect a good pension from him when my fooling days have passed. Indeed, he's told me so many a time. And I have my own quarters consisting of withdrawing room, bedchamber and another small room for a servant. So it isn't as if the prospect of me—'

'Somers, is there a point to this?'

'A point? Oh, indeed, my lord, there is. The . . . the point is that I wish with my very heart to make Marion my wife. And I anxiously await your permission, my good lord. For she loves me, and I love her. All very chastely.'

He never even took the time to ponder it. 'My Marion wed a fool? No. Out of the question.'

'But my lord—'

'I said it's out of the question, Somers. If that is all . . .'

'She can't marry Rodrigo. He was ill. They did nothing wrong.'

He stood. 'It is decided. You are dismissed.'

Everything slowed. The look of malice on Heyward's face, the very breath I exhaled, even the flickering flames in the hearth, everything slowed. All but my heartbeats, which had stayed in that same quickened rhythm.

I could speak to Henry. If I asked him, he would force Heyward to do it. He would do this for me. But then . . . if I did, this would make bad blood between me and Heyward and Marion and her father for years and years. He would never forgive me. And what sort of marriage was that?

Oh, how the pain of his refusal stabbed at my heart!

I couldn't do it. I couldn't go to Henry. I couldn't tell Heyward that I was going to do so. This was no cowardice, though Marion might yet call it so. But I couldn't have this man angry at his daughter, the bastard daughter he seemed to dote upon.

I girded m'self and bowed. 'If . . . if that is your wish, my lord.'

His gaze passed over me once before he turned away.

I dragged myself from his chambers and walked with a heavy heart through the corridors, not seeing at all where I was going. I could feel the other courtiers staring at me, waiting for Will to do something funny. For surely this long face I wore like a mask was only to hide my next caper. They never looked upon me as a man, with feelings and hurts. I was there only to entertain, to shock, to make a mad fool of myself. And why not? That *is* what I did. From the dawn of the day, to when the sun set. I was the king's dog, his puppet, his silly-arse fool. And silly fools have no heart.

I lingered outside Marion's chambers. I couldn't go in. I couldn't tell her that I had asked and had been refused in almost the same breath. It had been so swift, this judgment.

Just as I had finally girded myself, Marion burst out through the door and ran into me.

'Will! I was just about to go in search of you.'

'You shouldn't have bothered, my dear Marion.'

'Whyever not? You look terrible. What's happened?'

I took her hand, held it as if I would never hold it again. Indeed, it would not be *my* hand to hold. 'It was dreadful, Marion.' I shook my head in the thinking of it. 'I . . . I finally got up the blood to ask your father.'

She threw her hand over her mouth. 'What did he say?'

'He said what I thought he'd say all along. "It's out of the question,"' I said in a near perfect imitation of her father's voice.

She blinked at me. 'But . . . did you plead your case?'

'Of *course* I did!' I realized my voice was too loud and hushed myself. 'I did. I said that I made a good wage and was in the king's favor and that we loved each other. He wouldn't even entertain it for the span of a single heartbeat. We're doomed, Marion. He won't consent.'

'Then . . . we shall have to marry in secret.'

My heart soared for that fraction of a moment . . . until, like Icarus, my hopes were only wax too close to the sun. 'My love, I can't marry in secret in direct opposition to your father. And without Harry's permission. The king wouldn't like it. He might sack me. He might have me arrested. Then what would become of you?'

She bleated an exasperated sigh. 'Why did you have to be a fool?'

'You would have loved me less.'

'I might have done,' she said, wiping the tears from her face.

I couldn't stand her grief and enclosed her in my arms. 'Oh, Marion. What's to be done? Will you be forced to marry Rodrigo and go away to Spain? I suppose it wouldn't be so bad for you. They have oranges in Spain. And the weather is not so cold as in England.'

'I don't want to leave you. I don't want to leave England, oranges or not.'

'At least I was first on the list.'

'You'll always be first.' She turned in my embrace and sobbed.

Too many eyes were looking upon us, even if they were

servants, and I shuffled her into her chambers and let her dampen my shoulder.

I left her after some time. I promised to think of a solution, but cuds-me, my mind was a blank on it. It was later that Marion was to accompany Lady Nan's ladies in the gardens. She was to help them in their embroidery, for she was a master of it. Henry didn't need me, so I thought it best to be nigh. At least we could look at one another. And I could ask Nan's lady-in-waiting how exactly she knew that Kendrick's mother was Spanish. For it had gone completely out of my head. How did one find such information? I suppose one could look into church records. Where was Kendrick baptized? Or had the church burned down from such a devil as Kendrick getting holy waters?

Nevertheless, I found the ladies, all sitting under the shade of a tree, the lesser ladies sitting with Marion, while Nan's favorites surrounded her more closely. Mark Smeaton was playing his lute, so I had no need to entertain. I had forgotten my instruments in any case. I was at loose ends indeed today.

Instead, I sat near Smeaton and just hugged Nosewise, giving him the love I would have given Marion.

At last, I let the pup roam, and the ladies loved to pet and pick him up. Nosewise was a smart hound, for the ladies always had some treat to give to him. Oh, to be a dog. Of course, only if you were a mongrel could you choose your own bitch. Hunting dogs and family dogs had to be minded well, and couldn't court just any other dog they fancied.

I glanced at Lady Nan and she seemed satisfied to hold court with the ladies around her, laughing, jesting, gossiping. Once or twice, she looked toward me, no doubt expecting me to leap up and start some cavorting jest. But I wasn't in the mood. By Heaven, I was glad Henry didn't need me, for I would have had to pull the fool out of a great, dark well. And I didn't know if I could pull that hard today.

I leaned back on the grass, feeling the lovely sun on my face, but then it made me think of Spain and poor Rodrigo. And Gonzalo, for I had not yet found his killer. Nor my blackmailer. Or had I? For surely that had to be Lady Jane.

But why just that one note and not another? Why coy threats? And to threaten those I love? For I *was* guilty and they need not even prove it. All they needed to do was say it were so, and where the king could hear of it. Why hadn't she come for me yet?

I glanced again at Marion. She had such a soft face, with only slightly arching brows that often shewed her cleverness. Her eyes – such dark eyes with the mysteries of the world within them. Her auburn hair framed her face, as did the French hood she wore. Such a delicate face, so deceptive to the lioness in her heart. And a lioness in the bedchamber as well. Had I been more attentive . . .

It happened so fast. Marion leaned over to the lady beside her – Lady Jane, as it happened – pointing out some stitch, and then just as suddenly leaned away to answer a question of the lady on the other side of her. Something sheared the wind and Marion fell back with a cry. Then Lady Jane beside her jerked hard against the tree. Red blossomed on the embroidered kirtle bodice and there was the unmistakable crossbow bolt just sprouting from it like a flower. And then she slumped.

Screaming all around me. Shock. Fear. I jolted to my feet and looked in the opposite direction, the place where the bolt surely originated. Someone was running. Without thinking I sprang from my place and ran after him.

So many arranged bushes and topiaries. So many little fences and hedges. But between it all, something fell to the ground behind him. He was not a courtier, for he wore a dark gown of some kind. Was it . . . was it a cleric's gown?

I scooped up the object . . . a crossbow! I clenched it in my hand and leapt through the bushes, scratching my face and hands, where I only just spied him retreating into the palace. He turned his face once to see if someone was pursuing him before the shadows consumed him.

The carefully trimmed beard and mustache. The eyes I could not forget.

Father John Kendrick.

FIFTEEN

By Heaven. Kendrick. The scoundrel priest. He . . . he *murdered* Lady Jane! Had she told one too many persons of his Spanish connections? My mind played it over and over again. And from the angle I had witnessed it . . . but no! The notion was incredible. But seeing it yet again in my head, it was undeniable. It had looked to me that the bolt had originally been aimed at . . . at *Marion. My* Marion. 'Oh *Jesu!*' I ran. I threaded through the trees, between the hedges, and leapt over the last one and swooped in, dropping the crossbow and taking Marion in my arms.

'Oh Marion, Marion.'

'Will. Oh, blessed Holy Mother.'

I held her at arm's length and looked at her. Her sleeve was torn and there was blood. 'Marion!'

'It grazed me. The bolt. It killed Lady Jane. If I had not moved in that instant . . .'

I pulled her in again and pressed my lips to her temple. 'Marion,' I whispered. 'That bolt . . . was for you.'

She startled and tried to pull away, but I tightened my hold. 'Becalm yourself, dearest. You're safe now.'

'Who, Will? Who would do such a thing?'

'Steady yourself. It was Father Kendrick.'

She pulled away to look me in the eye. 'It's him. He's the blackmailer. He's the murderer. Oh, Will.'

'But this is a delicate business, my love. It was Lady Jane who threatened my loved ones. I thought she was the blackmailer. And so she might have been. Perhaps she had him do this deed, but the hand of God intervened and Kendrick accidentally took *her* out of her mortal life instead of you. Aye me.' I wiped my hand over my face. 'But if I let the guards get him, and *he* is the blackmailer, he will expose *me*. I'm at my wit's end. What shall I do? I can't have him trying to kill you, and killing others arbitrarily. And then casting me from court. I'd have no life after that. I certainly couldn't marry you.' A sob choked any further speech and I turned away from her, facing a tree. It was better than facing her. For now it all seemed rather cowardly at that.

The guards clattered forth. Some ushered Lady Nan away, whilst the others stood around the rest of us. A man in a physician's gown and white cap under his black hat knelt at Lady Jane's side. There were other men who gathered around him. I recognized them as part of the privy chamber. They searched around and their gazes landed on me.

Gird yourself, Will. I marched toward them with the crossbow in my hand. 'Somers,' said Francis Bryan, Chief Gentleman of the Privy Chamber – and with an eye gouged out at a joust but that many said God Himself took in debt – turning to me. That gouged left eye was covered with a patch, thank Christ, but with his dark beard, he had a most forbidding manner. One could always rely on him to change his opinion to match the king's. Very often I called him a weathervane, even to his face. Today, I did not. 'What have you to do with this?'

'My lord.' I held up the crossbow. 'I found this while pursuing the killer.'

'You?' said Roger Ratcliffe, Gentleman Usher of the king's chamber. He jammed his fist in his hip, sweeping back his coat of many pleats with its puffed sleeves, nearly as puffed as he was. 'What are you doing here?'

'I go everywhere, my lord, as you well know. Here. Take this.' I urged the crossbow upon him but he refused to handle it.

'Give it to the serjeant-at-arms there,' he waved vaguely. 'What else do you know of this?'

'I know that the bolt was intended for Marion Greene, Lord Robert Heyward's daughter.' I swept my arm with the crossbow toward her. And how small she looked with her face white with fear.

'Heyward's daughter, eh?'

'Yes, and when she drew back, the bolt barely missed her and hit poor Lady Jane. Lady Marion was grazed.'

'Are you certain of that, Somers?'

'By my life, sir.'

'I can see that. I've never seen you look so grave.'

'I . . . I think it is the same who killed that Spanish man from the ambassador's retinue. And tried to kill the same's groom only a day ago.'

'What's this?' He looked around, as if someone in the melee of weeping women and running guards could answer the question. 'What are you saying, Somers?'

'Just as I have said, my lord. There is much going on here that is connected.'

'A conspiracy, you say. And what makes you think that? Who are you to make these assumptions?'

'A clever man who is observant, who has walked into these events by God's own Providence.'

He stared at me, as did Bryan with his one eye, before he snapped to. 'I think I'd best talk to the Captain of the Guard. Here, give me that, Somers.'

He gestured for the crossbow still in my hand and I gladly handed it over to him. 'Did you see who did it as you were in pursuit?'

It seemed that it took me a long time to answer, but it must have been mere seconds, for he didn't remark on it. 'No, my lord.'

Coward, Will. But it wouldn't do to incriminate myself, would it?

He said naught more to me as he swaggered toward the Captain of the Guard with Bryan in tow.

Marion and I were there for some time. I told my story again, telling the guard and then *his* serjeant, and then the sheriffs's man. Some time during all this, Marion's father arrived. He glanced at me with his usual disdain and took his daughter into his arms and led her away. I didn't mind. Maybe he was taking her to his apartments. I'd feel better if she was there and out of harm's way. Because now I had to find Kendrick and put the dread fear of God in him to answer to me. I could not let another innocent die because of my fear of being exposed. To Hell with that. If I were thrown from court, then so be it.

*   *   *

My best chance was to talk to Lady Nan's ladies-in-waiting, but they were all in a disarray. And where was Lady Nan? I needed to talk to her to discover what she had seen.

Good God, Will. You're the sarding jester. You can go where you will. I had to tell m'self that, for I was as flummoxed as the next man in these matters. So I asked here and there of the courtiers where Lady Nan was, and I was finally told that she was in her apartments and was not to be disturbed. Well! That had not stopped me before.

I made my way to her rooms and a guard stood at the entry. He stared straight ahead and moved only his eyes toward me. 'What do you want?' he asked out of the side of his mouth.

'I wish to see Lady Anne.'

'She will not be disturbed.'

'But she called for me.'

He mulled this for an eyeblink or two before he looked to the left, then the right – all without moving his head, mind – before he jerked his head, meaning that I should go through.

I bowed to him, and hurried through the door.

In the withdrawing room I could already hear her, talking furiously with a sob to her voice. I burst through the door and was surprised to see Mark Smeaton, clutching the neck of his lute and trying to offer her calming words.

She swung toward me when she heard the door and the sudden flash of hope died when she recognized me. 'Oh. It's only Somers.'

'*Only* Somers. My dear Lady Nan.'

And then she seemed to remember that I had been a witness and she stalked toward me. 'Will, what happened? Is Lady Jane . . . is she . . .'

'She is, lady.' I crossed myself and lowered my face. She did so too. 'But I must talk to you of these very matters.'

She wrung her hands. 'I don't want to talk about it. Such a terrible thing.'

'But I must, my lady. You see, I think the bolt was meant for another. Your embroidery mistress, Lady Marion.'

She fixed a quizzical expression on me. 'Who?'

I held the anger back. Lady Nan was like any other courtier, I told myself. She paid no attention to underlings unless
they were important to her, and Marion couldn't possibly be
important to *her*. But today, I would make her so.

'The embroidery mistress. The one instructing Lady Jane
Perwick. She was sitting beside her.'

'The ginger-haired one? Oh yes. I know her. *She* was the
target, you say?'

'I believe so. You see, she was in the path of the bolt, when
she suddenly drew back. If she had not moved – which I am
certain the killer hadn't thought she would – then *she* would
have been struck.'

'I see. And why should someone wish to harm this lady?'

'Er . . . that, I do not know. But she is a dear friend of
mine. And I must know who could have done this.'

'Ah.' Nan sat in her chair and rested her delicate foot upon
the footstool. She glanced toward Smeaton and abruptly waved
him off. Dismissed, he scowled at me and strode quickly to
the door. 'You are worried about her,' she said.

I swiftly got down on one knee to her. 'Oh yes, my lady.
She is most important to me.' For all the lower courtiers must
have known that we were tight friends. And Lady Jane knew
it too, since she did her nosing about. Then nosing put me in
mind that Nosewise was missing again. Faith! I knew that the
pup would show himself before long. I didn't need to worry
over him. I was worried over Marion.

'Will!' she must have said for the second time.

'Blind me, Lady Nan. I've been in my own head.'

'You have. I have never seen you so distracted. Come, sit
by me.'

I took up the stool that Smeaton had lately vacated and sat.
To my surprise, she took my hand. 'Poor jester. Poor fool.
Everyone thinks you are only the one thing, and no one remem-
bers that there are layers to you, as there are layers to any
man . . . or woman, when it comes down to it. Is your embroideress well?'

'Yes. Wounded slightly, but she is well. Her name is
Marion.'

'Like in the tales of Robin Hood?'

'Aye. The daughter of the Yeoman of the Records, Lord Heyward.'

'Oh.' And the tenor of that meant that she recognized Marion's status as a bastard. 'And she is dear to you. Is she your sweetheart?'

'Aye.'

'The things I am learning today. That the king's fool has a sweetheart.'

'I am a man like anyone else.'

'Not quite like anyone else.'

'Mayhap.'

'Dearest Will. For now I shall always think of you this way, with your brow so strained and heartsick, no longer the fool who torments me.'

'I have not tormented you of late, lady.'

'No, you have not. Not since we became friends.' She patted the hand that she held. 'What shall we do? How can we find this one who would have harmed her?'

'I already have my ideas.'

'Then you are a clever man. What do you need of me?'

'Did you see anything? Did you hear anything beforehand of anyone making a threat?'

'Alas, I was preoccupied. I only looked up when one of my ladies screamed.'

'And saw no one leaving the scene?'

'No, for I was just as shocked as anyone else. And then guards came to usher me away to safety.'

The door burst open and Henry stood in the doorway. At first, his face was masked in concern . . . and then he saw Lady Nan holding my hand. And his face changed again.

Nan rose and curtseyed low and I merely sat on the stool, like the fool I was.

She hastened to Henry and touched his hand, gesturing towards me. 'Your Grace, poor Will.'

'Poor Will? I was told you were in danger and that one of your ladies was killed. What is "Poor Will" doing here?'

'My lord, he was a witness and he says . . .' She got in closer to him and tried to get up on the tips of her toes to tell Henry's ear, 'Will thinks another lady was the intended target. His—'

I quickly shook my head, beseeching that she not mention my relationship to Marion. So it is that women are more attuned to subtle gestures and she understood immediately.

'Will's friend, Lord Heyward's daughter.'

'Lord Heyward? What nonsense is all this?'

'It's not nonsense, Hen – my lord. For your Will is much aggrieved. He was there. He saw it all happen.'

Finally, it reached his heart. His face softened and he looked upon me with tender eyes. 'Will, my lad. Are you all right?'

I shrugged. 'As well as can be expected.'

'Come, lad. Come here.'

I rose and shuffled toward His Majesty. He scooped me up into an embrace, that mountain of a man, and I was well and truly hugged. 'You are excused from me for today. I want you to comfort your friend and do not think of your duties. They can be belayed for a day at least.'

'Thank you, my kind lord.'

'Anything for you, Will. Now be off with you. I worried over Lady Anne and I must do my own comforting.'

He had done me a good turn. What other servant would have received even half his graciousness? I bowed low to him, and then to Lady Anne, and I took my leave of them both.

I tried to get to see Marion in Lord Heyward's chambers but, as I suspected, I was turned away. Marion would surely tell him what I had said about her being the target, and then Heyward would hasten to marry her off to Rodrigo and pack the two of them off for Spain. But what if this was all part of a Spanish plot to begin with, one that Gonzalo tried to foil? What about her safety then? Maybe it was best Heyward sent her away from court in England. Maybe . . . maybe it was best for all of us.

I dragged myself from the guarded door and I suddenly heard the clatter of claws on wood. When I turned, Nosewise was barreling toward me. I patted my chest and he leapt up and landed there.

'Little pup, where have you been? I am in sore need of

you.' I hugged him and kissed his muzzle and he lapped at me with that tongue and joy in his eyes. 'Good boy,' I said to his fur. 'Oh! You are in need of a bath, my lad. For you stink indeed.'

I took him back to our lodgings and fed him before I called for a servant to bring me hot water.

My own washtub would do, and I removed my doublet and rolled up m'sleeves and carefully regulated the heat of the water before asking him to jump in. He did so with all relish and got himself good and wet, splashing about in ecstasy. A washcloth with some soap was what I used to scrub him up and he even seemed to enjoy that too. I added a little rose water – it surely could not hurt – and when I brought him out, he got me drenched when he shook it off, but he was quivering and so I grabbed my flannel and scrubbed his fur as dry as I could get it. 'I shall have to get you your own flannel, I see. I can't have the laundry thinking I have this much hair on me. A crooked back is quite enough to live with.'

He was happy and dry and smelling much better. 'When you lie down with courtiers, you will end up smelling like a dog, my friend.' He licked my face and scrambled around the room. 'Out again? You've just been out, and only God knows where. All right. I must investigate in any case. But let's leash you this time.'

I found the leash under my bed (did *he* put it there?) and attached it to his collar. 'Let's go.'

Thus leashed, I was just another courtier taking his dog for a walk. The afternoon was drawing late. And I had thought the king would not take his meal in the banqueting hall, but preparations were being made after all and I had no wish to be in the servants' hall this day anyway. So I returned to my lodgings to bring my basket of nonsense, for even though Henry had given me the day off, I was like the worker in the field and this was no Sunday.

Soon, all the candles in chandlers were lit, the linens were laid, the Yeoman of the Pitcher House had brought trays of jugs and goblets for servants to set upon the high table. The salt cellars were last to be laid, for King Henry's was a lavish creation in silver and shaped like a Welsh dragon – for he had Welsh heritage – while the lesser tables had a small dish with a spoon. And the farther tables none at all.

I had a stool set *before* the table in front of Henry because I ate from his plate so that I could talk to him, and my very own goblet was laid – the one that Henry had called to be made for me, with a jester carved out in relief on the side . . . in silver. I stood before that plate, merely looking at it; my own stool, my own trencher, my own goblet, right in front of the King of England.

But Henry would be pleased to see me, despite his having been gracious. He would know I was grateful to him for the offer but that I loved him best. And I did.

Giles Duwes, the lutenist, was tuning his instrument and sitting to the side on a raised platform. Close enough but not too close as to obscure the king's view of the hall nor the hall's view of the king. That was *my* job.

He looked up and caught my eye and I gave him a wave, which he acknowledged with a nod. I sometimes asked him for advice about that tune or this, for he had been trained where I had not been. He was generous with his time with me. Not everyone was in competition at court, though it seemed that even the mice in the pantry were at odds. For Henry was a musician himself and he enjoyed Giles's music and that of his son. I could never replace them. And, as far as I knew, they'd never replace me, not being as foolish.

Gradually, courtiers began to arrive. First the lesser ones closer to the dais, and then the others farther back, and finally the head table.

Before I was brought to court, I thought that everyone, including the least servant, ate with the king, for I'd heard tales how the royal court's hall was so big it could stand the whole population in it. And while that might be true, protocol – I had since learned – changed that. There were outer chambers. The great watching chamber was for Gentlemen of the Privy Chamber and some household officers. Most other servants, grooms and pages served at all the tables . . . and got what was left over in their own hall.

We were all admonished not to eat in our own chambers,

for we were a society of the king, and as any good Christians, we were to eat communally and share of what we had . . . though the servants on the bottom of the rung would grumble that they never quite shared fully with those of the highest rungs. Indeed, the king and his highest courtiers could eat in private. Who was to naysay them?

I suspected the reason that we weren't to eat alone in our chambers was to discourage vermin. In that case, I suggested to the Board of the Green Cloth – that auditing body of the entire Royal Household – that each person at court should be issued a cat. The suggestion was not appreciated.

But forgetting all that, here was Will Somers, eating off the king's plate and even the king could not naysay me. Though sometimes Henry did swat at me with his spoon when I went for the best morsels.

As the seats filled, no one was allowed to eat until the king arrived. We could smell the wonderful scents of food under their lids. Henry's tables never lacked, and our appetites were whetted indeed. Even mine, strange to say. I wanted the wine for my goblet. No ale was necessary at the king's table, though Henry did like his ale as well.

At last, he arrived to trumpeting and cheers. I don't know that all men loved him as I did, but they had to admit that King Henry presented a fine specimen of the male body. Strong, tall, with a ready smile, and great wit. A composer, a musician, a dancer, a jouster . . . Yes, he was all a man or a woman could want in their king. Even if he had his odd notions about marriages and heirs.

He waved to his courtiers and then ignored them as he sat, and Giles played his lute softly.

'Will,' said Henry as the wine poured into his goblet and then into mine. 'I thought you'd be gone from here. I gave you the day.'

'And a kind and generous thing it was, Harry. But when I saw the banqueting hall prepared for you, well, I couldn't stay away. You cheer me as much as I cheer you.'

He smiled with tenderness in his eyes. 'Ah, you are my good Will, aren't you?'

'I do my best, sire. And that reminds me. Do you know

why men stay babes all their lives? I know many a wife will swear to that.'

'No, you silly ass. Why is it?'

'Because they never pass an opportunity to suckle at a woman's teat.'

Henry cast his glance to the women at the table, who tittered under their hands, while he let out a loud guffaw, pounding the table with his hand. He recovered and, chuckling, he wagged a finger at me.

I wetted my throat with wine.

The king was served larks on sticks, a pork pie, two roasted pigeons, slices of beef in gravy, and the hartichoak in a bowl, one of his favorites, a beastly thistle drenched in honey. My knife stabbed at one of his pigeons which I hoist to my plate. I cut off a leg and shook it at him.

'You know, Harry. I think you would have been happiest as a yeoman farmer. *I* would have been such had you not snatched me from obscurity.' Either that, or picking at wool for Master Fermor. I scooped some salt with the tip of my knife from the silver dragon nef, and sprinkled it liberally on the pigeon.

'Maybe, Will, you'd be surprised to note that I myself had thought that many a time. How the cares of state sometimes weigh a man down, and how pleasant it would be in the country, looking out across the landscape of my farm, and plowing a field with the good smell of the turned earth in my nostrils.'

'A poet farmer,' I said, taking a bite of the pigeon.

'But Your Grace,' said Suffolk, the king's brother-in-law, 'you as a farmer? The kingdom should be the poorer for it.'

'Am I not a tiller of the land anyway?' said Henry. 'But it is my courtiers that sow the seeds—'

'—of contention,' I quickly interjected. I reached over to his plate and made a grab for the pork pie, but Henry tapped my hand with the flat of his knife. 'I think I should have liked to see you as a farmer, Harry. You appreciate the land. I can see you getting your hands dirty. Not like these others who don't know what real work truly is.'

Suffolk didn't take the bait, but Thomas Howard, the Duke

of Norfolk, was ready to. He was a hawk, always pleased to stoop no matter what the prey was. 'You think that one must dirty one's nails, Somers, to do work? I assure you, the privy council does the good work of the kingdom.'

I chewed and spoke out of the side of my mouth. 'Forgive me, Norfolk, but a man that can't even wipe his own bum knows nothing of work.'

They all at the head table stiffened, even Henry. For he had groomsmen to do the task of the king's garderobe. Aye, and there he was at the end of the table, standing by, Sir Anthony Denny. And a proud job it was. I saluted him with my cup.

But in the end, Henry smiled. I think that if he could be a country esquire, he'd learn to wipe his own bum, and gladly.

'Let us not speak of bums whilst we cut our meat,' said Henry, with a warning eye at me. 'But I tell you what we shall do. Tomorrow, I propose a hunt.'

The head table fell silent, until Brandon, the Duke of Suffolk, spoke up. 'But Your Grace, it takes some planning for a royal hunt.'

'Not a *royal* hunt as such, Charles. Just . . . a few of us. A simple hunt. A *secret* hunt,' he said, where the whole court could hear him. 'We won't need all the dignitaries. After all, there's been a death.' He seemed to remember that as he said it and frowned. But then his usual jovial attitude prevailed. 'Just a few of us. And I want you, Will, to come too.'

'Me, Harry? Why do you want me on your hunt?'

'Because you've never been, and I want you to come. Say you will.'

Spoken as if I had a choice on the matter. I don't know that I'd enjoy seeing a majestic hart or boar speared, but Henry wanted me there for whatever reason in his head, and that meant I was to go.

I drank down my wine, thinking of all I still needed to do. That Marion was kept safe was my first concern, but now that Lady Jane was dead, was that a fear any longer? And Kendrick, that murdering priest. How could I leave Marion here while he was on the prowl? He killed Jane instead of Marion, so was there anything left to fear? Unless Jane confided all to him . . .

And I worried over Rodrigo's fate . . .

I slammed the empty goblet to the table like the pragmatic man I was. 'Of course I'll go, Harry! I am like Ruth in the Holy Scriptures: "wherever you go, I shall go!"' And God bless us for it.'

SIXTEEN

The next morning the hunt was quickly assembled. Henry wanted a humbler hunt, one far less ostentatious than his usual hunts, so that meant no stands to be built for courtiers to watch, no foreign dignitaries, no pavilions for the ladies, no musicians in accompaniment. Only certain courtiers were to be invited: his privy men, and also servants, cooks and several galapines to prepare the meals, two pavilions for larders and food preparation, five more for Henry and his men, pages for the luggage, and carts of faggots for the fires, men-at-arms for the hunting spears and archers for the bows and arrows, Gentlemen Ushers of the Chamber, members of the King's Wardrobe, Sir Nicholas Carew who was Master of the Horse along with the horses, horse grooms for tack and saddles, and an assortment of others who do this and that . . . and one court fool.

A humble affair in the Tudor fashion.

Henry had his favorite spot in the park surrounding Greenwich, only a few miles from the palace, and camp was set up. I wondered how any animals remained in the vicinity after the noise of setting up a camp with the fires and horses and such. But I was but a virgin when it came to a hunt, so how was I to know?

Sir Nicholas Carew was on his horse with a pennon on his spear, awaiting the king and the rest of us. A horse was appointed for me, and Harry had meant it when he said he wanted me to be in it, for he enjoined me to ride beside him with the Master of the Horse on the other side. This was a great honor for such a one as me, who was not nobility and never would be. For some reason, Henry had taken me under his wing and, treating me like a son, he wanted to instruct me on what a hunt was.

I girded myself and choked the reins, and then I apologized to the poor horse.

We rode out into the forest. Ah, but I did love the forest and the green plains of England. Not that I'd been to any foreign land, but I was a farmer's lad, and being caged in a palace made my heart ache for the open skies, the green and fresh aromas of farmland. And Henry loved it too, for he favored the wild lands, the parks for hunting and riding. He needed it as much as I, and I was grateful for the respite, notwithstanding my urgent situation back at court.

Henry usually hunted with a spear, but today he wanted to boast of his expertise with the bow. Not all his companions followed on this hunt today, but we did have at least eight fellows in our company. The dogs ran ahead of us, for the Master of the Horse had seen deer sign and we were following the tracks.

Henry followed close to Carew for several miles but gradually fell back, for he could well see that the dogs had lost the scent. He waved the other courtiers ahead and took another track, gesturing for me to follow. Again, he waved off the men-at-arms, for it seemed Henry's scheme was that he and I were to be alone.

We rode up a rise and suddenly had a magnificent view of a patchwork of farms with their hedgerows between them and acres of forest before it.

'It's a good land, isn't it, this England of ours,' said Henry, admiring the view, proud of his kingdom.

'It is that, Uncle. A beautiful thing. And up here, there are no cares, no worries.'

'No, there aren't.'

I turned to him then, studying that profile. Thirty-seven years old, fourteen years my senior, and not a gray hair on him. No wonder he looked on me as a son – the son he did not have but hoped to get from Nan Bullen. 'You're thinking deep thoughts, Uncle.'

'That I am, Will.'

'Do you . . . wish to unburden yourself?'

He turned his gaze on mine. There was amusement in his eyes. 'A man who takes advice from a fool . . .'

'. . . is that much of a fool himself,' I finished for him. 'And yet, you quote well your own fool.'

'Because my fool often has better advice than my councillors.' He glanced behind him, just to make sure none of them were nigh, and shook his head in weariness. 'How I wish I were a yeoman farmer.'

'Then do it, Harry. Steal away from this rabble. Sell the jewels on your doublet – for there are many – and buy a patch down there. That one? Or perhaps that one? Be free of the cares of state once and for all.'

'Don't tempt me, Somers.'

'Tell me your troubles, then, Your Grace. You know I am yours.'

'"Your Grace"? You never speak to me thus.'

I shrugged. 'I forgot myself. Tell me your troubles, Harry. And I will tell you to take sixpence and throw it to the crows. They know everything anyway and will give you their instruction.'

'Sixpence to crows? What babble is this?'

'If you will not babble to me, I will babble to you.'

He smiled fondly at me before he turned his mount in front of me and rode back into the wood. He slowed the horse's trot and walked him, listening to the birdcalls, the red squirrels in the trees, the badgers in the bracken. All the forest was alive in the colors of autumn; golds, yellows, oranges, and reds. Like a royal cloak, it was, magnificent in its textures and patterns.

In the shade, a chill breeze moved our hair and he suddenly stilled. He seemed to sense something. He knew. He was of a sudden the Wild Man of the Woods, the spirit of the forest, face made of oak leaves and acorns. And he knew – without yet seeing it – that a deer was nigh. He carefully took the bow from his shoulder and grasped an arrow from his quiver on the saddle.

I listened with all my might and could not do it, could not discern deer from squirrel. But from the thicket not more than ten yards hence, a buck with its crown of antlers emerged, like a great pagan god. He did not look at us for the wind was with us, taking our scent far from him.

Henry, with arrow knocked and the bowstring drawn back to his cheek, took aim.

'No, Harry,' I said softly. 'Let it be.'

He aimed still with a steady hand and spoke softly. 'Do you not favor venison?'

'I do, sir. But just for today, let us not think of this creature as our meat. Let us . . . merely enjoy his nobility.'

Henry hesitated, watching just as I was, as the hart picked his way over the fern, wide ears turning in search of an enemy. He raised his head and, like any king, slowly perused his court; the shadows, the oaks, the fern, and even the red squirrels. It seemed that all should bow to this creature who appeared to own it all.

It could be that Henry at last recognized his kin in this deer, for slowly, he released the string and lowered the bow. 'You are a most unusual man, Somers.'

'Aye, and that's why you love me.'

'What were you like as a child, I wonder?'

'Much the same as I am now, Uncle . . . only shorter.'

He chuckled and we watched as the deer ate his fill of moss unmolested. 'It *is* a noble creature,' he acknowledged.

'Yes, sire.'

After a long time of watching the deer, it disappeared at last into the shadows and I wondered if it were not some wild forest spirit instead of a creature of flesh and blood.

I followed Henry as he moved his mount forward in the opposite direction of the deer. 'No one has ever told me "no" like you do.'

'I must. Now that deer will be grateful and may grant you a boon someday.'

'The fantasies you weave.'

'It could be a magical creature, like a nymph or faery in disguise. Oh, you mustn't laugh, Harry. For one never knows. Don't you ever daydream of such? Have you ever climbed a hill and lain upon the grass and simply looked up to the clouds and saw . . . oh, such things as you could see in them?' For when we had a view of the plains and the sky, I could see mountains of clouds hanging like drapery in the blue heavens.

'Don't be absurd. Never was I so idle. My tutors would have whipped me.'

'Whipped *you*? A tutor striking a Tudor?'

He laughed, but then that laugh dimmed and a shadow crossed his brow as he lowered his face. His gloved fingers – shod in glinting rings – stroked his beard. 'If you will recall, I was not the heir . . . until I suddenly was.' He crossed himself and I followed suit. We were both thinking of that older brother of his, Arthur, who should have been king. And who had first been wed to Henry's current wife . . .

'My poor Harry.'

'Lying on the grass. Did you ever do such? Do *men* do such?'

'Oh, aye, sire. The common man does. Let's go now! Forget the hunt. Come away with me and *be* idle for a time.'

'Become a yeoman farmer, lie upon the grass, look at clouds, of all things. What notions you have this day, Somers. Besides, a king is not at liberty to be idle. His people would see that as slothful, and a king must not be that.'

'But a king must need it the most, eh? Lay aside your bow. Come with me.'

I could almost see it in his eyes, his working it through. *Could* he? *Would* he, even for an hour? But it seemed that the notion of it disappeared like smoke just as suddenly as it had appeared. 'What a tempter you are. Are you the Devil or a jester?'

I suddenly felt saddened for him, for he could never truly be a man like his subjects. For all the gold and comforts of his life, there was the other side of that coin. One of cares and sorrows, and . . . selfishness . . . and state. 'No, sire. I'm just a man. A man who had time to be idle . . . and watch the clouds.'

The king did fell a hart later that day, but not the one we saw, thanks to God's mercy.

His Master of the Horse directed it to be hung in a tree by its hocks, and it was carefully and expertly split down its underside, peeling away only enough hide to get to the bung and the entrails. The king's hunter efficiently pulled out the entirety of his insides and tossed them aside for the dogs, except for the heart, liver, and kidneys which he kept in a wooden bowl. The buck would hang in the larder by the kitchens for about two weeks until his meat was good and seasoned. And his antlers might grace a wall at Greenwich somewhere.

I watched the proceedings with mixed feelings, for, being raised in the country on a farm, I was well acquainted with butchering, even done many a pig m'self. But this time, living at court with all its intrigues, I well knew a man could be done this way too. If he were a traitor, he'd be hanged, then cut down before death to be castrated, then sliced like a tailor's seam, his guts pulled out and set aflame before his eyes. Because a traitor to the king was never to be tolerated. He was to be reviled and treated like a piece of butchered meat, and left for the crows to feast upon, deprived of holy blessings.

And then, I wondered if Henry – in his way – felt much the same, like a traitor to his crown. That he had failed his people by not giving them a son, and he hadn't really wanted to give up Queen Catherine but knew he must do the disgraceful thing for the good of his people.

I wondered what was truly in his mind on it.

Or was I being too naïve, this lad from the country?

His cooks prepared a fine dinner of lamb, cheese pies, and an assortment of other fancies for his table in the afternoon. Henry enjoyed the chase and cornering that deer, and it seemed he had forgotten our talk of that morning, but much later by the warm, crackling fire that cut the dark of the night when the others had gone to bed, he sat close to me and we took turns pouring from the wine jug, finishing it and starting on another. He chuckled and put a hand on my arm. 'You are a good companion, Will.'

'It is my sole desire, Harry, to be a good companion to you.'

'But you are the *best* companion,' he said, with a slight slur. 'I know the others always agree with me to keep me happy. "Yes, Your Grace." "You're correct, Your Grace." "What a brilliant sentiment, Your Grace." Bollocks. It is in their best interests not to rouse anger in me by naysaying me. Sometimes

I notice it. More often than not . . . I don't.' He chuckled at himself. 'But not you. You tell me the truth. That's why I trust you above all others.'

'I am gratified to hear it. Perhaps you should raise my wages.'

He lightly cuffed me across my head and chuckled.

'I didn't mean it,' I said. 'Unless you think it is a good idea, Harry.'

He shook his head and smiled. 'I know you didn't. That's why I *will* do it, you pillicock. You are the truth I seek above all others.'

Shocked, I said, 'Surely there are clerics to tell you the truth. Your own confessor?'

He took a gulp of wine and wiped his mustache with the back of his hand. 'I don't know, Will. These are the men who should speak the truth above all else, in the name of God. But some of them . . .' He let the sentence hang there . . . as much as some of the men he and I were thinking of *should* hang.

'And so,' he said, almost seeming abashed. 'I wanted you to know.'

I grazed my knuckles good-naturedly against his shoulder. 'I know, Harry. I am the most blessed of your subjects. I alone am allowed to call you "Harry" to your face. I know the trust I keep in the hollow of my hand. And I will not fail you. You are in my keeping, you know. I consider it a solemn vocation.'

'I am in *your* keeping? Well. That is the truth of it. *I* am the one blessed.'

We fell silent, the crackling of the fire our only companion. 'Oh dear.' My voice broke the stillness. 'We've become maudlin in our drunkenness.'

'We aren't drunk,' he said.

'My head begs to differ.'

He laughed and then seemed to remember the others were asleep and hushed himself, forgetting that he was king and could do whatever he liked. 'Will, your jests make me laugh and I do not wish to awaken anyone, for I am content in our quiet time this night. I do not want to be interrupted by anyone telling me I should get to bed.'

'You can tell them to go to the Devil.'

'And I do. But I do not wish to be disturbed from this moment.'

I smiled and emptied my cup. The king filled it again for me. 'Me, too, Harry. I like this.'

The king sighed. 'Wasn't this a splendid day?'

'Aye.'

'And do you know . . . I was almost tempted. Almost, I say, to your offer to rush away from it all, to gallop down to the nearest farm and offer up my jewels for it. Almost.'

'You'd make a fine farmer, Harry. You understand the land.'

He chuckled.

I glanced at him, his profile edged by firelight. 'Would you have? With a little more prodding from me?'

He smiled and gazed at me sidelong. 'I reckon we'll both never know.'

I sat back and shivered, looking up past the treetops. 'Aye me, will you look at that sky?'

He lay back his head against his chair and marveled, as did I, at the blackness sprinkled with thousands upon thousands of stars, like a bejeweled gown. He pointed upward as we both observed a shooting star streak across the heavens.

'Look at that, Will,' he breathed. 'Do you suppose it is a good omen?'

'I can't believe that anything this night, at the end of this perfect day, could be anything other than a good omen.'

'I think so too, God will it.'

'Then let's drink to it, Harry!' He clapped our goblets together, spilling a good deal of the contents onto our hose and shoes, and drank up.

An icy breeze came up and he hugged his leopard pelt around his shoulders. I had to make do with a fox fur. 'Will,' he began, sounding sober, 'everyone has an opinion about who is under my bedclothes, but I know nothing of *your* bedchamber. Is there some lady who has caught your eye? You are young yet.'

By the grace of God, an opening. The perfect moment to tell him of Marion and her recalcitrant father. If Heyward could see me now in intimate conversation with the mightiest monarch in Christendom, what would he say to that! Would he still think wifing his daughter to a fool was worthless?

I opened my mouth to say, but the dim, sober part of me told me to pause. *Remember, Will, you aren't going to talk to Henry about it. And you recall why, don't you?* Because it would put a wall up between Marion and her father. Her stubborn, irrational father who refuses to learn anything about me, who doesn't like me simply because I am a fool by profession and have no title other than that.

What was I to say to Henry, then?

'Oh . . . here and there, sire.'

'No one in particular?'

'Who would love this silly face and this crooked back?' I hoist my cup to my lips again. Though once, I had thought I was not worthy of love, but my quick humor brought women and men to my bed. They may not have noticed my face upon first look, but they took a second look when I made them laugh.

'Nonsense, Will. I see the way maids look at you.'

I smiled. 'You have?'

He nodded with a wide grin, the lubrication of wine brightening his eyes again. 'I have.'

'So you see? What need do I have of a sweetheart . . . or a wife?'

'You dally? For shame.'

'What is good for the king is good enough for his jester.'

'A king has a different role.'

'In the end, we are all men. We are the bee, flitting from flower to flower. And we are all fools.'

'You must not get yourself into trouble, Will. I am the king. I cannot be prodded by several gruff fellows in the dark corners of court, defending the honor of a sister or daughter.'

'Ah. Then you know such things occur?'

'Of course I do. And many a man has pleaded with me to help them with a lady.'

'Oh?' As casually as I could with an unsteady hand full of a goblet of spirits, I rested my chin on the other hand. 'And, er, what is the outcome? Say, when a father will not grant a man the leave to wed his daughter . . . or some such. And the suitor pleads to you.'

'I tell them that my influence in the matter will cause rifts in the family. That a father must know best for his own daughter.'

'Oh.' And so Providence had saved my skin once again. My conscience would not let me speak, and it had been the right choice, after all. But my heart still ached.

Suddenly, I was weary of this hunt and just wanted to return home. To court. To Marion.

'Perhaps it *is* time to go to bed,' I said, slowly levering myself from the chair.

'Will you not wait with me for a while?'

I shivered. Was this not what a saddened Jesus asked of his Apostles the night before his death? But Henry had nothing of that kind to fear. Only more sessions with noisy lawyers and clerics, with obtrusive cardinals and bishops, and always Lady Nan asking over and over, 'When, Henry? When?'

So I fell back into my seat and patted his hand. Poor old king. Poor old jester.

SEVENTEEN

Three days we were gone from court, and Henry's privy councillors were glad to have him back, as the petitions and Secretary Knight's notes piled up.

I worried that Marion might have been sent away or wed already whilst I was gone . . . but thank Christ she was not. She was back in her own apartments, but now there was a page guarding them. I pushed the unfortunate boy aside and marched in. '*MAR-i-on!*'

She came through the door from her bedchamber and glared at me. 'Where have *you* been?'

'In the king's company.'

'*You* went on the hunt?'

'Aye, I did. Spent a lot of time with His Majesty.'

'Oh.' She sat in a chair by the fire and gnawed on a finger-nail. 'And did you . . . speak of such private things as . . . as . . .'

I knelt beside her and took her hand. 'I thought about asking him to tell your father that, fool or no, you were to marry me. I knew he could force your father's hand. But . . . in the end, I did not.'

She took her hand back. 'Why, Will?'

'Because . . . because I knew it would cause trouble between you and your father. And definitely between *me* and your father. I couldn't do that to you, Marion.'

'I'm with child, Will.'

That stopped everything; my heart, my breath, my blood circulating – no. The latter was not true, for it roared like a waterfall through my ears. 'Marion,' I whispered, taking back her hand. What did I expect? We did spend a lot of time in each other's arms, in each other's beds. 'That . . . puts another chess piece on the board.'

'At least, I think I am.'

'Would you tell this to your father?'

'Not until I was certain.'

'He'd still hate me.'

'But we would be wed.'

I rose from my position and released her hand. 'When will you be certain enough to tell him? At the child's birthing?'

'I can be more certain before that.'

'Very well. We'll wait, then. Rodrigo—'

'Rodrigo has been sent back to Spain.'

'What!' Three days. Three little days I was absent and suddenly my world had turned over. 'When?'

She sighed and bit that nail again. I pulled her hand from her mouth. She'd bite them all to the quick if not told to stop. 'Yesterday. Father went to the Spanish ambassador with his plea, and they quickly bundled him off on the next ship. He left a letter for you.'

She rose and went to her table, taking the letter from her secret drawer. She handed it to me and I opened it.

Dearest Will, God keep you and bless you,

I am sorry I cannot tell you in person, but circumstances have made it impossible. I shall not have to marry your lady but I return to my homeland in disgrace, or so it is scattered abroad. Do not fear for me, for I shall find another place with another worthy. In the current day, it is no great sin to err in the English court due to the circumstances surrounding the Great Matter. Such is the philosophy of our gracious king and emperor, Charles V. I know you will keep fighting for justice for my lord Gonzalo, and I commend your care to the Holy Virgin to that course. Content yourself that you are doing the best you can. I shall pray for you and always think fondly of you.

Your loving friend,

Rodrigo Muñoz

I folded the paper and tucked it into my doublet. 'Well, that's that,' I said sorrowfully. I would miss him.

'My father still talks of sending me away. I have still refused him.'

An ache was coming upon my head and I rubbed my brow. 'Christ, Marion. If you carry my child, not only *should* I marry you, but you must know that my heart dearly *wants* to marry you.'

'And if my father still refuses?'

'*Then* I shall ask Harry.' I knelt before her again. 'But first, I must confront that swine Kendrick.'

'He's a killer, Will. He's not afraid to hurt people. I'll not have him hurting you.'

'Me? I fear for *you*.'

'You silly-faced fool. I shouldn't want to live if something happened to you.'

It was a strange thing to perk up to, but I did. 'You love me . . . that much?'

Her hand cupped my cheek and her eyes grew tender. 'Of course I do. And more. You are my sweet man.'

I reached up and kissed her, and once tasting that sweet nectar, I rose, embracing her tightly, kissing her deeply. We were thus engaged for a time, and it would have moved to her bed ordinarily, but I thought better of it. Reluctantly, I released her and stepped back. 'We . . . cannot. Not now. I *must* find Kendrick.'

'Yes. My brave, brave jester.'

Brave jester, or idiot fool?

I sought out Wolsey. I had heard that in the early days of Henry's reign, young Wolsey was heaped with many honors by His Majesty. Henry had liked the man's industry, for Henry himself – as much as he talked of the cares of state – did very little in that regard. He liked his music, his dalliances, his exercise of riding and fighting, but he did not like to read documents and he abhorred writing letters. He truly should have been a farmer.

But of late, Henry no longer trusted his cardinal. He could not secure a divorce from the pope, and in his failure, Henry did not deem him dependable. Wolsey's minions – like farm animals – were slowly taking over the farm and the farmer was the last to know.

I was told by servants that Wolsey was in his apartments,

but there was a crowd of courtiers surrounding it, all waiting to see him. Many were turned away.

'Waiting for something, Somers?'

Like a snake, he came upon me without a sound, and like seeing a snake, I jumped. Cromwell.

'Good master, I seek . . .' What could I tell him? For wasn't it Cromwell who told me Kendrick was no longer welcomed to the cardinal's presence? 'I . . . seek Father Kendrick.'

'Strange you should say so.'

'Why strange, my lord?'

'Because no one has seen him for some days.'

That *was* passing strange. 'Is anyone worried about it?'

'Only you. And why does it concern you so?' He took a step closer. I resisted taking a step back.

I studied him, my adversary. For he was the instrument for engineering the exchange from our good Queen Catherine to Lady Nan on the throne. Could I trust him? Every pore in my body, every vein screamed that I could not. So instead, I blurted, 'It has been said that Father Kendrick's mother was Spanish born.'

'Yes. I believe that is so. We . . . had only just discovered it.'

'Do you think he was a spy for the Spanish?' I said as innocently as my eyes could achieve.

It did not convince Cromwell. 'I think you know already, Somers.'

'But truly, Thomas,' I began, falling back on my presence as a fool, 'this spying and this condition of his being missing. Does none of that trouble you?'

'I am not troubled.'

'But . . . missing! That could mean mischief.'

'Could it?'

'Come, Tom. You are as wily as I am. Can you not tell me?'

'And why, Master Somers, should I do that? Why should I tell the court jester of the serious matters of court politics?'

I suddenly made an elaborate shrug. 'You know me well, Tom. You know that I use all the information I can find to taunt and to shoot my barbs. I should like to taunt Kendrick. Oh, very much so.'

I watched his face, and it was like machinery, like the gears of a great clock, each tooth of each gear moving inexorably to the next tooth and the next, moving on until it struck a great chime. This was all on his face, and I had the feeling it was on mine too, for we were not so different, Cromwell and I. We could discern men from the mere look of them, and detect their weaknesses and their faults. But we differed in what we did with that information. I merely wanted to bring their faults to the light of day to make merry, to make fun, and to put them in their place.

But Cromwell was a ploughman, planting them deep into the furrows they themselves made . . . and burying them over.

'If I should find out something more about him,' said Cromwell, 'say . . . something scandalous, I would make certain that he disappeared . . . forever.'

'Forever is a long time. Perhaps this silly jester has information of that kind. But it might implicate someone else who is an innocent and like to lose their place in court. That is my dilemma.' *My* place. But I could not hand him an arrow to target me, of course.

'I see. This . . . innocent. Is their value to court greater by their presence or their absence?'

The man was an accountant, seeking to find the worth of men on his tally sheet, to see how they could be used or bought. 'Their value is very much to the greater good should they *stay* at court, Tom.' I lifted one hand heavenward and placed the other on my heart. 'I give my oath before God Almighty.' The truest prayer I ever made.

He blinked slowly like some great toad. Finally, he huffed a sigh. 'I do believe you, Somers. Will you tell me then?'

I got in close, closer than I wanted to, and with the grace of God to uphold me, I told him quietly, 'I saw him with a crossbow run from the scene of Lady Jane Perwick's murder. I followed him and picked up the discarded crossbow. And I have reason to believe that it was he who also murdered Don Gonzalo de Yscar.'

His eyes widened. I do not think Cromwell was often surprised, but this time he was. 'Is this the truth, Somers, or is it some elaborate jest?'

I crossed myself. 'It is on my honor and my love for His

Majesty that I swear the truthfulness of what I have witnessed and discovered.'

'You've done well, Somers. You have it on *my* honor that I shall do everything I can to apprehend him. Does he know you know?'

'Aye, Tom. That's why I feared to say. What if next time he aimed for me and hit the king?'

His face blanked, but in a way that gave me courage. 'Never fear, Somers. I am in your debt.' He bowed to *me* – God's body! – and took his leave through the crowd and into Wolsey's presence chamber.

That's done it. Your fat is in the fire now, Will. No going back. I had told him. And what if he discovered about Will Somers's penchant for buggery? He'd use it to use me, he would. But I had to take that chance.

I made my way through the court, dodging some courtiers whom I did not want to entertain, and in so doing, I found myself near the quarters of the queen. At present, because of the roiling dust of the Great Matter, it was a lonely and unused part of the palace, for visitors were no longer allowed. Two guards stood at the door, except one left with a quick trot, probably off to the necessary. The one remaining seemed bored. The queen and the Princess Mary had been shifted to what was now a dark and lonely corner, the loneliest of Greenwich.

I could not pass up the opportunity, so I sauntered into the corridor's light. The guard finally had something to do and he watched me carefully. I smiled and came up to him, glancing up and down to his crimson coat and breast plate on his chest. 'Good ev'ning, friend. Why do you stand alone at an unoccupied door?'

'It's not unoccupied . . .' and then he stopped his mouth, for he had spoken the unspoken.

'Truly?' I said, inspecting the door as if I were an architect. 'It does seem unoccupied for such a busy court, for no one seems to come or go. Who lies within?'

'Nobody,' he said, and even winced at the stupidity of it.

'Nobody? But you said it was occupied.'

'I . . . God's teeth,' he rasped. 'Go away, Jester.'

'But I am a curious lad, and now here lies a mystery. It is unoccupied and yet occupied . . . by Nobody. By St George. According to Odysseus, beyond that door lies a Cyclops!'

He clearly did not understand the reference, and I hadn't the time to tutor him. 'Look, friend. I know who is within, and you know who I am.' I closed on him, speaking frankly. 'Dear, dear sir. This was my family . . . and I miss them. May I please spend but a few minutes in their company? It will not harm you and may, in fact, show your mercy to the Almighty.'

He glanced around. He surely did not wish to accommodate me, but he was young, younger than I, and he had not yet been jaded by court.

Finally, with a screwed brow, he rasped, 'Hurry you now. I'll not wait to get you out again.'

'Bless you, bless you.' I didn't hesitate to grab the handle and open the door to the antechamber, closing the door behind me. The first person I encountered was Catherine's lady-in-waiting, Maria de Salinas, Baroness Willoughby. I had not known she was still at court, hidden away with her dear friend.

She burst into tears when she saw me and I bowed and took her into my arms. 'Dear Lady Maria. It is only Will Somers. No need to weep over it. I don't look that bad, do I?'

'No, you fool,' she said in her still thick Spanish accent. 'It is because you look that good. That good to see you again.'

'I don't have much time. I only wanted to give my salutations to the queen and Princess Mary.'

'The queen. So *you* still call her so. There are many at court who will not. Come, Will. You are most welcome.'

She ushered me through, and there was Queen Catherine sitting in a chair by the fire, doing her embroidery, and young Princess Mary sitting across from her, how they always used to be. How plump and aged Catherine looked, and little wonder. She was only a few years older than Henry, but now seemed to look like his mother.

'Look who has come to visit!' trumpeted Lady Maria.

Catherine glanced up, and her face, so swollen and solemn, lit up like a beacon. 'Will Somers!'

Princess Mary dropped her embroidery. She was twelve now, and charming of face and aspect. She came running to me and I found myself encased in her puffed sleeves and woolen bodice. She wept. 'My sweet Mary,' I cooed to her. 'My sweet girl.'

She had been sent away from court to Ludlow three years ago to establish her own court, but Henry had brought her back only two years ago. And yet, that's when this whole business began. I feared she'd be sent away again, and soon.

She did not wish to let me go, but Catherine bid her release me. Reluctantly, Mary did so.

I looked to Catherine and she held her hand out for me to kiss. I fell upon my knee and took it, and it was then I realized that tears were on *my* face.

'We have missed you, Will.'

'Oh, my dear, dear lady. I have missed the two of you as well.'

'Why are you here? Has . . . has my lord sent you?' She said it incredulously, for his cruelties to her had only seemed to accelerate. She was not allowed the festivities of court, and at any day, I expected her to be sent away.

'Erm . . . no, my lady. I came on my own authority. I was passing by . . .'

'Oh, Will,' and in her heavy accent, it came out more like 'Weel'. 'You should not have risked it.'

'It was well worth it, for I miss the both of you.'

'And how is my lord husband?' Slowly, with shaking hands, she went back to her embroidery, but it seemed that she could not pull a stitch.

'Aye me. He is Henry through and through. Nothing has changed.' And by that I hoped she interpreted what I meant to convey; that the annulment was still proceeding, that Lady Nan was still at court, and that her hopes had little chance of succeeding.

She nodded her head.

I wanted to comfort her, make her understand that it was not personal . . . but when one's husband turns away from a twenty-year marriage, how much more personal could it be? 'It is . . . politics, my lady.'

'Not everything at court is political . . . or should be, Will. Sometimes . . . sometimes love is stronger.'

'Henry doesn't love her. Not as he has loved you. He was made mad by Wolsey . . .'

'It is difficult for me to believe a man of God could come between a man and his wife.'

'Alas, my lady, Henry is not just any man. But I don't have to tell *you* that.'

'No indeed.'

Princess Mary either didn't understand our conversation or chose not to hear it. It seemed instead that she couldn't wait for her mother to stop speaking. 'Sing us a song, Will! I have longed to hear your songs again.'

'Oh, my lady. I don't have my cittern.'

'I have a lute!' She jumped up in her high spirits and grabbed her lute from her bedchamber. She rushed it to me and I barely got a hold of it when she let it go into my hands and she returned anxiously to her seat. She was as prodigious with the instrument herself, and likely played better than me. But a song from her Will is what she wanted, and that she would have.

I broke into a lively execution of '*Helas Madame*'. I did speak French but wasn't so good at it. So I rendered the words in English:

Alas, my lady, whom I love so,
let me be your humble servant;
your humble servant I shall always be,
and for as long as I live, I will love only you . . .

Princess Mary was delighted, smiling in a wide grin the whole time. But Catherine seemed sadder upon hearing the words. At least the child could be cheered. For it must be confusing for a daughter whom Henry once called 'his Pearl' to be forced into the life of a prisoner by her own father. There was even some talk of declaring her a bastard, to make certain any heirs from Lady Nan would be the *only* heirs. How would it be to be called a bastard, knowing you are not? Marion was a bastard. It was fact. But her father loved and cherished her, and he had no other heirs. How would it be to one's heart?

I finished the song and Mary clapped enthusiastically, while Catherine gave her nod to me.

'I cannot stay long, my lady. But . . . may I ask you? You must see your own confessor, but had you aught to do with a Father John Kendrick? Has he come to see you at any time?'

Catherine looked up past her kennel headdress and thought. 'A dark-haired priest with a beard and a sour disposition?'

'Aye, lady. That would be him.'

'He came only once, but I did not like him. I know it is a sin to say so about God's own anointed, but . . .'

'Madam, in this case your instincts were correct. I think God has turned His back on this priest. What did he say to you?'

'He explained that he had Spanish blood and that I could trust him. But as you say, my instincts did not believe in that trust.'

'So right you are. He . . . *is* a spy . . . and a murderer. I am glad you turned him out.'

'I have put my trust and my faith in my longtime confessor Fray John Forest. He is a good and faithful priest of the Observant Friary.'

'Thank the grace of God for that, madam.'

The door opened and, though Lady Maria tried to stop him, the guard who had stood at the door had come to fetch me. 'You are done here, Jester.'

'Oh, please,' begged the princess.

But I took her hands and bowed to her. 'I was only allowed to tarry briefly here, my dove. I am glad I was able to sing you a song.'

She sniffed and seemed to straighten. 'When I am queen, you will be *my* jester. I so vow it.'

My poor Princess Mary. She was never to be queen.

I smiled anyway and nodded. To Queen Catherine, I knelt and kissed her hand, and then I bent my forehead to it for a long time. For she had been like a mother to me, mine being gone for some great many years now. Her other hand dropped to my head, and she murmured a Spanish blessing. It saddened me, this brief visit and this parting. I doubted I would ever find a way to return before she was sent away. And when I lifted my head, her eyes knew the truth of it.

'Farewell, my dear ladies. I wish you every blessing from God.'

'He has been kind to us in His mercy,' she said, as by rote. For as far as I could see, the Almighty needed very much to be more present to the queen and her daughter.

As their doors were closed to me and the guard urged me on my way, I wondered if my visit was a good thing or a bad one. It was like the tender dainties marched past the servants' dining hall only to be served to others. Such hunger and desire, never to be quenched.

As I stood in the corridor, I felt at a loss. Where should I go now? To where should I turn? Henry, Henry. You have made a stable boy's mess of this marriage business. Better to have a daughter to be bartered to a crowned head of Europe and take her place as Queen of England, than this foolery and battle with the pope. What good outcome could there be?

Angry at the situation with the queen and Princess Mary, I wanted to strike out. I couldn't strike out at the king, but the next best thing was to confront Kendrick. That was foremost in my heart. I even laid my hand on the bodkin at my belt. But I thought better of it. He was two murders up on me to my none. But if there was anyone who needed murdering, it was him! I could get the courage to do it. But would it be the best use of my cunning?

I decided that, no, it would not be. I needed more information all around. Something was missing in my mind on it. If Kendrick was after killing my Marion, I needed to know why, for it had to be more than to keep me quiet. Murdering *me* would be the only thing to stop my tongue. For it would not now keep me quiet, no indeed, and with Cromwell on the trail like a mastiff, Kendrick was sure to fall, and soon. What I needed instead was to talk to Nan's ladies-in-waiting again. They had secrets to tell me, I knew they did. After all, it was Lady Jane who informed me about Kendrick's Spanish blood. I had to go back and loosen some tongues with the charm I knew I could muster. Time to return to my lodgings for my lute and my dog.

*　　*　　*

It was Nosewise who did the trick. That little pup was a boon
to me and his nosing his way into here and there. My lute
was also no little thing to easing the hearts of the ladies, who
had been turned to fear from the murder they witnessed, for
all the court was in mourning for that lady, even as Henry –
sometimes oblivious to the needs of others – had gone on his
hunt to enjoy himself. But ladies are ladies, and their lives at
court are made up of service to *their* lady – Lady Anne – and
they were a close society. Their daily fare was gossip and their
meat was even more gossip. Sometimes it was false, but sometimes it was true, and it was for the recipient to ferret out the
truth from the lie.

I was all ear when it came to talking with the ladies, for
they were sure to tell me things they would never tell any
other man. Perhaps they viewed me as a eunuch in the harem.

If they only knew the truth of it.

I played my music and even sang, but mostly I made up
rude rhymes to entertain. I noticed certain ladies making their
way nearer to me, and suddenly, I found myself surrounded
on either side by Lady Bess Holland and Lady Jane Parker,
Viscountess Rochford. I noticed that Lady Nan was mostly
entertained by Mark Smeaton sitting closer to her and to some
of her more favored ladies.

'Why are you beautiful ladies sitting near old crook-backed
Will Somers, and not with Lady Anne and handsome Mark
Smeaton?' I asked.

Lady Bess sighed. She was plain-faced of all the ladies, blunt-
nosed and wore too much jewelry. One must never wear more
jewelry than the lady you are waiting upon. 'All she wants to
talk about is the murder. And I don't wish to discuss it anymore.'

'Why not? I would have thought that this is the juiciest
meat of all.'

'No. It was terrible. And I don't want to think about it.'

'And you, Lady Parker?' Now *she* had a sweet face, like a
child's, with lovely blonde hair under her French hood. 'Do
you wish not to think on it?'

'It was dreadful. It could have been any one of us.'

'Could it? I have a mind that someone else was the target.
Someone who moved at the wrong time.'

'Who?' they both enquired, leaning in.

'Lady Marion Greene, Lord Heyward's daughter. The embroideress.'

Lady Bess straightened the velvet of her veil. 'Who would want to kill *her*?'

Her utter disdain for Marion coursed through my mind. But then I paused and mentally slapped my head. I was so set that Marion *was* the target because of Lady Jane's threat, that I didn't stop to think of all the reasons she wouldn't be. 'Do you think it *was* Lady Jane Perwick who was the target, then?'

'She's dead, isn't she?' said Lady Jane.

'Lady Jane!' said Bess.

'Well . . . you're thinking it too.'

'But I didn't speak it.'

'Then why do you think—'

'I don't want to talk about that,' said Bess, threading her arm in mine. I stopped my lute playing. At least the chatter in the room was loud enough to mask what we were saying. And Smeaton's music-playing further drowned out our speech.

'Then what *do* you want to talk about?' I settled in with the two of them, very close on either side. My cod was liking it, even as I worried over Marion. 'Tell Will all about it.'

Bess giggled, but tried to keep it behind her fingers. After all, one of their own had been recently murdered. 'You're just as bad as we are, Master Somers.'

I glanced about the room. Some of the ladies were taking it very hard, in fact. They kept to themselves and were as quiet as mice. Lady Jane Seymour, for one. Perhaps she had been in mourning for her last lady, Queen Catherine, just as I was. It must have been strange for her to be made to change allegiances to Lady Nan. Just as I had had to do. Indeed, I felt for Lady Jane Seymour.

Nan Cobham also looked morose, as did Ursula Marbury, Gonzalo's former lover. Pale, she was. Perhaps the murder reminded her all too close of Gonzalo's.

Margery Horsman was also with the other listless ones. But those around Lady Nan, and the two jackals beside me, seemed to be able to dismiss it from their minds. How privileged they were to be able to do so.

I hadn't quite been listening to the two of them as sharply as I should have as I scanned the others, but Bess was saying, '. . . and if I were Lady Anne, I'd be paying more attention.'

Wakening to her voice, I asked, 'And what mean you by that?'

If she got any closer to me, she'd be in my lap. 'Because Lady Anne holds off the king to keep his interest. But he is a man, after all, and that means he must find his ease elsewhere.'

'With you, Lady Bess?'

She threw her head back and laughed and only stopped because Lady Nan was glaring at her. She cleared her throat behind her bejeweled hand. 'No, never. I'm a bit afraid of him.'

'But others are not,' offered Lady Jane.

I squirmed a bit with my hips touching theirs. 'You are not telling me that one of the ladies here has, er, been spreading the king's sheets right under Lady Nan's pert little nose?'

'We *are* telling you that,' said Lady Jane. 'And you'll never guess.'

'No, I won't.'

'You'd be so surprised,' said Lady Bess. 'It's always the quiet ones.'

'And who here is most quiet?' for I could not believe that any of them were.

They looked at one another across me, silently communicating as women seemed to do. 'Why, Master Somers,' said Lady Jane. 'Don't *you* know? It's Lady Ursula.'

EIGHTEEN

Lady Ursula? The same lady who mourned the loss of Gonzalo? But spent the rest of the time in the *king's* bed?

I glanced toward her with mouth agape. What had I done coming from tame Shropshire to here? This was Rome before the Fall. Everything at court stemmed from iniquity. Even Marion and I were not spared, for we had not waited for the marriage bed. And I had all my sinful dalliances. Maybe I was perfect for court after all, for this particular court, a court of dragons and devils. Christ save me.

Ursula's face was white, surrounded by her dark hair and a French hood, with gold biliments closest to her hair and white frill, framing her face nicely. Ursula's countenance was dainty and sweet . . . like Henry seemed to like them. Aye, I could see him wooing her right behind Nan's back. Henry, Henry.

But if so in love with Gonzalo, why this? I slapped my forehead. She had had another lover! I recall it now. And I had quite forgot to discover it. Because she had lied about being in Gonzalo's bed . . . because he had been with *me*. And that lover was Henry? Fie on a woman's heart, and fie on Henry's cod! What was I to make of this? I was just a jester. My only vocation was to make merry, to sing songs. I was not a lad to indulge in this labyrinth of lies and sin.

I glanced at Ursula again as the ladies beside me jabbered on with this and that. Oh, what a dangerous bridge you walked, Lady Ursula. Between Nan Bullen and the king. Which was the greater threat to you? Gonzalo was gone, no wedding there. Was she setting her sights higher? Surely not. All of court knew she was Gonzalo's intended, perhaps his lover, and that would make her unsuitable to be Queen of England. But if she could convince Wolsey that Gonzalo was all a lie, was she a better case than Lady Nan as queen? Did Henry fancy her? Or had her liaison been brief, only to console him? Just the one night? Mayhap she felt guilty at her dalliance with the king, and Gonzalo's death had been her punishment from God for her infidelity. Such things happened. And it explained her morose expression. I tried to discern it from her face, its blankness, its sadness . . . and could not. Her mask was in place and not like to slip. Maybe I wasn't as clever as I thought I was.

Nosewise ran up to me, sitting up, and paddling the air with his paws. He yipped at me, and the ladies were charmed. 'You little beggar,' I said. 'Is it that you want a treat? Is that what I am to you, a mere repository for your delicacies?'

He yipped again, much to the delight of the ladies. Even Nan smiled, perhaps relieved to have something else to concentrate on besides death.

'Very well,' I said, reaching into a pouch at my belt. I kept little bits of broken wafers in there, king's seal and all. I raised up a crumb and twirled a finger to make the cur whirl, and he did. I tossed it to his jaws and he snapped it up.

'What else can he do?' asked one of the ladies.

'Oh, he is marvelous clever.' I stood before the dog with my hands at my hips. 'What happens to you if you displease the king?' I said sternly to the dog, wagging a finger at him.

Nosewise fell over in a faint, seemingly dead.

The ladies tittered and laughed. I shot a glance toward Lady Ursula. She did not look amused. Instead, she gathered her things and swept hastily out of the room without taking her leave of Lady Nan.

It was later that I sat in Marion's chamber. We were both unusually quiet, even as her servant went about cleaning this and that.

'That will be all, Michael,' she finally told him.

Michael bowed and left the chamber, closing the door behind him. I lifted my face to Marion. 'I haven't found Kendrick yet. Cromwell says he's missing.'

'Maybe that's a good thing.'

'I cannot feel that it is. But Marion. What if . . . what if that arrow was *not* meant for you?'

'Then I would praise God.'

'Of course. But what I mean is, your safety would not be in question any longer.'

She walked to her sewing frame by the hearth, ran her fingers along the cloth, and slowly sat. 'I thought you said Kendrick was trying to get to you through me.'

'I said that because it was on my mind. But it doesn't make much sense when you think about it. Why not just . . . kill *me*? And no one has threatened *my* life that I know of.'

The needle was in her hand when she paused, hand hovering over the cloth. 'True. And why has he not spilt what he knows about you and Gonzalo?'

'Aye, that has been troubling me. To keep me quiet? But I haven't been. And if to wait for a better time, just what *would* be a better time? I feel that I have missed something important through all this rumination. I mean, Lady Jane's threatening you and me . . .'

'She's now dead. But what of Kendrick? He's still dangerous.'

'Aye, that he is. I set Cromwell after him. Told him that if this priest is after me, he might kill the king by mistake. You can be sure Cromwell and the king's men are after that doleful priest.'

'Let us hope so.'

I rose and walked to her, looking over her shoulder at her exquisite embroidery work of flowers and conjoined letters. An H and an A. She flicked a glance up at me and then away, back to her work. We both knew who this was for. 'And, er, how are you feeling?'

She took a deep breath and sighed it out. 'I'm *not* with child, as it happens.'

The stab of disappointment was deep and . . . unexpected. 'Oh?' I said neutrally.

'My monthly arrived. I am not with child.' Her eyes welled and I dropped to my knee beside her.

'Sweet Marion. We will wed someday, and then you *will* have my child. My silly-faced and possibly crook-back child. I . . . I crave it now.'

She reached blindly for my hand, found it, and squeezed. 'I love you.'

'I love you, too.' I pulled her to her feet and embraced her, let her sniffle on my shoulder, mourning a child that had never bloomed within her. 'It's foolish, I know,' I whispered to her hair under its veil, 'but I desire a daughter. Is that strange?'

'Not for you,' she said with a giddy laugh. 'It would be just like you to go against all convention.'

'But I *love* women.' I held her, for her fingers gripped at my doublet and would not let up. Babes. Such needful creatures. Who knew that such would be the end of queens, and fortunes would depend upon it? That Henry was so enamored of the idea of a male heir that he would upturn his own marriage, stand against popes and the Holy Roman Emperor, against kings . . . and even perhaps God Himself?

And yet ours – Marion's and mine – had been a mere ghost of our own imaginations.

Then again . . . I thought of Lord Heyward and how we were still under a cloud. For if there was no pregnancy, there could be no leveraging a wedding.

What folly. What wretched folly.

I surprised myself by wiping at a tear in my eye and pushed her back, giving her cheek a kiss. I had wanted that babe. 'Yes, I want a girl. I want what the king has and does not want. And . . . in that vein . . . well, I went to see the queen and the Princess Mary today.'

She jerked back and glared at me. 'Will! That was very foolish of you.'

'I'm a foolish man. But the opportunity presented itself.'

'Oh, Will! Do you have a desire for death?'

'I was not thinking of death. I was thinking how I missed Her Majesty and the princess.'

Her glare softened and became something more tender. 'Oh.'

'They were my family, Marion,' I said softly. 'I was far from home when I first came to court. And not like to see my father again. And everyone here was strange and queer. This royal family were my comfort as much as I tried to make merry for them. Families should not change but for death. This is all unnatural.'

'I know.' She held me and now I breathed on *her* shoulder.

'It was good to see them. But sorrowful, too.'

'Do you think the king will ever relent?'

'No, my dear. That is the one thing he hates to do; admit he was wrong. And anyway, now he is bewitched by Nan Bullen. He wants her.' I glanced at the door to make certain it was properly closed, and then I flicked a glance at her embroidery with its intertwined H and A. My lips were at her ear. 'But he doesn't wait in celibacy. It seems he still seeks his solace with other women. And I was told by some of Nan's ladies that lately he had chosen . . . Lady Ursula.'

'What?' she cried, all hushed and husky. 'Gonzalo's lover?'

'It is true. So why was she lamenting her lost love when her sights reached much higher? She was with Henry when she lied and told me she was with Gonzalo.'

'When Gonzalo was with you.'

'Aye. I have not seen her look particularly smug. If she were in Henry's bed, I'll wager it was once only. She does have a sour look about her. I thought it was sadness over Gonzalo, but now I think . . . I think it might be discontent.'

Marion smoothed out her kirtle absently. 'There is one thing I know about some of the ladies of court, and that is that they are flowers in secret gardens that welcome many bees.'

I shook my head and went to the fire. I picked up the iron and jabbed at the glowing wood in the grate. 'There is gossip aplenty at court, this I know. But I wondered how much of it was true. Apparently, most of it is.'

'Will, there is one way to see if I was the target or if Lady Jane was. I must go about court unescorted.'

'And *be* a target?'

'Yes. It's the only way.'

'Your father won't like it. *I* don't like it.'

'But you'll be nearby.

'That won't help if it's another crossbow bolt.'

'What else can we do? We must be sure, mustn't we?'

I joined her at her embroidery frame again and pressed my hands to her shoulders and then slid my arms around her, my cheek resting against her head and French hood. 'Maybe, if I cannot find Kendrick, I should find out about Lady Jane. That might be better than you parading about court with a target painted on your belly.'

'I'll allow you to go on this course for a brief while, but then I must try my scheme. I can't live in this uncertainty.'

'Aye, my love. I agree. You are my brave Marion, aren't you.' I kissed her temple, but she reached up for a better kiss and I did indulge her. 'Will you watch Nosewise for me?' I asked.

'Of course.' How that pup loved Marion.

I left the two of them together, and off I went in search of some answers about Lady Jane.

Lady Nan was pleased to see me in her company. She must have taken this as a sign she was becoming more welcomed to court as the king's future wife. Well, that couldn't be helped. I looked around for the gossiping ladies and I noticed Ursula was not in attendance. Mayhap I should talk to her. Skirt around Henry's bed, of course, but see what she *would* talk about.

Off I went to what I believed was her lodgings. Aye, they were down this corridor. Of course, all these courtiers had their own houses and estates sometimes quite far from court, but here it was they had to live, or not too far away up the Thames in London. They had their *Bouche* of Court, what Henry would pay them to live with him – lodgings, board, even a candle, ale, and wine allowance. Their clothing was the thing that cost a pretty penny, for you could not be seen in company of the king unless your clothing was nearly as fine as his was. Though *not* as fine. And never finer. There were sumptuary laws to consider. Only certain nobles were allowed to wear certain furs and certain colors. And the king wore the best of all.

Though the king provided for *my* cloth, it didn't need to be fine and jewel-encrusted at all. In fact, that would not have been allowed, due to my rank. I liked my woolen doublet and hose, my plain coats, for they were comfortable and more suited to all the capering and tumbling I was required to do. And I had cut off all the bells now, so I could come up unawares to my victims and surprise them with a jest, a jeer, or a jaunty song. Henry hadn't noticed or didn't deign to remark on it. Most times, I didn't even wear my fool's hood. I often tumbled about without my coat, only in doublet and hose. Perhaps I'd start a fashion.

I came at last to Lady Ursula's chamber. There was a guard, but he knew me well and allowed me in. 'But,' he said, 'she is with her confessor. Have a care.'

Her confessor, eh? She'd be needing him.

I passed through the antechamber with its furniture and furnishings, tapestries and fine coffers, but as I passed through to her withdrawing room, I could hear noises of an unusual kind. She was moaning. Good Christ, was her priest whipping her for her sins? But all at once, I realized what a fool I truly was. For that was not the sound of punishment, not as I had come to know it.

I smiled. So someone disguised as her priest was in there with her, for now I could hear a man's sounds of moaning. What brazen fellow should go to her chamber when she should have been attending Lady Nan, and in the mid of the day! What saucy creature was this?

There was no chaperone, no matron to guard the virtue of this 'maid'-in-waiting. I crept closer to the door. I needed only open it a crack to see who it was, unless the swines had closed the bed-curtains. I grasped the door handle and gently, softly, pulled it just the merest of cracks so that I could set my eye to it.

I clamped the sound of my gasp behind my hand. For there was no mistaking what Lady Ursula was up to with her skirts gathered up around her waist and her naked legs wrapped around her lover.

And that lover!

The blushing, bleating face of Father Kendrick! Going at it with the fervor he should have reserved for his religion.

NINETEEN

I carefully closed the door and further tiptoed through her rooms and out.

'Was she still in confession?' asked the guard.

'She and her priest were, er . . . devout in their attention,' was all I could say. I moved away from her lodgings' door, but then I thought, *Aha! I can confront Kendrick. All I need do is await his coming out.*

Faith! I wish I could wash my eyes to get the sight of that from my mind. Priests were supposed to be celibate. It was one of their vows. Of course, the vow of poverty was seldom kept. Our Wolsey had his great houses and jewelry. And there was many a priest who secretly had a wife. Religion was like a big meal: it was lovely to look at, and you felt yourself happy to be seated before it, but more often than not, it was never filling enough.

I waited in my darkened corner, and with that flash of Ursula's shapely leg, I could only think of Marion. She was an enthusiastic lover, and it did make me wonder why she hadn't got with child before now. I knew that women had their remedies for such things. They always whispered about it. But maybe . . . no. I mustn't think of such. That she was barren would be a forbidding jest to play upon so good a woman. God would not be so cruel. For if there was anyone who loved me as she does, I knew I should never meet them. And the fact that she wanted whatever misshapen child I could produce said more about her character than any angel from on high could shout in exultation. I was a lucky man. Of a sort. If her father would never agree to our marriage then . . . Faith. What *would* we do?

And then – strange man that I am – I thought of Gonzalo, and his handsome face, and his vigorous lovemaking. And Rodrigo's eagerness in the sheets. And Edward's, who was always available for a tumble. But I didn't love them as I loved Marion. My sin was as crooked as my back, and such I would take to Purgatory, for I have never spoken of it to a priest in the confessional, which is, in itself, a sin. And I take the bread of Christ, wondering sometimes what it is all for. Should one such as me reach the gates of Heaven? A lad of Shropshire who liked his bedding often and with a variety of partners? In the end, I must let the Almighty sort it out.

I heard the great clock in the courtyard chime the hour, the half-hour, and wondered with some amount of envy if that scoundrel Kendrick had the stamina of a bull . . . or was he merely lingering. Or asleep. And then I wondered if this was the only way out. Surely a man who knew he would be caught would not stroll through the corridors.

I scrambled down the hallway and shot through the doors to the courtyard, counting windows. But would he come this very public way either? So I ran out of the front gate and around the building. And here was where I didn't need to count windows, for there appeared a man climbing over a garden wall to the surrounding landscape, and he wore a long gown like a cleric, and I could clearly see his white legs as he hoist that gown to do his climbing.

He was disappearing into the park around Greenwich and I put heel to ground, chasing after and over the wall.

He knew nothing of stealth, for I could well hear him stumbling through the brambles and breaking every twig there was. When I leapt, my hands seized arms and I dragged him to the ground in a heap. He cursed some of the vilest oaths I had ever heard from layman *or* priest, and especially when he discovered who it was that had entrapped him.

'Will Somers, you cursed crooked little troll! You whoreson! You cock lorel! You cross-biter!'

'Tut, tut, Kendrick. If I were you, I'd lessen my sins, not compound them. Now shut it.' And I slammed my hand over his vile mouth. I sat upon him with his hands stuck beneath his weight and mine. 'We have some talking to do. For I saw you kill Lady Jane.'

He had been fighting me, but now he stilled, his eyes round like a gold crown piece.

'I'll take my hand away because I want answers. You will behave now, my lad, eh?'

He gave a shallow nod.

I lifted my hand away from his mouth and pulled his dagger from its sheath. He watched me with narrowing eyes. 'Now. There are things I need to know. Why did you kill Don Gonzalo de Yscar?'

I watched his face carefully, especially his eyes, which speared right through me. Oh, there was evil there . . . but also . . . confusion. 'You're a fantasist, Somers. I did no such thing.'

'Come now, Kendrick. You can only hang once. Best to confess it all.'

'I tell you I did not kill that Spaniard!'

'And why should I believe you?'

'Because . . . I had no reason to kill him.'

'Oh, but you would have? Had you had a reason?'

He breathed out slowly. 'If it was needful.'

Such cold words from such a cold man. 'But you are half Spanish.'

'And so?'

'You don't deny it?'

'You seem to know the truth of it. My mother.'

'And you spied for Spain?'

He turned his face away and would not answer.

'Were you the one sending me a blackmail missive?'

He jerked his head back to look at me, brows raised. 'Blackmail? Believe me, Somers, if I had some information worth getting coin from you, I'd trumpet it loud and often at court.'

'That was before they didn't have you for murder, of course.'

His wild face stilled. He seemed to remember again who had whom.

He spoke more soberly, quietly. 'I sent you no missives.'

'So why did you kill Lady Jane? What had you against her?'

'Nothing. I had nothing against her.'

'Then was it . . . Marion?'

Kendrick drew back, perplexed. 'Who is Marion?'

'Marion Greene, the daughter of Lord Heyward.'

'I don't know who that is and I little care to know.'

'Then by all the saints in Heaven, Kendrick. Why?'

He turned his face away from me. 'I will say no more. I have decided already to leave this place.' A tear came to his eye.

'Do you miss court so much? Or is it . . . a certain lady you will miss?'

He jerked his head toward me. And with that, he lurched so mightily that he dislodged me and I tumbled back. By the time I righted myself, the miscreant was long gone into the trees.

'Cuds-me!' Would the king's men find him? Not before Cromwell's men found him. He was not long for this world.

I tossed his dagger away into the underbrush. His answers were singularly unsatisfying. If he could be believed, then he didn't murder Gonzalo and he was not my blackmailer. But if not him, then who? Lady Jane? If so, I'd never now know. This was a complicated puzzle far beyond my means.

I stalked back around the walls and entered through the gate again, the guards barely giving me a twitch of a whisker. What to tell Marion? What to do about these murders? Why did he murder Lady Jane? Was it because she knew about him and Ursula? 'Now there's an idea,' I muttered. If she had threatened to expose them, then that was a pretty bit of gossip staunched. Maybe Henry wouldn't like the idea that he had a priest's leavings. He certainly wouldn't like the idea of a priest bedding anyone at all, including one of Lady Nan's ladies. Very much including. And dear me. I wonder if Lady Ursula – if it came to Henry's attention – would be imperiled. It wouldn't do for jealous Lady Nan to get wind of one of her own ladies romping about in Henry's bed. Wretch. He had only himself to blame. You don't dip your quill into the same inkpot where all the other ink – damn, that metaphor was getting nowhere; as nowhere as I was getting with this.

How were other such murders solved in the realm? Did the miscreants give themselves up? They'd have to. I was beginning to despair that Gonzalo would never get his justice.

But by St George I *would* find his killer. And when I did, I'd write to Rodrigo. I was certain he'd want to know.

What to do now? It was best that I see to Henry, see if he needed me, and as soon as I might, I'd return to Lady Nan's ladies, see if Ursula had returned to her presence. I wondered what excuse she'd come up with. And also I needed to see what Lady Parker and Lady Bess had to say on the matter. For I would wager they didn't know about this priest who made his way freely through the bedchambers of court.

I found Henry in his inner privy chamber, meeting with his privy council. And what faces they wore! By the mass, each time they met with the king – and, of course, Cromwell, telling them the state of things – they all seemed to grow morose at the news, long-faced, like mules. It was about the Great Matter, certainly. Naught could make their faces as sour.

The king sent me a look that told me straightaway that I wasn't wanted. I gamboled around the table before I left. Good. I'd rather spend my time in Lady Nan's company . . . and how times had changed on that score! Now I was a frequent guest to her cabal of ladies, though she mistook the reason why. Yet, if Henry was to have his way – and I couldn't imagine he wouldn't – I suppose I'd best be in Lady Nan's good graces.

My poor queen. My poor Princess Mary.

Lady Nan was outside in the garden again, but this time, two guards were set around them at every entrance, and even above at the parapets. She liked being out of doors and even I felt safe with so many men-at-arms. Kendrick was gone. He'd not be back if he had any sort of intelligence. Or if he did return, he'd be on the end of a rope. Either way suited me.

No sooner did I bow to Nan and take a seat – with my lute and my basket of foolery at my feet – than she asked me to play . . . much to the sour face of Mark Smeaton. As I played, he fidgeted. I hoped that he would join in, for I knew he knew this song, but as he would not, I began adding my own comical flourishes to it, and the ladies lauded it so that he took personal offense, jumped to his feet, bowed to Lady Nan with some sort of excuse, and took his leave.

I finished my song with my own words that fitted the melody: 'And that's what scares musicians most . . . that they can't compete with a fooooool!' stringing out the last note as long as I could.

They laughed and clapped and I was content. But not so was Lady Ursula. She looked just as miserable as she had since Gonzalo's death. What cause had she to be so sour? She had the vigorous attentions of Kendrick . . . unless he had told her his farewells with their latest pony ride. But perhaps it was because she could not gain the attention of Henry, the fickle man. I cast about for my gossipers, but they were sitting behind Lady Nan and could not in any casual manner make their way toward me.

I stayed a while, walking about the seated ladies, making rude rhymes about what each lady was embroidering, and making a proper fool of myself, when I saw the futility of my staying. And I also needed the necessary.

I bowed to Lady Nan, bid my farewells, and, taking up lute and basket, headed for the easements at the main gate, near the river. I found myself a cozy seat among the many. That bean soup I had for breakfast was coursing through me and it was time to relieve myself of it. But soon I was joined not too many seats away by two lower courtiers, more sirrahs than sirs. Not the richest of men, they seldom dined anywhere near the king, but I was able to hear their talk because of the way the jakes was built. It was at the west end that one could hear what all speakers at the east end were saying. Some builder's clever business, or perhaps it was quite by accident. In any case, it was my favorite relieving-spot for this very reason.

'You owe me two pence,' said the one.

'Eh?' said the other.

'Our wager of the king's pleasure, remember?' said the first.

'Oh! And what did you hear?'

'Not only hear, me lad, but saw it plain. I told you about Lady Ursula.'

'Aye, and you got nearly a groat out of me for that one.'

'She kept tarrying near the king's lodgings for days after-ward. She thought he'd call on her again, I'm certain.'

'Did he?'

'No. You know that he burns for that Bullen woman.'

'And she's clever, holding her maidenhead dear.'

'I know it. There's some that say that mayhap she doesn't . . . for other men.'

'Why? She's almost got the prize in her hand.'

'Oh . . . a moment.'

The first man gave up the most boisterous of farts. A real trumpeter, that one.

He settled in again and rested his arms on his thighs.

'Do you think Lady Nan knows of it?' asked the second.

'Not a chance. That Ursula is still a maid of honor. She'd never be if Nan knew it.'

The second one did his business with a flourish, and then proceeded to wipe his bum with a little wool.

'But that's not the juiciest bit,' said the first.

These gossips were worse than any women. But I supposed they needed to entertain themselves in some way. With teeth clenched, I kept my bowels still so I could hear every word.

'Go on, then.'

'Well.' The first leaned into the second. 'The king may not have needed Lady Ursula to stand in for Lady Nan, because he had another to his bed. You'll never guess who.'

'Don't keep me waiting, lad. I'm almost done here.'

'Now this one I almost think the Lady Nan had a hand in.'

'Well?'

The first one smiled wide. 'It's the *dead* one. The one recently slaughtered by a crossbow bolt. That Lady Jane Perwick.'

'No!'

'I saw it m'self. Saw her sneaking out through the with-drawing room, right out of the king's bedchamber, and the king himself, waving her off.'

'Poor Lady Jane. But hold. What are you saying about Lady Anne and all?'

'I think she found out. I think she got herself someone to do her bidding.'

'You mean got someone to kill the lady for her? That's deadly cold.'

'As cold as the grave. Here, hand me some of that wool.'

And just like that, my world tilted again.

TWENTY

After those two nose-bodies left, I had a chance to think, as well as to empty my bowels: *Henry did spill it about court, didn't he? But now I'm confused, because what was Kendrick doing killing her, then? Because it would get in the way of the marriage of Lady Anne and Henry? Yet, was not Kendrick a Spanish spy and trying to kill such a marriage? Or* was *he? And what of Ursula?*

Bollocks! This was stuffed and tangled more than Wolsey's braies.

I was getting something terribly wrong, I knew it. I wished Rodrigo was still here to talk to, but at least my Marion was here. For now. Henry wouldn't need me for some time, so I was free to see her. At least, if her guardians would allow me access.

I finished my business in the latrines, washed my hands and hurried through court, stopping now and again to make a jest or jibe as the courtiers expected. I didn't want them to think I was hurrying to some personal errand. The less they had to say about *me* the better.

And wouldn't you know, when I turned a corner going too fast, I bumped into Wolsey himself in all his bulk. It was like running full tilt into a bolster.

He almost landed on his bum. I wasn't as lucky.

'Somers!' he choked out. 'By the rood, why are you careering about the court as if your hose were afire? Such a fool!'

No one helped me up. They stood as angry pillars surrounding the old porker, and glared down at me. Cromwell was among them, at his right shoulder, peering over the man to gaze at me, more becalmed than all the rest of them put together.

I rose with exaggerated movements, brushing off my coat and carefully arranging my basket inside the crook of my arm again and picking up the lute, glad that it had come to no harm. 'Well, Thomas, I tell you. Some be fools by nature, the same that we call idiots. Others be cunning and crafty fools, those who cannot thrive by their wisdom and seek to live by their folly. And such a one, it may be imagined, is your Will Somers. Or . . . were you referring to yourself in this instance, Your Grace?'

His face reddened. And it was a pleasure to see it. I darted a glance at Cromwell, and his expression – as always – was mild, but with the merest of twinkles in his eyes.

They shoved me aside, His Grace and his cadre of priests and courtiers, frowning in long faces at me as they passed. I wasn't fooled. Those were the precise men who would be laughing as uproariously as the next when they were in the king's company and enjoying my escapades. That is, as long as the king was laughing.

I sent up a prayer for Wolsey's own fool, Patch. He and I were good friends. It could not have been easy making merry in *that* company.

I hurried to my own quarters to relieve myself of basket and lute, and when I turned around, I nearly jumped out of me own skin when Edward emerged from the shadows.

'You've been avoiding me.'

'Hang you in your teeth, Edward! I have not been avoiding you. I have my matters to attend to. And you frightened my soul from me. How did you get in?'

'I serve the court and clean it. I have the keys.'

'You mean you stole them from the Lord Chamberlain.'

He frowned. 'Mayhap.'

I wiped the sweat from my brow and landed my hand upon his bosom. More softly, I said, 'Harken, Edward. I did not forget you.'

'Then take a moment now.'

Before I could reply, he wrapped his hand around my neck and hauled me in for a sloppy kiss. Ah, but Edward's kisses were a bonny thing. And before I could comment about *that*, he'd dropped to his knees, and pulled open my codpiece.

Well . . . I couldn't very well push him away when he was so engaged. It wouldn't be polite. And neither would it take long, in any case. So I let him minister to me as he ministered to himself and . . . Lord! His mouth was paradise.

'Edward, I need to sit or me legs will give out.'

He wiped his mouth and sat beside me upon the bed. We both set our hose to rights and lay back. 'Edward, you mustn't be so . . . so passionate.'

'You like my passion.'

'I . . . well, aye. I do. But just at this moment . . .'

He crossed his arms tightly over his chest, even as he lay supine. 'You put me off.'

I rolled to face him. 'Nor should you be jealous. You know I have many lovers.'

'And I don't have to like it.'

I grabbed his chin and kissed him hard. 'I won't settle for one man.'

'But you'll settle for one woman.'

'I have. You know it well. And I will not hear you speak ill of her.'

He turned his face away, but at least his arms unloosed and fell to his sides. 'I love you, Will.'

'Ah, Edward. I love you too, in my way. But I love many.'

Grumbling, he turned halfway back toward me. 'They say that you'll marry her.'

'If I can. The way I love Marion is different from the way I love you and the others.'

'But why? Can't you just . . . be mine?'

'God has made me in this particular way, Edward. I can't seem to fight what he has made. Or perhaps the Devil has made me, crooked back and all.' He frowned, looked to be on the verge of tears. I laid my hand to his cheek. 'But I will always seek you out. Marion is very understanding that way.'

He nodded. He did know it.

'She's clever, is Marion,' I said.

'God 'a mercy,' he whispered.

'Just be patient.'

'Oh, then . . .' He slowly sat up and rubbed his messy hair. 'Then I can no longer gloat, can I? I was going to.'

I sat up with him and noticed the laces of my doublet had

loosened, so I tied them. 'What were you going to gloat about? Which is, incidentally, a very nasty habit.'

He lowered his face. 'It's about the Lady Marion.'

'What about her?'

'She's got her servants packing, hasn't she? They've brought in coffers and she's going away.'

My heart stumbled. No! She couldn't be. That damn father of hers!

I leapt off the bed and darted through the doorway before I skidded to a stop, turned around, and came back to Edward. He was straightening his clothes and looking miserable and red-faced. 'I'm sorry, Edward. But you know how it is with me and Marion. I don't want her to go.'

'I'm sorry too,' he said to his feet.

'I must go.'

'Go on, then.'

I kissed his cheek and flew out of the chambers again.

I headed toward Marion's apartments but slowed to a stop. What good would that do to go to Marion's and talk to her? If her father forced her to go, go she would. I had to talk to her father, plead my case again. And . . . beshrew me! He *had* to listen to me or I *would* go to the king. I needed my Marion and she needed me, horrible man that I was with my many sins dragging behind me. But I mustn't think of that. I must gird m'self and talk sense to the man.

All this and more I said to myself in my head as I made my way through the corridors and halls, past courtiers, past the many guards stationed here and there, and finally to Lord Heyward's apartments.

Once I reached it, I was told he was elsewhere, so I followed his path and found him in an alcove talking with courtiers in the serious manner that men at court did; furtively, with brows drawn down, straight-lipped. Never was there more need for a jester in their midst.

I capered, made jests that lightened their mood. But not Lord Robert's. No, of course not. He endured my presence likened to a stone gargoyle: stiff and grimacing.

Then I stayed out of the way so that all the business amongst them could conclude, and waited until Lord Robert was alone.

He watched his fellows retreat, and without so much as an eyelash twitching in my direction, he set off to God-knew-where at nearly a trot.

'Lord Robert!' I shouted after him. But he pretended as if he hadn't heard me. I ran after. 'Lord Robert!'

Without slowing, he said in a clipped puff of air, 'Yes, Somers?'

'I need to speak to you urgently on a personal matter.'

He kept walking and my ire rose to the surface and I forgot my place for that moment. I halted and said loudly, 'Will you stop and talk to me!'

That did it. He halted and swiveled toward me with a shocked expression.

I didn't falter. I straightened my doublet and adjusted my coat with its few pleats and stalked toward him until I was nearly nose to nose. 'I say again, my lord. I am an honest man, a favorite at the court, with the ear of the king. I earn a goodly sum, enough to buy a house for a wife. And I care deeply for your daughter, sir. By my life, I do. And she cares as deeply for me. I ask for your permission to marry her, to keep her safe, to love and cherish her as befitting the kind, Christian soul she is. I ask it not as a fool by trade, but as a *man*, my lord. A man of integrity and obstinacy. Traits that you yourself seem to hold dear.'

His eyes raked over me in disbelief. Who the devil was I to speak to him thus? Only a man looking to get a wife. Just a man. With not the straightest of shoulders. Could he not see past my motley and my foolish aspect?

He stood thus for a long time, more than was comfortable. His eyes flicked here and there, looking for those at court who liked to spy and gossip. I didn't see anyone.

Staring down at the ring on his finger as he rubbed his knuckles, he frowned. 'I can see that you have a genuine affection for my daughter, Somers,' he said softly. 'And, God mend me, she for you. But love may not be enough to sustain a couple in this cruel world.'

'But we have more than love, my lord. I have the surety of farmland in Shropshire to inherit. And as I said, my finances are such that I can afford a modest house in London. This is surely more than most men in the lower reaches of the court can expect. And . . . though I am in the lower reaches, I . . .'

He raised his palm to me and leaned against the wall. Heyward was always a robust man, at least in the four years I have been acquainted with him. But now I worried.

'Are you well, sir?'

He nodded, pulling at the fur trim of his coat's collar. 'I love my daughter,' he said. 'Some men think it folly that I love a bastard child who cannot give me the alliances I would have otherwise sought with a son or a daughter who was fully legitimate. Her status does not offer her much of a chance in that regard. Surely you understand that, Somers? I will not live forever. I cannot protect her forever. I need a man of integrity to do that.'

'I know, my lord.'

'Look at the court,' he rasped. 'Look at the state of marriage when a king can put aside a legitimate marriage, blessed by the pope himself. What woman is safe?'

I crept closer to keep our conversation intimate in such public surroundings. I made my face as sincere as its silliness could be. 'I . . . I do understand, my lord.'

'It's no longer politics, Somers. It's personal. It's personal to me.'

'I do know that, my lord. I . . .' God blind me! His words suddenly struck me like a thunderbolt, stabbing deep where I could feel it, waking me as if from a slumber. 'It's personal,' I muttered. '*Not* political. Just like Queen Catherine said. By the rood!' My head shot up and I blinked at Lord Heyward. 'I have to go. I'm sorry.'

I fled in the other direction, back toward Marion's rooms, with the sound of Lord Heyward yelling after me, 'Somers! Get back here! *Somers, you whoreson!*'

TWENTY-ONE

It was just as Queen Catherine said. Some things are not political. They come from the heart. I had to talk to Marion. I had to stop her before she fully packed and went away.

I held to the wainscoting at the corner of the corridor to keep myself from plowing into the wall. It helped me to slow down and then speed up, rushing past the servants and guards at her entryway.

'Marion!' I cried, hurrying through her dining chamber, her withdrawing room, and finally into her bedchamber.

She turned a shocked face to me, stilling as she folded the linen shifts in her hands. 'Will?'

'Marion.' I looked about at the women helping her and the serving men carrying out her coffers. 'Stop packing and stop . . .'

Nosewise jolted up from his little pillow and jumped at my legs, barking.

Frustrated, I called to the servants to 'put down that coffer. Now!' They looked at me perplexed, but since I was someone they recognized, they obeyed me. Nosewise continued to bark. 'Get out, all of you. And you!' I said to one of her maids. 'Unpack those things at once.'

She looked to Marion and, with a hopeful smile, Marion nodded to her. Nosewise followed the last maid out, barking at the poor creature, who closed the door, leaving us in peace. Even that cursed dog shut his muzzle.

'Marion, you are safe. No one is out to get you. Oh, I've been such a fool! I mis-saw everything, mistook everything. I've been so wrong.'

'Will, you aren't making any sense.'

'It was never political. Never a spy mission gone wrong.' I fell into a chair and laid my head back. My melon spun with all the information in their puzzle pieces finally fitting together.

I jumped up, took her arms, and dragged her into her own chair. 'Harken, Marion.' I ticked it off with each finger. 'Gonzalo is killed by an unknown person and I receive a threatening missive. I follow the missive's instructions but nothing comes of it. I am thoroughly warned, though. But, like the fool I am, I'm just relieved that naught happened, never thinking beyond the fact that I am spared. Oh, I did give it thought here and there, but there was nothing to be done.'

'But Will . . .'

'Wait, Marion. Wait until I've told it all. It wants spilling out faster than I can say. Because of Gonzalo's high rank and because he is a Spaniard, we instantly thought it meant that it was a political crime, that his was an assassination. And then we went down that crooked path of thinking in that vein. No wonder I stumbled here and there, confusing myself further. But! What if politics had naught to do with any of it? What if it had everything to do with . . . jealousy?'

'Who was jealous?'

'Just so. *Who?* It wasn't Kendrick, though he committed murder. But Kendrick didn't kill Gonzalo. I asked him straight in the eye and he denied it. But he never denied killing Lady Jane. He didn't even know who *you* were.'

'He confessed it? To you?'

'Well . . . I was holding a knife to his throat.'

'Will Somers! Oh, my brave, brave fool.'

'Aye.' I sat up, preening a bit. Must take my laurels where I may.

'Then who, Will? Who was jealous of Gonzalo enough to kill him?'

I leaned in close. 'Lady Ursula.'

'Oh no,' she said dismissively. 'That doesn't serve.'

'But it does! Look, she is Gonzalo's lover and she somehow finds out about our one night. In jealousy, she kills him and tries to blackmail me. But when it came down to blackmail, she has no more need of it. She doesn't care anymore. Gonzalo is dead, her revenge secured. She forgets me, has no need to continue with my like. And so naught comes of it. Remember the night we waited in the garden? She would have had to reveal herself and she must have thought better of it.'

I watched Marion's face carefully. 'I see how that can be,' she said carefully.

'And – a pence for a pork pie – Kendrick is her lover.'

'What? The *priest*?'

'I saw it with my own eyes, and poor devils those eyes are for seeing it.'

'But how does it fit that Kendrick killed Lady Jane?'

'Ursula was the king's lover.'

'No!'

'Aye. She *was*! And maybe set her sights high indeed. But I've been told that Henry took her to his bed but once, and she expected more. And when the king did not attend to her as she expected, she discovered that *Lady Jane* took her place on his sheets. Jealousy! She didn't want to kill her herself, but had her pup Kendrick do it. He was so besotted with her that the fool actually did it. And now he's on the run.'

She put her hand to her mouth in surprise. 'God's blessed mother,' she whispered to her fingers.

'Aye. So it was jealousy that pushed her on. Jealousy of me, then jealousy of Henry.'

'And she used poor Kendrick for her foul crimes.'

'For all we know, he *might* have killed Gonzalo, for all his lies on the matter. It doesn't much bother. He's on a short path to Hell, and I hope he gets there soon.'

'Oh, Will. She could have just as easily killed you.'

'I think that dog saved me. Maybe she was afraid that Nosewise would have attacked her. And by the mass!' I slapped a hand to my head. 'That was why Lady Jane . . . Oh, Marion, I *had* got it all wrong. Lady Jane was, in her way, trying to get out of me if *I'd* seen her leaving Harry's bedchamber. She wasn't threatening me, nor had she known about me. It was all about her tryst with Henry, and she wanted to know if I'd keep quiet about it. If only she had plainly said . . .'

'You know why she couldn't.'

'Aye. She wanted to know if she was safe from the wrath of Lady Nan. What a wretch I have been.'

'What are you going to do?'

'I'm going to confront Lady Ursula. I want her confession.'

'But she can still make things bad for you.'

'Marion, it's a chance I have to take. After all, I confronted your father only a few moments ago.'

'You didn't.'

'I did.'

'And . . . what did he say?'

I looked around her rooms. They were comfortable, certainly bigger than mine. We spent many a sweet evening in these rooms, in her bed. But I also liked the soft evenings when we sat together by the fire, sipping some warmed wine, she darning the heels of my hose, and me telling her stories of my life in Shropshire. I loved listening to her little chuckles, and seeing her shaking her head with an, 'Oh, Will.' It was those times I would miss the most if she left. And my heart would be torn apart. No amount of darning would mend it.

'He said he loved you more than any legitimate daughter. And he worried that no one would care for you when he died.'

'Did he . . . did he agree to let you wed me?'

'I . . .' Good Christ! I ran out on him before he could say. And left him angrier at me than when I met him.

I gingerly rose to my feet. 'Er . . . we didn't quite come to that. He . . . I mean I . . . Oh whore's teeth! I got an idea about the murder and ran straight to you . . . never letting him finish his speech.'

She jolted up and stomped her foot. 'Will!'

'I'm sorry! I should have let him speak his piece. But you know how I am.'

'I know now that I will never marry you.'

'Oh, don't say that. He might yet yield. That's why I must get this damned Ursula woman to confess it. I will yet be the hero.'

'Is *that* what you wanted from this? For vainglory?'

'No. For justice. For Gonzalo. But if hero I be, then your father might be more inclined toward wedding his daughter to a court jester. Don't you see, Marion?'

'I see that you'd better let me get back to packing.' With a reddened face, she turned away from me, stiffly taking her linens and folding them into a pile.

'You're not truly going, are you? I couldn't stand it if you did.'

'Then maybe you should have thought of that before declaring yourself a hero, Will Somers.'

Limply, I watched her concentrate on each crease and fold of her linen shifts and stockings. She refused to look at me further, and so I trudged out the door. The servants were all still standing about frozen, glaring at me as I left her chambers. What had I done? Had I lost her for good? No. I refused to let her go. I'd get Gonzalo his justice and I'd pin that Ursula woman to the wall. She had to pay and I was going to make her pay.

I scrambled back to my lodgings – looking behind the drapery for Edward – and sat myself at my table with paper and quill:

> *Greetings Lady Ursula Marbury,*
> *Certain things have come to my attention concerning*
> *Father Kendrick and you and two Spaniards of our*
> *acquaintance, as well as Lady Jane. It is imperative that*
> *I talk with you immediately about these things.*
> *Your servant and Christ bless us all,*
> *Will Somers*

That ought to get the cobwebs out.

TWENTY-TWO

I sent for a servant and he took the missive to the lady. I waited over an hour, two hours – all the while worrying that Marion was on her way to Heyward's manor.

Finally! A servant arrived with a message. I broke open the wax seal and read through it. 'Meet me on the parapet near the clock tower.'

I read it again. At the parapet? Clock tower? What was this?

I set the paper down at my table, opened the inkpot and scribbled what I was doing. And then I left it there. Because if I should *not* return, I wanted someone to know what had happened to me. And who did it.

I wanted to hasten, and at the same time I dragged my feet. Was I going to my doom? Did *she* have a crossbow? *Almighty God*, I sent up the prayer. *If you ever loved this poor jester, protect me now. Help me get justice for Gonzalo and Lady Jane.*

I found the stairs. One step, two steps . . . I climbed as if climbing the steps of a gallows. I traced my hand along the stone wall, feeling its roughness under my fingertips, the coarse chiseled marks left unsmoothed by masons of long ago. At the top there was a door left ajar. I crept to it, slowly looking around the corner.

And there she was, standing at a crenellation, the wind whipping at her veil and sending it behind her, skirts flapping.

I adjusted my doublet and rose to the top step, walking through the entryway.

She turned only her head to look at me with a cold, steady gaze. 'Master Somers.'

'Lady Ursula.' I bowed most eloquently as one does at court.

She lifted her hand, showing me my missive she had crumpled in her hand. 'There were brazen accusations in this letter.'

'Indeed. They came from careful consideration, my lady.'

'You have no proof.'

I sagged. Perhaps this was not to be the heartfelt confession I had hoped for. But I soldiered on, for there was little left to do. I couldn't imagine telling this tale to the Lord Sheriffs and being believed. 'I have the proof of God's witness, my lady. And of some timely bits of news. You see . . .' I kept a good distance from her, not knowing if – in her farther hand – she sported a dagger. Mine was still in its sheath and, being no fighter, I doubted I could brandish it in time to save myself. 'You see, there are certain things I know. That you and Don Gonzalo were lovers—'

'As were you and Gonzalo!' she rasped between clenched teeth.

I stilled. With a bracing breath, I nodded. 'Aye. You know it well. So your . . . your blackmail note said.'

She turned her face back to the view of the countryside. And what a view it was. On one side was London, with its many tightly gathered roofs of red clay, its smoke from hearth fires, church spires spearing upward from one street to the next, the gray Thames snaking its way throughout and disappearing round a bend in the distance. And on the other side, flat plains of green divided by hedges or stacked stone, gentle sheep grazing without a care in the world, absent the thoughts of what was transpiring above them on this parapet.

'Such vile sin,' she whispered.

'So some say. Some also say that congress with a priest is a sin.'

Slowly, she turned her head and fixed her steely gaze on me. But since she didn't speak, I went on.

'I don't understand why you killed Don Gonzalo. One would have imagined you would go for me . . .' I stepped farther away from the parapet's edge. 'But you did kill him with a dagger to his throat. An ugly, messy death.'

She neither confirmed nor denied and so I went on.

'Methought it had more to do with his spying for Spain. I never suspected a jealous lover. And indeed, this thought was reinforced by the attack on Gonzalo's varlet, Rodrigo. Why try to kill him? Did you discover that he, too, had been Gonzalo's lover?'

Her eyes narrowed, and they were glazed with the moisture of unshed tears. 'Once I saw you with him, I knew.'

'Ah. You put two and two together. At least Rodrigo survived. I nursed him and the Spanish ambassador sent him back to Spain.'

She sniffed but that was all the comment she made.

'And then there was Father John Kendrick.'

Her gaze slid back to the countryside.

'I suspected him of the murder and attempted murder, because he was a suspicious man on his own. I found him in Don Gonzalo's rooms, sniffing around his papers. I assumed he was spying on Gonzalo. But *I* had obtained the papers he sought.'

Her lip curved downward in a sneer. 'I doubt that.'

'It is true, lady. The letters seemed to implicate Don Gonzalo in spying on the king . . . but that was later found not to be true.'

'You found nothing. Father Kendrick was looking for . . . other letters.'

'Oh? Perhaps having to do with you and he in a . . . personal nature?'

'John and I were lovers. You already seem to know that.'

'I did accidentally spy the two of you . . .' I shuddered at the vision of them in my head. 'So what was he looking for . . . Ah! Love letters? Did Don Gonzalo find love letters between you and your priest?'

She heaved a great sigh. 'Yes. And Gonzalo confronted me about them. There was to be no betrothal.'

'One wonders if there was ever to be one. I mean, after all, if a lady gave it up to a priest and to her own betrothed, how many others might there be?' I slowly approached, aiming my barbs carefully. 'A man must know that the offspring from such a match is his . . . There was the king too, after all.'

She flicked her eyes toward me and quickly away.

'Aye, the king in secret,' I said. 'Oh, what a disaster it would have been had Lady Nan discovered that.'

'Henry promised me—'

'Don't be a fool, Lady Ursula. The king did not go through all of this with clerics aplenty and the pope for the Lady Anne just to put her aside . . . for *you*.'

Her fist closed on that paper ever tighter. And I closed on her ever nearer. I was going to subdue her if I had to punch her in the jaw to do it.

'Was it one night, my lady? Two? He merely needed to relieve himself, and what better way than on a convenient lady. After all, he also chose Lady Jane Perwick when he tired of you.'

'That's not true! He didn't tire of me. He was waiting . . . waiting . . .'

'For Pyramus to find Thisbe? Oh, dear Lady Ursula. That was not to be. You yourself were a maid of honor to Lady Anne. Surely you saw the difficulties. Putting away a lawful wife, a *queen* is hard work. Look how Wolsey's brow grays on it. Look at all his ministers and councillors. Look at the delegation from Spain and how they fretted. And dead Gonzalo, who had remained stubbornly neutral in order to be effective here at court.'

'The king promised me—'

'Henry *lied*, my lady. God love him as I do, but he *lied*. He lied to get you into his bed, as he lies to get any woman into his bed. He is the *king*. He may do as he wishes, *hurt* whom he wishes. As close as you are to the inner workings of court, I am surprised you never reckoned that.'

She turned full to me then, and this hurt from Henry seemed to be the worst of it. It was all over her face. Not Gonzalo's infidelities with me or Rodrigo, but this supposed promise Henry gave to her for her privileges in the bedclothes. I almost felt sorry for her.

'And you discovered that Lady Jane had taken your place with Henry. And you forced your lover John Kendrick to kill her for you. Why did he do it? Was he so besotted with you that he would have done anything? Or did you blackmail him as you tried to do with me?'

'I will ruin you, Jester. I *will* tell the court . . .'

'Tell them what?' I said, feeling bolder. 'Tell them that you decided not to kill me as you had done your lover, but to blackmail me instead? Will you kill the king because he put you aside?'

'I would never—'

'"Never," lady? Never? For I have never killed nor will I ever for jealousy. But *you*! You have killed twice, tried to kill thrice. Where will it end? Will Lady Anne be your victim next?'

Her face was covered in tears now, and her grimace was as ugly and as twisted as her soul. 'No. But *you* will be.'

I wasn't prepared, though I should have been. For her other hand did have a dagger in it, and she rushed me. I grabbed the wrist with the knife, but her other hand raked my face with her nails, reaching for my eyes. We struggled. I thought I could easily disarm a woman, but she was strong, strong in her anger and pain, like a devil, she was. I used my strength to wrench the knife from her to drop it to the floor, but when I did, she reached across me and pulled *mine*.

Now I was in real fear of my life. *Christ help me!* She was using both her hands on the hilt to aim for my heart. Her eyes were wild, her mouth gaping. She was the very image of a demon out to take my soul.

I grabbed *both* wrists, fending it away, trying to think how I was going to stop her now, when my foot slid to the embrasure and my heel hung over the edge. I made my way slowly to the safety of the merlon, but she now saw her chance. If she could push me over, her troubles would be done.

I doubled my efforts and with my hands firmly on her wrists, I swung her with all my might till she crashed into a merlon. That seemed to weaken her, but she had not released her hold on my dagger. She tried to pull me toward the embrasure, but I knew her mind on it. I held her firm, kicking at her legs but damn those skirts! I could not tell where they were.

I saw her lips twist in a maniacal smile. I was too close to the embrasure. She put her weight behind it when she lunged, shoving me.

But God Almighty did love this fool, for somehow, my foot stepped back, braced against the merlon, and my hands with their iron grip of her wrists swung her whole body . . .

And there she went, through the embrasure and into the air. I opened my fingers and with my dagger still in her hands, she plummeted over the side and landed flat on the gravel courtyard below, moving no more.

She was splayed like laundry, like a drying shift on the grass, arms this way, skirt that way. She was still looking up at me, but the eyes were glass now, seeing naught. Guards came running and knelt.

And then, as I leaned over the side and breathed hard, they looked up at me.

TWENTY-THREE

It took much time to convince the guards to take me to Henry. They brought me to the inner privy chamber, not daring to bring me further in; as soon as Henry heard what this was about, he waved his guards away, though I knew they were directly outside the doors.

He stood before me, his ginger brows frowning over his eyes, his fists at his hips. When he wrestled, he took such a stance before his attack. I had never been so frightened. If Henry didn't believe me, all would be lost. I prayed as hard as I ever had.

'Lady Ursula was a murderess,' I croaked.

'So my Captain of the Guard told me that you told to him. Explain.'

I swallowed. My throat was dry. Dryer than the deserts of the Holy Land. 'And so . . . I shall try to explain it all. Lady Ursula was the lover of Don Gonzalo. But she was jealous of his other lovers, for she thought – possibly mistakenly – that she and he were to be betrothed.'

'I never would have allowed that. No more Spanish marriages.'

'I can understand that,' I said feebly, 'but this was her thinking. She discovered he had a lover and so, in a fit of jealous rage, she killed Don Gonzalo. And she tried to kill his varlet for . . . for . . .' *Think fast, Will!* 'For hiding this lover from her, for bringing the lover secretly to Don Gonzalo.'

Henry's brows unloosed, became not so gnarled. For this game of secret lovers, he knew well. And he relied on the silence of his groomsmen to *keep* it a secret.

'Where is this varlet now?'

'He . . . Rodrigo Muñoz was sent back to Spain.' Should I tell him about Marion and how her father tried to marry him to her? No, best not to tangle my own lover into it if at all possible. 'But Brother Fulke with the Observant Friars can attest to his injuries, for it was he who nursed him in his hour of need.'

Henry's brow ticked again, for I knew that the Observant Friars were staunch supporters of the queen. It couldn't be helped.

'We will see about that anon. Go on with this tale.'

I latched on to his word, 'tale'. 'Aye, Harry, for it is an exciting tale, alongside that of Roland or Gawain.' I fell easily into my prattling role. For now I was trying my mightiest to entertain Henry. For an entertained Henry was a generous one, a *forgiving* one. 'I pursued this murderer of Don Gonzalo—'

'Why?' he interrupted.

'What's that?'

'Why were *you* set to pursue the murderer of a man you didn't know from a foreign court?'

'But I *did* know him, sire. Earlier, after I had played for the court, he asked me to teach him some English songs. For his lover – Lady Ursula, you will remember – is English, a maid of honor to Lady Anne. We spent nearly a whole evening making music.' Not quite a lie, but in the manner of a *tale*, after all.

I saw Henry visibly loosen his distress. For music was something he well understood. He composed his own music, and good tunes they were.

I saw my opening. 'I taught him some of *your* songs, Harry. How could I not? They are very popular here.'

And with that, Henry was mine.

'And so she killed poor Don Gonzalo and tried to kill his servant Rodrigo, for we had become friends, saddened over the Spaniard's death. But Ursula wasn't done with her murderous jealousies. For she was the lover of yet another. A man of . . . high estate.' I raised my brows.

Henry shuffled uncomfortably and turned away from me. He sat in his great chair and waved for me to go on.

'A man of . . . *very* high estate. But alas, this man, though promises he did make to her, had no intention of fulfilling them. Well, that is neither here nor there. Men are always doing such for the love of a lady, true? And so Lady

Ursula got herself yet another lover, the priest Father John Kendrick.'

'*What?*' He leapt to his feet.

'It is true, Harry. This Kendrick was likely Spanish. In Wolsey's office, no less. He had a Spanish mother and ties to Spain. He was working against you, sire.'

Henry fumed but waved at me to continue.

'This woman was as fickle as they came. This man of very high estate was well rid of her, for in her jealousy, I am certain she would have tried to kill *him* next.'

He put a hand to his throat and slowly lowered back to his chair.

'I see your distress. It is a distressing notion. But with this priest-lover who was besotted with her, she convinced him to kill the person she believed was yet another rival for the affections of this man of very high estate . . . and he then killed Lady Jane Perwick for her.'

'This is outrageous,' he growled.

'Oh, Harry. You don't know the half of it. Now. I saw John Kendrick slay the lady. I saw him running away and he dropped the crossbow. I saw him with my own eyes almost as close as we are to each other. I might have lied at the time about it to the Captain of the Guard, to keep the honor of a priest and the Church out of it. But I confessed that to Wolsey. Well, to Cromwell, who no doubt is hot on his trail. He will be brought to justice if he has not slain himself. A true sinner of the vilest kind, ignoring his vows of his office and committing, oh, several sins against the Ten Commandments; murder, coveting, bearing false witness . . . so many. And with the evidence of these women, lovers of the man of high estate—'

'Get on with it.'

'I reckoned the woman had to be Lady Ursula Marbury. I sent her a missive telling her she had better confess all and she sent one back, telling me to meet her on the parapet. I left that message in my quarters so that someone could find them as witness to . . . well. If I had succumbed to her. And when I confronted her with all the evidence – all of which she never denied, as God is my witness – then she rushed me, first with *her* dagger, and then with *mine*. We fought. And she was so possessed of a devil that she had preternatural strength and she tried to push me off the battlement, but with the help of the Almighty Who Rights All Wrongs in Heaven and on Earth, I was given the strength to finally subdue her and . . . and . . .' It was finally catching up to me. I had killed someone. True, it was in self-defense, but I was no killer. I sobbed the rest. 'I threw her off. Oh God, Harry! I had to do it . . .'

I don't know how it happened but he had suddenly enclosed me in his arms. I was enwrapped by furs and silks and sweat and ruffles, by His very Majesty, and he comforted me, seeing how distressed I was. I wept onto his silk-covered breast.

'There, there, Will. You are so gentle, aren't you? And you fought for your life as anyone would have.'

'I couldn't let her get to you, Harry,' I sobbed. 'She was the Devil. You would have seen it.'

'It's all right, Will. The Captain of the Guard said they found her with your dagger in her hand.'

'Harry, Harry . . .'

He held me, rocked me like a babe. I felt a kiss on the top of my head. And I felt loved as no one had ever been in the realm. Loved by the king himself, and instantly in my mind, I felt the same as Ursula must have felt. If, for only one night, the King of England had loved you, and there was nothing as magnificent as that. I empathized . . . for only a moment. For her motivations were all born of evil, and for that, I could not ever condone it.

'You are blameless,' he said, his voice bold and steady. He lifted me up and took me with him to the door. He opened it and all the faces of guards, privy council, grooms, and other courtiers waited without in his presence chamber. 'He is blameless!' the king declared in a loud voice to shake the rafters. 'Will Somers is innocent and saved the life of the king.'

I sat in Marion's withdrawing room, crowded with servants and friends. I told the tale again, leaving more out of it this time, and lifted my cup to slack my dry throat. Everyone had their cups, both wooden goblets and pewter, as they anxiously listened and drank, listened and drank.

I felt better in telling it a second time . . . well. It was the third, for I had had to tell the Captain of the Guard first before he would have ever taken me to the king. Will Somers was exonerated, and his secret would be kept, and that was what was needed.

'How come you had such a hard time fighting her off, Will?' asked one of the lower courtiers.

'She was possessed, that's how. She was strong in her embrace of the Devil, she was. Oh, I could see it in her eyes, the hellfire, the demons. I almost went over m'self. God Almighty reached out of Heaven to keep me in the palm of His hand is what saved me. Verily.'

I glanced over at Marion, and though she was enrapt as any of the others, there was just the merest glint in her eye that said, 'Just how much of this tale is true, Will Somers?' And I could honestly tell her, 'Too much, my love. Far too much.'

There was a commotion at the door and everyone parted for some courtier. I jumped to m'feet when I recognized Lord Heyward.

Quickly, the crowd dwindled and they all disappeared, closing the door after them. With the room emptied, I glanced about and saw that the people had been sitting on Marion's coffers and other luggage. She was still leaving.

I whipped my head toward her. I'm certain I was bleached white, for I could feel my cheeks drawing colder.

Heyward paced slowly about the room, fingers trailing over clothing and goods in some of the open coffers still to be packed. 'Word has traveled through the court, Somers,' he began, 'about your miraculous fight for good over evil.'

'It was a miracle true, sir. The hand of God, it was, that saved me.'

'You have not boasted of it. I have heard enough to know that. That is . . . very commendable.'

'Aye, my lord.'

'And you saved the king from harm.'

'I . . . I took a life, sir. I . . . my heart is sore on it.'

He glanced at me then, his brow questioning. And then like the king, he came over to me and laid a hand on my shoulder consolingly. 'It is not an easy thing to take a life, Somers. No man should be proud of it, either in battle or in any other circumstance. God gave each of us the gift of life, and who are we to take it? But in the course of doing our duty to our king, it sometimes becomes necessary. You did not shirk your duty. And in this, I am . . . proud of you.'

For the second time that day, my throat choked with a warm lump, and I could not speak.

He patted my shoulder and finally dropped his hand to his side. 'I think, under the circumstances, if my daughter still wishes to remain at court, then I give my leave for her to do so.'

'My lord,' she gasped and rushed to him, embracing him. He easily curled his arm around her, and kissed her forehead. He truly did love his daughter. It was there on his face.

'And . . . I have agreed to . . . to *consider* this betrothal between the two of you. *Consider* it, I said. I have not yet given my leave for it.' And he pinned me with his narrowed eye.

'My Lord Robert!' I gushed.

He set his daughter aside and looked me over. 'See that you conduct yourself well, Somers, and I may have a decision by the end of the year.' Keeping his eyes on me, he withdrew from the room and a servant closed the door after him.

I turned to her. 'Did you hear that, Marion!'

'By God, Will! You are a miracle worker!' She threw herself into my arms.

Good Christ. And all it took was a little murder.

AFTERWORD

Will Somers was Henry VIII's real court jester. He came from Shropshire to Henry's court in 1525 at about twenty years old, and stayed there the rest of his life, through all of Henry's wives, through Edward VI's brief reign, through Mary I's, and into Elizabeth I's. He was beloved by the whole family and loyal to the last. A jester could get away with quips no other courtier could. It was understood. They were allowed to. Oh, they could be beaten or kicked for it as other men in high places treated *their* fools, but the most that could happen was being sacked from the job.

Little else is known about him. How old he was exactly, if he ever married, or anything else. And no, we don't know if he had a dog though there is a painting with him and a dog. There is also a painting of him with a monkey. I'm sure we'll see that creature in later volumes.

A man who could be anywhere in court, privy to some of the court's highest secrets? What better person could there be as an amateur sleuth?

Henry was a difficult man to parse. There is the outer Henry, the one most of us see in history books or depicted for good or ill in dramas – a vain, vicious man, and absolute monarch, single-minded in his need for a male heir. But as with most people, there is the inner Henry, a much more complicated individual. He was staunchly religious, even being called *Fidei Defensor*, 'Defender of the Faith', by Pope Leo X. He wrote treatises on the Catholic religion, and even against Martin Luther and his Protestantism. That soon waned when Henry's 'Great Matter' – that of his divorce from his first wife, Catherine of Aragon – could find no foothold in Rome. Henry had received a papal dispensation specifically to *marry* Catherine in the first place because she had first been married to Henry's older brother Arthur, who died not long thereafter.

But Catherine couldn't give Henry a son as heir, and this became what he felt was an obstacle to a successful reign; that he couldn't leave a king after him, only a woman to be queen. (And why was this a problem? It hadn't been done in England, except for the twelfth-century Empress Matilda, the daughter of Henry I, William the Conqueror's son – and a civil war ensued to depose her. A queen might also be at the mercy of whatever husband she chose, the man being the head of the household. Naturally, Englishmen didn't want to be ruled by a foreign prince, especially if the queen died in childbed. Probably chiefly one of the reasons Elizabeth I never married.)

Henry said he had no right under God's eyes to marry his brother's wife (and that's why God punished him by not giving him lawful sons. He did have at least one bastard son, Henry Fitzroy, who died when he was about seventeen). This sentiment might have been heartfelt . . . at first. But Catherine's opposition to the divorce, that she was lawfully wed to Henry and their daughter Mary was not a bastard, caused the Tudor monarch to double down. When the pope refused him his divorce, Henry broke with Rome and became the head of his own Church, the Church of England, as monarchs of England have been ever since (except for Mary I's reign, when she tried to bring Catholicism back to England, and for King James II, who was the last Catholic king. Having become Protestant, there was no going back.)

We mustn't forget that at this stage of his life, Henry was not the fat man of the famous painting, nor the tyrant he was yet to become. But instead, a very handsome man, six foot one, young and strong, a poet, a composer of music, a patron of the arts. 'His goodly personage, his amiable visage, princely countenance, with the noble qualities of his royal estate, to every man known, needeth no rehearsal, considering that for lack of cunning, I cannot express the gifts of nature that God hath endowed him withal.' So said lawyer and Tudor chronicler Edward Hall. Henry was the last medieval monarch and the first Renaissance one in England, spanning the two eras. I'll be exploring the many changing human faces of Henry as the series goes on.

As for Anne Boleyn, there were many spellings of her

surname, 'Bullen' being one of them, as spelling was not yet codified. But courtiers – as well as Will in this book – refer to her somewhat derisively and call her 'that Bullen woman' or 'Nan Bullen' in a familiar, rustic, and insulting way. There is no proof to the myth that Anne 'Frenchified' her name from 'Bullen' to 'Boleyn' to be fancier, because both spellings were in use in letters and documents of the time.

As you can imagine, there are fictional people in this book. Fictional people who murdered fictional people. There must naturally be leeway when concocting a murder mystery. Don't be looking for Father Kendrick, the Spanish gentleman Don Gonzalo de Yscar, Anne's ladies-in-waiting Lady Ursula and Jane Perwick, Brother Fulke, or Marion Greene and her father Lord Robert Heyward in any documents. They are fictional. I tried, to the best of my ability, to populate this series with the real people of Henry's court. I promise to point out the false ones in future afterwords.

Let's get back to Will. My imagination has always been captured by the figure of Will Somers, ever since I was a kid. 'A Jester? A Jester? A funny idea a Jester.' That's a quote from the Danny Kaye film *The Court Jester*, a film known for its humor and clever patter songs, but not the least bit of historical accuracy. No, I've known about Will a long time (because I was a nerd kid and consumed with historical novels and history because my family were rabid Anglophiles).

Some of the nonsense Will spouts in this novel is indeed attributed to him, and some I made up. You can have fun deciding which is which. But never let it be said that the Tudors would ever pass up a good fart joke.

I know what you're thinking. Was Will Somers bisexual? It's purely my own speculation on his character. He had to have been an extraordinarily interesting individual, with a lot of wit, verve, and confidence. Does *this* make him bisexual? Quoting bestselling author Louis Bayard on his book *Courting Mr. Lincoln* where he poses the question that Abraham Lincoln was gay, he said, 'When all is said and done, do I need Abraham Lincoln to be gay? No. I just need him to be something more complicated than he's been allowed to be. I would argue we all need that.'

Thanks, as always, to my hubby Craig for the encouragement and suggestions. Thanks also to my readers for making sure I did, finally, write this series. And grateful thanks to Kathie Dapron for giving my Will Somers mascot the coat and jester hood he deserves. You have magical fingers!

The next book in the series, *The Lioness Stumbles*, finds Will with another murder a little too close to Queen Anne Boleyn. She fears the killer is trying to implicate *her*, and begs Will to solve the crime. Read more about this and my other series at JeriWesterson.com.